"W

A corner of those soft, warm lips tipped unsteadily upward. "If you have to ask then I guess I'm not doing it right."

Oh, he'd done it right. No worries about that.

"Why you're doing it at all is the question."

"I guess that's just my way of thanking you for making a breakthrough with my sister."

Her body still felt flushed and her lips still tingled, a sign that what had just happened was wrong in too many ways to describe and that she was in way over her head.

"A simple thank you will suffice."

"Maybe. But a simple thank you isn't nearly as much fun . . ."

By Candis Terry

A BETTER MAN
TRULY SWEET
SWEET SURPRISE
SOMETHING SWEETER
SWEETEST MISTAKE
ANYTHING BUT SWEET
SOMEBODY LIKE YOU
ANY GIVEN CHRISTMAS
SECOND CHANCE AT THE SUGAR SHACK

Short Stories

SWEET COWBOY CHRISTMAS
SWEET FORTUNE
(appears in CONFESSIONS OF A SECRET ADMIRER)
HOME SWEET HOME
(appears in FOR LOVE AND HONOR
and CRAZY SWEET FINE)

CANDIS TERRY

a
better
man

A SUNSHINE CREEK VINEYARD NOVEL

AVONBOOKS

An Imprint of HarperCollinsPublishers

AVON BOOKS
An Imprint of HarperCollins*Publishers*
195 Broadway
New York, New York 10007

This one is for the teachers
who encouraged me in my early years.
For the teachers who go above and beyond
with knowledge, patience, and compassion.
And for Claudeen Bergeron,
one of the nicest and best.
May your lessons and voices be heard
and appreciated for generations.

Chapter 1

The pungent scent of sweat-soaked bodies and the ice beneath Jordan Kincade's skates filled his nostrils. He devoured the energy, the thrill of the game, and the barely controlled chaos like a perfectly grilled steak. Queen's "We Will Rock You" and anticipation vibrated through the jam-packed arena as he skated to face-off with his opponent on a power play. The Carolina Vipers might be down by a goal, but he knew the high-decibel, foot-stomping boost from the home crowd would pull them through.

It always did.

After an earlier vicious cross-check delivered by Dimitri Pavel, Jordan—much to the crowd's delight—racked up five for fighting. Now it was time to cut the shit and focus. He couldn't allow Pavel's toothless sneer to tempt him into chalking up any more penalty points. There was just too damn much at stake.

"Gonna vipe smile off dat pretty face, kinky man."

Pavel spat when he spoke, a habit that tempted his opponents to dodge the spray and miss the drop. Jordan, who had mercifully retained all his own teeth, imagined it was hard to speak properly when you had the gums of an infant. Still, Pavel could have strings of snot hanging from his nose and Jordan wouldn't care. He didn't dodge anything if it meant he'd lose the face-off.

"Your saggy jock calls bullshit," Jordan shot back. Yeah, okay, the bait had been too strong to resist the smack talk. So sue him.

Like a wolf focused on its prey, Jordan's attention sharpened as the ref lifted his hand and dropped the puck in front of Jordan's skates. Jordan wasted no time in pushing the biscuit across the ice into Tyler Seabrook's stick. The center took control. Dodging sticks, skates, and elbows, he managed to set up a shot in the sweet zone. Jordan snagged the pass and slapped it through the five-hole before the goalie could get his glove on it.

Red lights flashed behind the net and the horn blew, signaling the goal. The crowd leaped to their feet in an ear-splitting roar as the players came together for congratulatory slaps on the back. Nothing felt better than a team celebration after an important goal. The one he'd just scored had been vital and hopefully took the burn off the penalties he'd drawn earlier. With the score now tied, the Vipers would have to quickly score once more or win it in overtime. The chances of either were iffy.

The shift change gave Jordan a chance to catch his breath and rest his legs. During a regular season game he didn't usually tense up. But the closer they got to making the playoffs, the more he tended to tighten every muscle to the extreme. By the time he made it home tonight he'd feel like he'd been hit by a bullet train. Once his team claimed victory and made it into the locker room, he'd need to have his favorite masseuse make a house call. Lucky for him his favorite masseuse came with a pretty smile, long blond hair, a taste for fine whiskey, and preferred to work in the nude.

A smile curled his mouth as he watched Beau Boucher press his opponent into the corner boards with a glass-quaking thud. The hulking defenseman used his weight and muscle to steal the puck and slide it across the ice to power forward Scott O'Reilly. O'Reilly sank it into the net so fast the goalie barely saw it flash by.

With only two seconds remaining on the play clock, the Vipers bench emptied and the entire team roared onto the ice to celebrate the win. Unless a miracle materialized for the other team in the next blink of an eye, the Vipers were one step closer to the Stanley Cup.

Hallefreakinglujah.

After a loss a locker room could be as silent as a crypt. Tonight, the noise level and celebration escalated to ear-splitting.

Jordan did his best not to grin like a raging fool during his post-game recap with the reporter from the *Observer*. Exhilaration tingled through his chest. He loved this damn game, his team, and right now he even loved Coach Bill Reiner, who openly admitted that he was an unlovable SOB. Didn't matter. Hope remained alive. Every man on skates in this room could imagine the coveted silver Holy Grail of hockey pressed to their lips.

Interview complete, Jordan had time to celebrate with the guys before everyone dropped their jocks and headed for the showers. Plans were already being made to take the party to the team's favorite sports bar. Turk's Ice House provided cold beer, perfectly cooked finger steaks, sharp darts, and plenty of pretty ladies who didn't mind if the newest rookie sported a purple Mohawk or wore his jock strap on the outside of his jeans. Hazing could be hell, and Turk's was always more than happy to add a little extra torture to the newbies.

Tonight it didn't matter if you were the captain, a veteran, or the newest kid on the ice. Tonight they were a team and tonight they'd celebrate as one. Come tomorrow they'd all be back to kicking ass in practice and preparing for the biggest games of the season.

Near the lockers, Boucher tangled rookie Colton Dahl up in a headlock, and Jordan laughed. Damn, he was happy. Just out-of-his-mind fucking happier than he'd been in a long time. Things had been going great for a while now. If he were a superstitious man, he'd be worried that his string of good luck was about to break. But he wasn't even the type to grow a good-luck beard during the playoffs like the other guys. He didn't hesitate to walk under ladders, and he didn't flinch when a black cat crossed his path. The vibe he had going was pretty sweet, and he planned to do everything in his power to keep it on fast track.

Grabbing the back of his jersey with one hand, he pulled the number eighteen shirt over his head. A flash of purple and black briefly covered his eyes before he tossed the stinking material into the hamper and hung his pads in the locker. Before he could sit down to remove his skates, his cell phone rang.

He debated answering it.

Somehow the bleached blond princess he'd tangled legs with last week had gotten his number. Not that he didn't appreciate her willingness to go above and beyond between the sheets, but Jordan didn't have a want or a need to tie himself down to any woman. Especially one who had dollar signs in her eyes and envisioned his ring on her finger. Still, there were others who could be calling. And with five siblings it could be any one of them.

Grabbing the black case, he glanced down at the caller ID.

Ryan.

His big brother rarely picked up the phone. Usually the man was too busy helping their parents run the family vineyards back in Washington State and being a single dad to his nine-year-old daughter. Then again, maybe Ryan had seen the game on TV tonight and was calling to offer his congratulations.

Jordan poked the ANSWER button. "Hey, big brother. Did you see the game?"

"I caught the first period."

"Only the first? What's the matter?" Jordan laughed.

"You couldn't stand seeing me waste another five locked up for rearranging Pavel's big nose?"

"Jordy." Ryan's tone twisted through the pit of Jordan's gut. "I'm sorry. I didn't call about your game. I've got some bad news."

The knot tightened. "How bad?"

Ryan's silence on the other end of the phone sent a chill up Jordan's back. Behind him the locker room celebration continued to blast at full volume. "Hang on a second. Let me go out into the hall. I can barely hear you."

Jordan shoved open the swinging doors and stepped into the much quieter passageway between the locker room and the coach's office. "What's going on?" With five siblings it could be anything. In the past, it often had been. There had been Ethan's close call with a wildfire, the burns Parker received when a skillet of grease blew up, Declan's near fatal crash on a California freeway, and Ryan's bone-breaking fall from the roof of the winery. Nicole, their baby sister, seemed to be the only one in the family who didn't break body parts on a regular basis.

Ryan cleared his throat. "There's been an accident."

"What kind of accident? Is Riley okay?" Jordan asked, immediately feeling the familiar guilt that he didn't get to see his niece often enough.

"She's fine. It's . . . Mom and Dad."

His heart skipped a beat. "Are they okay?"

"They hired one of those tour helicopters to fly them over Molokai." Ryan's voice hitched. "It crashed."

"What?" Disbelief sent Jordan's fingers jamming

through his hair. Their parents had gone to Hawaii a few days ago to celebrate their thirty-fifth wedding anniversary. They'd been looking forward to warm sunshine and tropical drinks. "Did they . . ."

"They're gone, Jordy. There were no survivors."

Jordan's throat closed like an iron fist had wrapped around his windpipe. He couldn't breathe. Couldn't think. Couldn't move. For a second he had to bend over and brace his hands on his knees to keep them from buckling. To keep his stomach from rolling like he was fighting titanic ocean waves. He couldn't even remember the last time he'd spoken to either his mom or his dad at length. And now . . .

In a distant echo he heard his brother calling his name.

Agony pounded the breath from his lungs as he returned the phone to his ear. "I'll be on the next flight home," he told Ryan.

"Let me get things figured out here a little more. Someone needs to go to Hawaii to claim the bodies and arrange to have them flown home," Ryan said in an unbelievably calm tone.

Ryan had always been the strong one, the one with a spine of steel in most any situation. Didn't matter if Jordan was known to be a tough son of a bitch on the ice, Ryan was the one who managed to stay composed in the most stressful situations. Hell, even when his wife had left him high and dry with a little girl to take care of, Ryan's steadiness never cracked. Jordan admired the hell out of him.

"I'll be on the next flight home," Jordan repeated.

"What about your game schedule?"

"Fuck the game schedule. I'll see you tomorrow."
Hands shaking, Jordan disconnected the call and swallowed the nausea pooled in his throat. No doubt his brothers could take care of everything so he could focus on winning the Cup. But that silver trophy wouldn't mean shit if he abandoned them right now. He'd put his family in second place too many times in the past.

He didn't know if they really needed him, but he sure as hell needed them.

Beyond the swinging metal doors to the locker room the celebration commotion continued. But for Jordan, life as he knew it had vanished.

Chapter 2

Whoever said you can't go home again hit the nail dead nuts. In a house that had never quite felt like home, Jordan sat on the leather sofa in his parents' living room surrounded by those who shared his last name. The siblings he'd once lived and laughed with now seemed like distant relatives amid the suffocating grief and grave silence.

Their parents had been the glue that held the foundation of their family together, even if their footing had gotten a little shaky over the years. They'd been a loving, united front and always managed to put a shine on something that might seem a little tarnished. Knowing those who'd given him life would never be around again to share a moment or ask advice was unfathomable and created an ache so deep Jordan could barely breathe.

Tears burned his eyes as he lifted his gaze away from his clenched fists. Across the room, Declan, his fraternal twin—a multimillionaire workaholic—sat in a tufted leather chair poking away at his smartphone. As though Jordan had called his name, Dec looked up. Their eyes met briefly before Dec's brows pulled together and he returned his focus to the phone in his hand.

A hard knock rattled Jordan's rib cage.

Fraternal twins or not, they used to be as close as two brothers could ever be. Not that they possessed that weird twin thing where one instinctively sensed the other's emotions from miles away. But they'd been connected. Even back in the day when, late at night, they'd whisper their dreams and plan their lives, their differences became starkly apparent.

Declan had been the more cerebral, whereas Jordan had been the more physical. Not that Dec couldn't hold his own in a punching match. He could. And Jordan had often sported the black eye to prove it. Dec had always been a planner and he'd been determined to become successful at whatever he chose to do. He'd never been afraid to work hard for it either. Jordan admired his brother's success in the financial world. He gave great monetary advice and had always made Jordan a profitable return on his investments. But that personal link—that brotherly connection they'd shared—had long ago disappeared.

Jordan had only ever had one dream—playing hockey and winning the Stanley Cup. As a kid he'd had no idea of the sacrifices his parents would make for him to achieve that dream. He'd been too busy haunting the Philadelphia ice rinks where they'd lived and talking up the players to find out everything he could about the game. As soon as he'd learned to lace up his own skates, hockey became his life. That single-minded focus had pulled him further and further away from the brother with whom he'd shared the womb.

Slumped beside him on the sofa, with his dark hair in need of a decent cut and wearing a beard that hadn't seen a razor in months, sat Ethan, youngest of the five brothers. As a wildland firefighter, Ethan probably didn't need to look GQ on the job, but Jordan couldn't help teasing him anyway. That's what baby brothers were for.

"Forget where you put your razor?"

Ethan flashed a smile that never reached his eyes. "Don't own one."

"No shit? Aren't they afraid your face will catch fire when you're out battling those blazes?"

"Guess they're more worried about the destruction to the forests." Ethan shrugged. "Go figure."

Point taken.

So much for humor.

Ethan had a serious job that took him away from home for most of the year. Still, he exerted a hell of a lot more effort in staying in touch than Jordan.

Parker, fourth born in the crazy mix of testosterone that had rattled around under their roof, came into the room with a plate of snacks. Like Jordan himself, Parker had been a bit on the wild side. In his teens he'd been more trouble than their parents had been able to handle. Still, the folks hadn't given up on him. They knew he possessed the intelligence to accomplish whatever he wanted in life. But for many years he chose to throw it all away. He'd eventually been given a parental ultimatum—a challenge that had turned him into a successful and talented chef who owned one of the most prosperous food truck businesses in the Portland, Oregon, area.

While his younger brother held the plate in front of him, Jordan's mouth watered. The growl in his stomach reminded him that he hadn't eaten since yesterday.

"How the hell did you whip these up so fast?" Jordan asked as he snagged a chunk of bacon-wrapped pine-apple and popped it into his mouth.

"I won *Chopped* because I'm good and I'm fast," Parker boasted.

"Yeah, and your last girlfriend complained about that whole *fast* thing." Jordan couldn't resist giving his brother some shit. Truth was he was damn proud of what Parker had accomplished without asking for help from anyone.

"Fuck you." Parker's response came with a grin.

"Boys. Language."

Jordan looked across the room where their aunt Pippy gave them both the stink-eye. Quite an impressive feat when the woman wore more black eyeliner than Lady Gaga.

For whatever reason, their aunt had never quite moved on from the 1960s. She wore gobs of makeup, psychedelic colors, and gigantic earrings that could knock you out if they swung too hard in your direction. Her neon orange hair had been dyed within an inch of its life and teased into a style Jordan had only seen on nostalgic TV shows like *Rowan and Martin's Laugh-In*. She was the complete opposite of their conservative, serious-minded mother—Pippy's younger sister—but no one could argue that she was entertaining as hell.

Next to Pippy sat the only female brave enough to be born late into an all-boy family.

Nicole was an ethereal beauty loaded down with a typical rebellious seventeen-year-old girl attitude. For what it was worth, Nicki scared the shit out of him. Jordan wasn't used to her outbursts and temper tantrums. Hell, he wasn't used to *her* at all. He'd been sixteen years old when she'd been born and he'd barely been around in those days. For the most part he'd bounced back and forth from the East Coast to the West Coast playing hockey and living part-time with his uncle in Philly. Getting to know his infant sister hadn't been high on his to-do list.

Today, that rebellious teen was in tears and Jordan felt compelled to cross the room and offer comfort. His sister's blue-eyed scowl had been the only thing to stop him. For whatever reason, she made it clear he didn't top her list of favorite people.

Paybacks were a bitch.

When Aunt Pippy wrapped an arm around Nicki's shoulders, Jordan should have been relieved that someone was there for her. Instead he only swallowed another serving of guilt.

Absent from the room was Ryan's adorable young daughter, Riley. At only nine years old she'd suffered too many losses. The most devastating had come when her mother abandoned her for a career in Tinseltown. The former Laura Kincade's big claim to fame thus far had been a toilet paper commercial in which she looked into the camera, grinned, and breathlessly exclaimed, "It's deliciously soft." Jordan had never thought to associate toilet paper with *delicious* but they could have used a case of the stuff to clean up the shit storm Laura had left behind.

As a family the Kincades had moved to Washington State after their grandfather passed away and left their dad the vineyards. At least that's what the parents had said when they'd decided to rip their five boys away from their suburban Philadelphia home. Later it became clear the move had also been to get him and his brothers away from trouble. Seemed most of them had been good at that. All of them except Ryan, who'd always been mature and responsible beyond his years.

Jordan looked across the room where their oldest sibling and general manager of their family vineyards took the lead for the reading of their parents' will. Dark brows pulled tight over his trademark blue eyes, Ryan scanned the somber faces surrounding him.

"Aside from the circumstances, it's nice to have everyone together," Ryan said, his pained gaze dropping like a wrecking ball on Jordan's mountain of guilt. "I know Mom and Dad never shared much information on the state of the winery business. They figured you all had your own lives to live and didn't need to be worrying about the day-to-day goings-on here. You might have wondered and you might not. Either way, Mr. Anderson is here today to let us know their final wishes."

Their final wishes.

Jesus.

The knot in Jordan's stomach tightened over the bacon and pineapple appetizer he'd just devoured and made him queasy.

The short and stocky attorney stood and withdrew a stack of papers from the folder in his hands. He reminded Jordan of an older version of *Seinfeld*'s George Costanza. Unfortunately the man wasn't there to make jokes.

"Before I begin, I'd again like to express my condolences on your losses. I've known your parents for nearly twenty years. I respected and admired them. And I want you to know that if any of you have questions or concerns after today, please don't hesitate to pick up the phone."

Dread slithered up the back of Jordan's neck. If ever a stamp of finality to their parents' lives existed, the reading of the will would be it. He wasn't sure he was ready. Not because of the content, but because it truly verified the end. The enormity of the loss. The slap of reality that he'd never see his loving and supportive parents again.

The attorney read through the opening formalities in the document and then he adjusted his glasses and got down to the specifics. "Until she turns the age of eighteen, custody of Nicole Eloise Kincade is to be divided equally among her brothers. The vineyards, bed-and-breakfast, main house, and the complete property, which totals three hundred acres, are to be divided equally among Ryan Matthew, Jordan Daniel, Declan

Paul, Parker Gregory, Ethan Alexander, Nicole Eloise, and Riley Elizabeth Kincade. A lump sum of twenty-five thousand goes to your mother's sister, Penelope Margaret Everhart."

Aunt Pippy closed her eyes and bowed her head. Jordan didn't know if the emotion was from gratitude or a wave of overwhelming sadness.

The attorney cleared his throat and continued. "Regarding Sunshine Creek Vineyards, your parents requested that the property and its contents not be sold or any part be relinquished by any one party. It was their personal desire that the vineyard, in its entirety, remain in the hands of the Kincade family and be handed down to newer generations."

Like a storm cloud, silence hovered over the room as Ryan looked up, expression grim. "As much as I hate to ask . . . anyone want out?"

Across the room eyes met and darkened. Expressions remained solemn and unreadable.

Jordan swallowed hard.

As young kids, it had been all for one and one for all. Jordan had been the first to break that chain when he'd been drafted at the age of eighteen by the NHL and selfishly never looked back. His parents had always been encouraging, even when his visits home had become less and less frequent. Holidays had even become difficult. He hadn't made it home last Christmas because he'd had a game the following night. He remembered sitting in a hotel room, looking out the window at a snow-filled sky, thinking of his family gathered together around the tree, and feeling lonely.

The last time he'd actually seen his entire family had been before the season began last fall. Hockey game schedules were fast and frenetic. The season was long and grueling, with lots of travel involved. Still, he could have made the time and effort to come home. He hadn't and now questioned why. Had he just seen it as an inconvenience to fly coast to coast for a mere day or two? Or had he actually let the bonds with his family become less important than slapping a puck around the ice? It certainly wasn't a matter of finances. So deep down, what had really built that wall?

Family first.

Inside his head he heard his father's motto. The two simple words gripped his heart and wouldn't let go. Jordan believed he'd had perfect parents who had created a perfect marriage and a perfect family. Yet he'd let them all go, and now he felt like the stranger among them.

He glanced around the room to the clusters of framed images that told the story of who the Kincades were as a family. There were group photos of his parents, brothers, and sister at picnics among the grapevines or some other type of outdoor event. There were candid shots of his brothers grinning with their arms slung over each other's shoulders. There was a photo of his brothers playing tug-of-war with his laughing sister. And even more of Ryan with his daughter, Riley.

In each photo there were pairings or groupings of those Jordan should feel closest to. The only photo of him on display was from last year's team roster. The photo showed him sneering at the camera like he didn't

need anyone or anything in his life except the next
game, the next big win. It was the only photo in the
room with a single person in it. He blinked when he
realized how loudly it defined his life.

All the photos placed around the room showed his
family living life and having fun.

Without *him*.

His fault, not theirs.

Be careful what you wish for.

In that moment he realized what he'd missed and he
wanted it back.

"I'm in." He shot a glare around the room before
they scoffed. "It's what Mom and Dad would have
wanted. All of us together. Working to save what they
labored so hard to build. It's not fair for Ryan to try and
do this all on his own. He's a single dad with a little
girl to raise."

Yes, he'd been the worst about putting family first.
Hell, he'd never put anyone but himself in that top
position.

Right now his team was headed toward the playoffs without him. He'd never let his team down before.
He'd worked his ass off for years to win the Cup. But
he was thirty-three years old and for most of his life,
it had been all about him. All about hockey. All about
what *he* wanted, *he* needed, and *he* desired. He didn't
even know the other side of the coin. He didn't know
how to give unless there were skates on his feet and a
stick in his hand. He had a contract, and the team owner
and Coach Reiner expected him to return any day. The
team expected him back with his head in game-winning

condition. But right now all he wanted was to grieve his parents and reconnect with the people in this room.

"I'm in a hundred percent," he confirmed.

"We appreciate the sentiment, Jordy. And no offense, but your team is racking up the wins and it looks like they're headed to the playoffs." Ryan shrugged. "How can you be *in* with a schedule like that?"

Declan, Ethan, and Parker all shot him looks of doubt. Aunt Pippy sighed. Nicole glared. The attorney suddenly found the papers in his hand fascinating.

"I'll work it out."

Getting back in his family's good graces was all that mattered. Right now he couldn't pinpoint the moment or exact reason he'd backed off. Hopefully he'd have plenty of time to figure it out and correct the error of his ways.

He clasped his hands together, dropped them between his knees, and looked his wary family in the eye. "All I need is a chance."

When the drizzling rain stopped, Jordan stepped outside onto the large stone deck lined with potted plants and trailing flowers that overlooked the acres of sprouting grapevines. Once the fruit ripened they'd create the flavorful white and rich red wines his father had designed.

As a young man, Jordan hadn't been the least bit interested in how the wines were made. Yet his father had insisted that Jordan see and understand the things his grandfather had created. To know the hard work that had been put into the beginnings of something meant for generations of their family to appreciate.

Jordan realized now what his father had been trying to tell him. To teach him. And he'd let the importance slip away.

Never again.

Around him the vibrant green rolling hills merged with the meandering creek in a tranquil scene that brought a calm to his soul. When this place had belonged to his grandfather it had been modest. Nothing fancy. More like hippieville than a real business.

Jordan breathed in the fresh, rain-scented air, surprised when memories sprang up and a sting of misplaced jealousy stabbed through him.

Before he could dwell on it, the French doors opened and Ryan stepped out onto the patio carrying two glasses of wine. He set them on a nearby table and grabbed Jordan in a bear hug.

"Damn, it's good to have you home."

Immense pleasure from his brother's powerful embrace surrounded Jordan like a warm security blanket.

"It's good to be home."

"Those brothers of ours can't play hoops worth a shit. At least while you're here tell me we'll play a game or two and wipe the court with them."

"Done."

The backslapping ended and Ryan picked up the glasses. "Try this." He handed Jordan a glass of deep red wine.

"What is it?"

"Euphoria. The Cabernet Syrah Dad's been working on perfecting over the last couple of years."

Jordan's throat tightened as he held the glass up to the light. Swirled, sniffed, then sipped. "Nice notes of vanilla and chocolate."

"Yeah. It's almost there." Ryan drank from his own glass. "Still had too much of a peppery taste for Dad's liking."

"I'm sure you'll get it figured out." Jordan looked out over the property again and that sting of misplaced jealousy struck again. "Do you remember when we used to spend summer vacations here?"

"Yeah." Ryan chuckled. "I figure we climbed about half of these trees."

"At least." Jordan sipped the wine. "I remember hiking through the forest, wading through the creek, and pretending we were worldly explorers."

"Bunch of dumb kids is what we were." Ryan turned and leaned back against the stone fence. "You remember that rickety wire net we begged Grandpa to nail up to the side of the old barn so we could play hoops?"

"I remember being the only one tall enough to get anywhere near making a basket." Jordan squinted against the sunshine that suddenly peeked out from behind a fat gray cloud. "And I remember the campfires we built on the banks of the creek so we could toast marshmallows."

"Damn near burned down the forest a time or two."

"Remember when Grandma came out swinging her rolling pin at us, then made Grandpa finally teach us how to build a safe fire?"

They both laughed at the vision of their grandmother in her calico dress, apron, and sneakers.

"The thing I remember most about Grandma was

her waffles and blackberry syrup," Ryan said. "And the linen closet she'd clear out so we could build tents with her sheets and sleep out beneath the stars."

Jordan smiled and nodded. "And the ghost stories."

"Ah, damn." Ryan grinned. "I forgot about those. 'Bout scared the hell out of Ethan a time or two."

"It was a great way to spend a summer."

Until for Jordan, one day the fun had stopped and the work began.

While his brothers continued to spend weeks away from the suffocating Philly heat and humidity, he'd stayed behind to attend hockey camps. From the moment he'd turned thirteen, his summers had meant waking up at the crack of dawn and hitting the ice to accomplish his dream. Back then he'd never given a second thought to the fact that his brothers all remained together those summers, bonding, while he became a solitary and detached man.

Caught up in the day-to-day survival of the NHL, he'd never given much thought to the consequences of his dream or his actions. Hell, for fifteen years he'd never considered what he'd do after hockey. He'd never given a thought to where he'd live or what he'd do with so much time on his hands. God knew, thanks to the hefty paycheck he brought in and his financial whiz brother, he had plenty of money to do whatever he wanted and never work another day again in his life. But then what?

If he wasn't a hockey player, what was he?

If he wasn't a brother, *who* was he?

"I miss those days," he said.

"Yeah." Ryan drained his glass. "Good times. Is that what you were out here contemplating?"

"Naw. Mostly I was thinking about the multiple ways I've fucked up," Jordan answered honestly.

"How's that?"

"I walked away from all this." He waved his empty glass at their surroundings. "From all of you. Guess I've had my head up my ass for a long time."

Though Jordan was an inch taller and a foot wider than his big brother, Ryan smacked the back of his head.

"Ow!"

"You don't get to feel sorry for yourself."

"I'm not. I'm just sorry that I missed out on so much. Hell, I barely even know our sister. She looks at me like I've got two fire-breathing heads. I don't know what kind of music she likes. Or if she has a boyfriend. Or even if she gets good grades."

"Currently she doesn't."

"That sucks."

"Yeah. I can't imagine losing Mom and Dad are going to help her any," Ryan said. "She was pretty much Mom's little princess. Got everything she ever wanted except . . ."

"Except . . . ?"

"Dad's attention."

"You're kidding, right? After five boys you'd think Dad would have finally gotten what he wanted."

"I think Mom got what *she* wanted."

Jordan's head snapped up and he studied the grim look on his brother's face. "What the hell do you mean by that?"

"I don't want to get into this right now. We just buried our parents. It's not the right time or place." Ryan shook his head, then leaned his forearms on the railing and looked out over the vineyard. "Might never be."

"Not fair, Ryan. If you know something, you should share."

"I don't know anything. Just going by my gut."

"Well if your gut is grumbling about something other than Parker's appetizers, then you should definitely spill."

Ryan turned his head and looked Jordan in the eye. "Are you serious about being *in* to this whole thing a hundred percent?"

"I'm many things, but never a liar," Jordan said, knowing he couldn't get pissed about his brother asking such a question or doubting him.

"What about your career?"

Jordan shrugged. "I'll figure it out."

"Good to know. Because Nicki's going to need some guidance. Not that I don't love her and not that she isn't important, but I've got my hands full with business and dealing with Riley. She's devastated about losing her grandparents and she needs all my focus and attention right now."

"I can imagine." Jordan figured after being abandoned by her mother, little Riley didn't take losing people lightly.

"If you're truly going to stick around for a while . . ." Ryan reached into his back pocket, pulled out a folded piece of paper, and handed it to Jordan. "How about you be a good brother and handle this."

"What is it?"

"A good time guaranteed." Ryan touched two fingers to his forehead in a salute. "If you need me, I'll be at the office."

Jordan set his empty wineglass down on the patio railing, unfolded the note, and began to read.

"No. Fucking. Way."

Chapter 3

*F*or the second time in a matter of minutes, Lucy Diamond nudged the pencil holder on her desk a micro millimeter to the left. The movement was so infinitesimal no one except her would ever notice. She swept her hands across the ink blotter that covered the battered desktop, then settled a thick file folder in the middle. With a sigh, she flipped open the binder and reread the entry on the top page.

Most students took Lucy's creative writing class in their senior year because they thought it would be an easy A grade. A fun class where you didn't have to work hard or study things like frog guts or whether two circles both of radii 6 had exactly one point in common. No homework. Easy assignments.

And they were right.

For the most part it *was* a fun class, but during the three years Lucy had taught at Sunshine Valley High, her students had continuously been disappointed to realize it wasn't an easy A. And yes, there was homework.

Seventeen-year-old Nicole Kincade was a prime example of a brilliant mind with crappy follow-through. The girl had potential most didn't discover until their later years. But it seemed lately that Nicole was more distracted than ever. Quiet. Despondent. Teenagers were often moody and withdrawn, but when a normally bubbly, outgoing girl suddenly became introverted and sullen, red flags started waving. Lucy genuinely cared about the girl, thus the reason she'd put in the call to Nicole's parents.

Mrs. Kincade had informed Lucy that she and her husband were about to leave for a Hawaiian vacation, so she'd made an appointment to conference when they returned.

But they weren't coming back.

And that changed everything.

Lucy's heart broke for the family. Even more for Nicole, who'd already been living deep in a well of teenage angst.

A few days after Nicole's parents' funeral might seem the wrong time to discuss the future of her education, but Lucy believed it was important. Nicole was important. And finding out the reason behind her behavioral change was vital. Lucy was thankful and relieved to know that Ryan, the oldest of the Kincade brothers, intended to follow through with the meeting even though his burdens and grief must be overwhelming right now.

A quick glance at the clock told Lucy he was late,

but due to the nature of the situation she didn't mind. She'd wait until however long it took for him to show. To pass the time she got up and walked around the room, nudging the whiteboard eraser into place, straightening the books on a shelf, anything to keep her busy until the single dad, who now was most likely Nicole's legal guardian, arrived.

Behind her the door creaked open.

She turned with a smile that immediately faltered when she found not Ryan, but Jordan Kincade, standing in the doorway to her classroom, wearing dark sunglasses, a black leather jacket, a gray chest-hugging T-shirt, and jeans. At least a day's worth of scruff darkened his strong jawline, and the man looked like he should either be on the cover of *Badass* magazine or starring in a woman's fantasy.

An army of unwanted memories marched up the back of her neck. She pushed her glasses a little higher on her nose and breathed deep to calm the sudden onslaught of nerves.

The last time she'd seen the man he'd been a boy. A really cute boy who'd been nice to her, had even flirted with her a little, and then had rendered her speechless when during one of their tutoring sessions he'd asked her to the after-graduation dance. Of course she'd immediately turned him down because no way had he been serious.

Throughout high school she'd never had a boy ask her out. They'd barely even looked at her. She'd never gone to a dance. Heck, she hadn't even known *how* to dance.

Thanks to her father's inglorious swan dive into a never-ending bottle of cheap whiskey and her mother's choice to follow, Lucy didn't openly trust people back in those days. Her parents had given up on life and given up on her. Their lack of interest and constant berating hadn't served well as a confidence builder. Instead of each other, they targeted her with their ugly, slurred remarks. To survive she'd become a stealth ninja in the art of being invisible.

Invisibility offered her protection from the vicious words and heartache that often kept her awake at night. It made the mean girls at school look the other way. When someone else became their victim, Lucy felt a slap of cowardly guilt because she was thankful that at least it hadn't been her.

So for someone as good-looking and popular as Jordan Kincade to ask *her* to the dance when he could have had any girl in the entire school didn't make sense. It had to have been a trick.

Stubborn to the bone, he hadn't accepted her rejection.

He'd asked her again and again, flashing her a smile so honest and sincere she'd finally chosen to climb out of her cocoon and pretend she could be like any of those other girls. She wanted to believe that he could really see beyond her average looks, her thick glasses, and her thrift store clothes. She'd wanted to trust that he truly wanted to be with *her*. Not Priscilla O'Neal, who wore the newest fashions and had the ta-tas to fill out her tight-fitting blouses. Not Amy Henderson, who had a quick smile to match her fast reputation. And not

Leslie Meyer, who was gorgeous and was actually very kind.

After Lucy finally accepted his invitation she'd been so excited she hadn't been able to sleep. She'd broken into her college savings and bought a brand-new dress for the dance. She'd had her hair professionally cut and styled, and she'd learned how to apply makeup without looking like a streetwalker.

During the graduation ceremony, which her parents had been too drunk to attend, Jordan had caught her eye several times and given her a smile that had sent a crazy spiral of happy through her heart. After the ceremony ended she rushed home to get ready for the dance.

He never showed up.

Wearing the pretty blue dress she'd spent hours selecting, she'd sat in her room until midnight. Waiting. Wondering what she'd done wrong. Wondering if his invitation had just been a cruel prank. Feeling miserable in her teenage heart that she could so easily be disregarded. Feeling sad that Jordan Kincade had disappointed her by being just like all the rest.

Above all, she'd felt stupid for falling into the trap.

Sure, she knew her place in the school hierarchy. She was the quiet, smart girl everyone needed as a tutor but no boy wanted to kiss. She wore glasses, a ponytail of mousy brown hair, and an ever-present backpack of books slung over her shoulders. At the time she'd been more concerned with studying her way out of her living situation than she'd been with catching anyone's eye.

Some things never changed.

She still preferred glasses to contacts, felt more comfortable pulling her now red and gold highlighted hair back in a ponytail or messy bun, and opted for her trusty Keds over classic pumps. But today, she was a different person. Stronger because of the things she'd lived through. Smarter because she'd found a way to survive and come out the other side in a happy place. She knew *exactly* where she belonged, and that was teaching and helping students like Nicki. Which was why, right now, she was going to pull on her big girl panties and face the boy who had disappointed her head-on.

Lucy managed to pull herself together as Jordan removed his sunglasses and slid them to the top of his head. His smile lifted a masculine pair of lips that somehow managed to look cruel and sexy at the same time.

The boy had turned into a man times ten.

Tall and broad-shouldered, he had a chest that looked a mile wide. Judging by the smooth ripples beneath his snug shirt he was packing muscle, not pounds. Jeans, worn and frayed at the stress points, accented his long muscular legs and trim waist. His longish, nearly black hair gleamed beneath the overhead lights. And his sharp blue eyes focused intently on her.

It was all she could do to keep her heart at a normal pace and her legs solidly beneath her. If ever a man could be described as *delicious*, Jordan Kincade would be a menu's specialty of the day.

Too bad he was such a jerk.

"Ms. Diamond?" He came forward and stretched out his very large hand. "Jordan Kincade."

And clearly he didn't remember her.

Lucy smiled as a funny little tickle moved through her chest. Maybe this was going to be fun after all. Rarely was she ever given the upper hand or the opportunity to have even the slightest edge.

When he moved closer his warm palm engulfed hers, and her triumph died with a sizzle.

Close up she got a better look. She inhaled his sexy scent of worn leather and warm man. Every square inch of her female DNA perked up like it was party time. She hated to disappoint the little darlings but today was all about helping someone else.

"Please." She kept the handshake brief and formal before she disengaged and motioned toward the chair in front of her desk. "Have a seat."

He glanced at the standard school chair with a you've-got-to-be-kidding-me lift of his brows. When he sat down, the orange plastic chair creaked and seemed ridiculously small beneath the scope of his height and muscles.

Lucy took her own seat and noticed that the difference in chairs made her tower over him and seemingly give her another advantage. But when he leaned back and crossed an ankle over a knee, he appeared completely comfortable.

So much for one-upmanship.

"I apologize if I seemed taken aback just now." She opened the folder and pulled out Nicole's progress report as well as several exams and the few assignments Nicole had actually turned in. Late, of course, but complete nonetheless. "I expected your brother Ryan."

"He had business at the vineyard and sends his regrets."

She couldn't help noticing how very deep and smooth his voice had become. Like hot buttered rum on a cold winter night. He had the kind of voice a woman could imagine whispering sweet nothings in her ear while he caressed her in places that tingled beneath his touch.

"I understand." Snapping out of the fantasy, she imagined the enormous scope of duties Ryan Kincade must need to tend to after the death of their parents. Her heart sank a little further for the family. Especially for Nicole, who was so young and really needed the love and guidance of her mom and dad. "I hope you'll accept my condolences. And I sincerely apologize for having you come down at this sorrowful time to deal with what might seem insignificant but—"

"Anything regarding my sister is important, Ms. Diamond. Now more than ever." His brows dipped in a no-nonsense fashion. "So don't judge me when you don't even know me."

Oh, she knew him.

Knew he was the type who'd make a promise, then shatter it without ever looking back.

But that was then, and this was now.

"My apologies, Mr. Kincade. That was certainly not my intent."

His piercing eyes perused her face for a long, uncomfortable moment and she had to admit that the look did something funny to the beat of her heart.

Especially when with a slight tilt of his head he asked, "Why do you look so familiar?"

"Do I?" That erratic heartbeat kicked up another notch as she let go a chuckle to cover up what was really going on inside. "People say that all the time. I guess I just have one of those faces."

She pushed Nicole's schoolwork in his direction. "If you'll take a look at these projects, you'll see that even though she didn't complete the assignment exactly as it was defined, Nicole has an enormous gift."

"I'm pretty sure that's a lie."

"Excuse me?" Irritated, Lucy's gaze shot up to the slight smile curling his lips. "How can you say that without even reading anything? I guarantee your sister has a multitude of talent."

"I'm not talking about my sister's work. I'm talking about *you* just having 'one of those faces.'" He uncrossed his long, muscular legs and leaned forward without even looking at the papers she'd put in front of him. "So now I'm wondering why you sidestepped my question."

Good God, the man was intense. There was something in the combination of that nearly black hair that fell over his ears and his nape in perfect waves and those deep blue eyes that seemed almost otherworldly. She could imagine how he'd intimidate an opponent on the ice.

And it had nothing to do with his size.

But as far as admitting who she really was? Not going to happen. No need to dredge up a bad memory when all she really wanted was to help his sister.

"I apologize." Her heart beat erratically as she avoided the intensity of his gaze. "But I would like to stick to the subject of your sister's grades—or lack thereof—that may prevent her from graduating with the rest of her class. I genuinely care about her, which is why I noticed a problem way before the loss of your parents."

"And now you won't even look at me," he said. "Why is that?"

As he leaned in, his intoxicating scent came with him. Normally such things didn't affect her. Well, at least not with her colleagues, who tended to wear either too much aftershave or worse, too much body odor. Jordan wore his masculine scent like a sexual promise, and Lucy swore he should come with a warning label.

But back to business.

"In this assignment"—she pointed to the paper on top of the stack—"the class was asked to write their favorite childhood memory. Instead Nicole chose to write a review for a rerun of *Pretty Little Liars*. The review was entertaining, but that wasn't what she'd been asked to do. And I can't grade her on a movie review."

"Why not?"

Without thinking, her gaze shot upward and caught the hint of humor in his eyes. She was trying so hard to keep it together, when having the man so close was like having a buffet of tasty desserts spread out before her and each one was tagged with a "Do Not Touch" label.

"Because it wouldn't be fair to the rest of the class who'd done the assignment properly."

One corner of his sexy mouth tipped upward. "Maybe she didn't understand the assignment."

"She understood it perfectly." Was that a scar just above his right eyebrow? She wondered if he'd received that from a hockey stick, or maybe a lover in the heat of passion had cut it with the ring on her finger. Maybe he was married and his poor wife had caught him with another woman or . . .

"Ms. Diamond?"

"Hmmm?" Her gaze dropped back down to his eyes, and the captivating glint she found there suggested he'd caught her daydreaming.

"I asked if there was any chance Nicole could redo the assignment for a grade."

"Oh." She smoothed her hands over the folder, giving herself a moment to pull herself together. "Of course. And I actually asked her to do just that. But then . . ."

"Our parents were killed."

"Yes." Lucy sucked in a lungful of air. "I feel just horrible about discussing this right now. And I'm willing to let Nicole take as long as she needs to redo the assignments."

"But?"

"But she needs to do them before grading for the quarter ends. And I fear that, because of her situation on top of whatever was undoubtedly already bothering her, she won't."

"Are there any other options?"

"She could repeat the class in summer school. But that would mean she wouldn't receive her diploma with everyone else."

"I'm a little confused." Those huge hands lifted like he was at a complete loss when she thought she was making herself perfectly clear. "This is my first time dealing with someone such as yourself."

Exactly what did he mean by *that*?

"Excuse me?"

"I mean, you say you care about Nicole. You say you don't want to see her fail yet you also don't seem open to giving her an opportunity not to fail." He flashed a smile meant to disarm her.

How could a man appear so charming while delivering such an outrageous insult?

"Mr. Kincade, I hope you're not insinuating I should falsify Nicole's grades just so she can graduate. My goal is to teach, not to help a student learn to cheat the system. I believe that anyone who is given the opportunity for an education has the responsibility to succeed or fail all on their own. The state requires specific criteria to obtain a high school diploma. I have no control over that. And as much as I want Nicole to succeed, I can't and won't lie for her. However, I can and *will* do whatever is in my power to help her."

"Are you sure you didn't call this meeting with the hopes of getting my good-looking, single brother down here with an ulterior motive?" That dark brow lifted again and Lucy had to curl her fingers into her palms to keep from knocking him into tomorrow.

"Why, Mr. Kincade." She flashed him a disingenuous smile. "If you believe that, then you've taken too many hits to the head. And if that's the situation I can recommend a good doctor."

A laugh rumbled deep in his muscular chest. "I like a woman who speaks her mind."

"Yes. I'm sure that's different for you."

Another chuckle rumbled. "Meaning?"

"Meaning, unless someone has been living under a rock, your conquests are no secret to anyone who reads the trash magazines in the checkout line at the grocery store."

"And are you in the percentage of those who judge a book by its cover?"

"Meaning?"

"Meaning you don't believe any of those women have a thought in their pretty heads."

"I'm not a snob, Mr. Kincade. And I believe quite the opposite. Women like that are usually too smart to bite the hand that feeds them. Therefore vocalizing their thoughts can lead to disaster and disappointment."

"Are you flirting with me, Ms. Diamond?"

"*Flirting!*" And how the heck had he soared to that conclusion?

"Maybe it was your intent all along to lure *me* here."

She laughed. Snorted actually. The man might be gorgeous, but he bordered on ludicrous and delusional.

"How could I have possibly known *you* would come to this meeting? For your information, the original consultation was arranged with your mother."

His smile faltered and Lucy was immediately deluged with guilt for mentioning the poor woman.

"We seem to have gotten way off track, Mr. Kincade." While he again appeared to relax, she took a brief moment to catch her breath and grasp the real reason they were both in the same room again after fifteen years. It was her good fortune he didn't recognize her.

Because she wasn't entirely sure he couldn't see the effect he had on her. And that could spell disaster for poor Nicole. "If Nicole will redo the assignments I'll be happy to give her extra credit work."

"Is that all you can do to help my sister, *Ms. Diamond*?" He leaned back in the chair and casually folded his hands together.

Lucy hated when someone pushed her to her limit. Jordan had pushed beyond and blasted into Holy Shitville. Though the circumstances with the death of his parents never left her mind, she had to call it like she saw it.

"Let me ask you this, Mr. Kincade. What are *you* willing to do to help your sister?"

"What?"

Yeah. Gotcha, buster.

"You question my intentions and accuse me of making a play for your brother—or you—but let's be honest," she said in an amazingly cool tone. "Maybe you're not really the right person to deal with Nicole's problems."

His eyes narrowed just enough to let Lucy know she'd hit a nerve. Lucy folded her arms, steeling herself against the possibility of an explosion. "In fact, do you really even know her?"

"Of course I know her." His jaw clenched. "She's my sister."

"Is that so? Then who's her best friend?" Lucy asked.

"Her—"

"What's her favorite color?"

"She's—"

"What does she like on her pizza?"

"For—"

"Who's her latest crush?"

His hands curled into fists. "Are you going to let me answer?"

"Be my guest." Lucy leaned back in her chair and waited. Due to the current circumstances she hated to point out the obvious, but her main concern had to remain with Nicole. If he genuinely wanted to help, Lucy was prepared to do what needed to be done. But if his only plan was to march in here, make demands and accusations, and then go back to his life status quo, that wouldn't fly. She wouldn't bail on a young girl in need. Teenagers dealing with depression often took drastic measures, and Lucy had to do whatever she could to save this girl.

Seconds ticked by without Jordan's response. She could see him mentally grasping at straws.

She'd made him sweat.

Made him think.

Now it was time to throw out the life preserver.

"I understand you probably have a very busy life," she said in her most understanding tone. "One that hasn't allowed much time for getting to know all of Nicole's likes and dislikes. But I really am very concerned for her. This problem didn't just begin. It's been brewing for a while. I promise I'll do whatever I can to help find out the cause and do my best to get her back on track. I will stand by her and I will let her know she can trust me and feel free to discuss any matter with me."

This time his smile came with a sigh of relief.

After all these years and all she'd been through,

Lucy really thought she'd be immune to someone like him. She'd learned her lesson, right? But something inside told her Jordan Kincade might very well be swimming in the same deep waters as his sister. And that concerned Lucy even more.

"You're a very generous woman."

"Thank you."

He stood as if to leave.

"Thank you for coming," she said. "And since you probably need to get back to your job, have your brother contact me next week and I'll give him an update."

"I'm in town for a few more days, so I'll have a talk with my sister." He settled his big hand right next to where her arm rested on the desktop. When he leaned that six-foot-plus body down so they were nearly face-to-face, a spiral of heat shot right through her core.

Get it together, Lucy.

A flicker of something flashed in his eyes.

"As for you and me, *Lucinda*?" One dark slash of brow lifted. "I don't think we're done at all. So you can stop acting like we've never met."

The acknowledgment hit her with a jolt, and a gasp snuck from her throat before she could stop it.

"But we'll leave that conversation for another day. Because, as you said, today is about my sister." His deep blue eyes scanned her face one more time before he walked out the door.

Fifteen years ago, Lucy believed she'd washed the man out of her thoughts. Out of her fantasies. Out of her life.

Clearly she'd been wrong.

Chapter 4

Life definitely had a way of biting you in the ass. In that department, Jordan had been batting a thousand.

Not that treading deep water was new to him. Hell no. For the most part he had a tendency to put himself right in the middle of the shit storm. Anyone who questioned his talent in that direction could reference the 220 penalty minutes he'd already racked up this season. But those were game stats, and though those minutes gave the opposition power play advantages, he'd always found a way to come back in the game and score.

Making amends in real life wasn't so easy.

Lucinda Nutter.

Holy shit.

He didn't know what the whole "Diamond" thing was about, but hopefully he'd have plenty of time to find out. He hadn't been around much in his teen years because he'd spent a great portion of his time on the East Coast playing for minor league teams. Somehow during his senior year he'd been around long enough to make friends and play other sports. With the NHL on his radar, he hadn't been the best student. Which was why he'd taken it upon himself to hire someone to tutor him in the classes where he struggled.

And that was when he'd met Lucinda Nutter.

Today, sitting across the desk from *Ms. Diamond*, he'd tried to place the face that looked so familiar. Initially he couldn't recall anyone with that last name. Her refusal to acknowledge their acquaintance had piqued his interest enough for him to study her as he would an opponent.

There'd been something familiar in the flash of gold that lit up her dark brown eyes behind those glasses. Something in the tone of her voice. It hadn't been until she'd snagged her full bottom lip between her teeth and a dimple appeared in her right cheek that recognition dawned.

Ms. Diamond wasn't just a pretty package hiding behind a staid white blouse, black skirt, white sneakers, and dark-framed glasses. She wasn't just his little sister's creative writing teacher. She was Lucinda Nutter—the girl he'd stood up the night of their high school graduation.

No wonder she'd refused to acknowledge him.

Not that he'd been any prize back in those days, but she must have been crushed that night when he didn't show. Especially since he'd had to ask her several times before she'd agree to go out with him. The following day he'd tried to contact her to explain and apologize. Not surprisingly, she'd refused his calls.

He could hardly blame her.

He'd felt bad because he'd genuinely liked her. Lucinda had been able to hold her own in a conversation. She'd been smart, sweet, and honest. He always got the sense that she believed she didn't belong, and maybe that, more than anything, had been what connected him to her. With all the traveling he did and being away from his family so much, he didn't feel like he belonged either. To his surprise he'd found he'd rather hang out with her in the library on a Friday night than with a bunch of buddies looking for trouble.

But then he'd thrown it all away.

After several unsuccessful tries to apologize to her, he'd given up. At the time he'd been a selfish bastard solely focused on the NHL. Hell. He still was. But he'd been worse back then. He'd been trying to prove himself to those he thought mattered—the team owners and coaches. The moment he'd been drafted by the Chicago Blackhawks at eighteen years old, he'd forgotten all about her. He'd moved on to scoring goals, making money, and bedding hot women.

The sudden and horrific loss of his parents had shifted the order of everything. He hadn't been blowing smoke when he'd told his family he was all in. For the first time in his life he needed something more than the glory of slapping the puck between the pipes and the roar of the crowd. For the first time he felt the need to be more than part of a team that went their separate ways after the arena lights shut down.

He needed to be a part of his family.

Running into Lucinda solidified the necessity of

righting his wrongs. Unfamiliar territory, to be sure, but one he was willing to make happen. He believed in second chances. Hell, he'd been given more than that during his career. Now he had to make the most of the opportunity he'd been given, no matter in what ugly manner it had come. It was too late to make it up to his mom and dad, but there were still five siblings he could beg for mercy.

And there was Lucinda, who no doubt might be his toughest critic.

As he drove out of the high school parking lot and turned the rented Lincoln Navigator onto Main Street, he noticed there were still no big box stores in Sunshine. No one-stop shopping conveniences. Instead, time had pretty much stood still. As it had been when he'd been a kid, mom-and-pop businesses and cozy boutiques ruled both sides of the tree-lined road. A great majority of those shops were food-related, which didn't help the rumbling in his empty stomach.

Back in the day his parents hadn't been able to afford much in the way of dining in fancy restaurants. Which worked fine for the town of Sunshine, because at the time the most extravagant had been Ben's Burger Barn, a red-striped operation that touted twofer Tuesdays and all-you-can-eat fried clams on Fridays.

These days a place called Cranky Hank's Smokehouse sat in the old Burger Barn location, and the red striped exterior had given over to a rustic wood siding. Next to that sat Grandma Daisy's Pie Company, where a sandwich board on the sidewalk announced the specialty of the day was cranberry-pear tarts. From his left, the mouthwatering aroma of warm cinnamon rolls drifted from Sugarbuns Bakery.

Jordan remembered the birthday cakes his mother had brought home from the pastel pink building and the sugary rewards he and his brothers had received when they'd bring home a good report card. Straight ahead, the Milky Way Moose professed to have the smoothest chocolate in the Pacific Northwest. Jordan thought if he actually strolled down this street he'd probably gain ten pounds.

A little farther down Main Street, the Back Door Bookstore took up the small space at the corner of Main and Burgundy and sat next door to the local newspaper, *Talk of the Town*, while Sunshine Gifts and Treasures took up residence in the old Laundromat building. Above the store there was still the vintage Maytag Laundry sign with the figure of a washer-woman scrubbing clothes on an old washboard. Divine Wine and Beyond the Vineyards had tasting rooms located directly across the street from each other, like gunslingers ready to draw on the first patron to cross the sidewalk.

The building designs were a crazy mix of Cape Cod and Old West, with a little New Age thrown in to keep things really interesting.

If he continued farther he knew he'd come to the city park that ran along the shoreline of the Columbia River—a perfect place for wind sailing. And across the iron bridge was a new eighteen-hole golf course.

Surrounded by rugged mountains and rolling hills, the town was pretty and welcoming. Still, as a teenager there hadn't been much to do in a place with the population of roughly eight thousand souls. In those days Sunshine had been just a speck on the map on the way to Vancouver or Portland. Now the town operated as a tourist destination with a few first-class restaurants and elegant spas for couples to come for a weekend, relax, and get away from the grind of the big city.

The last of the shops on Main Street was Kid's Station School Supplies, which brought back one single thought.

Lucinda Nutter.

Holy shit.

As a precaution, Jordan headed to the baby dragon's lair armed with a bag of sweets from Sugarbuns. He knocked on Nicole's door and got no response.

Big surprise.

As much as everything inside him just wanted to shake some sense into her, he wanted this discussion to go well. Wanted to handle it right. Wanted his sister to know she could count on him and that he had her best interest at heart. Then again, he'd never done anything of this magnitude before, so who the hell knew how it would really go.

Hoping to keep his temper in check, he knocked again and waited for the delayed, grumbled acknowledgment before he turned the knob and entered Nicole's girly haven. Walls of deep purple could have been depressing were it not for the white iron bed covered with a black and white print comforter. A crystal chandelier

hung above the bed, and prisms of colored light sparkled on the white ceiling. All accents in the room were
either lace, feathered, or sparkly.

On the white Provincial dresser were perfume bottles
labeled "Pink" and "Juicy." Two words a brother *never*
wanted to put together when it came to his baby sister.

Everything in Nicole's room indicated that as the
only daughter and the youngest in the family, she was
probably a bit on the spoiled side. Still, she was a young
girl who'd just lost both her parents. And as much as
the son of those parents wanted to hide away to grieve,
life still needed to be reckoned with.

"What do *you* want?"

Well, that was hardly the greeting he'd hoped for.

Stretched out on her bed with her feet on the wall
above her headboard, Nicole tapped frantically on her
glittery pink smartphone. No doubt she was looking
for a rescue from having to talk with the dreaded big
brother.

"I brought you cookies." He held up the bag, not that
she was looking to notice.

"Seriously?" She huffed, still not looking at him.
"You think I'll fit into my skinny jeans if I eat that
garbage?"

"I think you look fine. And a cookie now and then
isn't going to kill you." He reached into the bag and
pulled out a lemon-frosted sugar cookie, hoping to
entice her. "Look, they're not very big. Try one."

"I'm not touching that after you've had your fingers
all over it." She finally sat up. Unfortunately it was to
turn her back on him and keep texting.

"Nicki. Could you please turn around so we can talk?"

"Nothing to say."

Accustomed to handling loud, obnoxious hockey players but highly unused to dealing with teenage girls in a snit, he wanted to groan.

Loudly.

"There's plenty to say." He bit into the cookie. "And these are really good. You're missing out."

She made a noise that fell somewhere between a scoff and a sniff.

Late afternoon sun beamed through the lace-covered window and danced across her long dark chocolate curls. The stiffness in her shoulders might have frightened weaker men, but Jordan faced two-hundred-pound sneering opponents on a daily basis. One little bit of a girl wasn't going to scare him away.

"I'm trying to be nice here."

"Why?" She spun around; narrowed those dark blue eyes that snapped with anger, hurt, and confusion; and aimed her daggers in his direction. "Everyone knows you're leaving, so why bother?"

Whoa.

Tempted to take a step back from the force of her anger, he did just the opposite and stepped forward. "In case you didn't hear me, I said I was all in."

"For as long as it gets you what you want. Then you're gone. You're always gone." Her eyes narrowed again. "You don't belong here. So why don't you just get the hell out now?"

Instead of turning her back on him as he'd expected,

she glared so hard it burned a hole right through the center of his heart.

He had no experience at this kind of thing. This was something his mom and dad excelled at. They'd had six kids to practice on. They'd put their hearts and souls into always doing the right thing, making good points, and practicing what they preached. Jordan had none of the above. And unless angels came down from heaven to help him out, he was flying blind on this one.

"I'm not going anywhere." He pulled out the chair tucked beneath her vanity, spun it around, and straddled it backward. He folded his arms across the back and tried to soften the hard features he used to intimidate an adversary on the ice. "I understand you're hurt right now and probably a little scared too. Losing Mom and Dad has knocked the wind out of all of us. But I'm not the enemy, Nicki. I'm your brother and I care about you."

"Bullshit."

How was it that one little slip of a girl could hit so hard with only words?

"It's true. I'm sorry I haven't been around. That's all on me. And I know I'm the one who has to make changes. But you've got to give me the opportunity to make them."

"I don't have to do anything. You already proved yourself the last seventeen years of my life." She folded her arms and glared at him as though daring him to prove her wrong.

He couldn't.

"You're right."

She blinked.

Yeah, that one took her back a step.

"I've been a bad brother." He shrugged. "I figured you had Mom and Dad and plenty of other brothers and you wouldn't miss me."

"You don't know jack about what goes on around here." Dark, arched brows pulled together over her red-rimmed eyes. "And by the way, if you're trying to convince me you're suddenly a good guy, that's not saying much for yourself."

"I'm not trying to convince you of anything. But one thing you'll learn about me is that I don't lie. It's a complete waste of time. When I've screwed up, I'll be the first one to admit it."

He didn't take her silence for submission. More than likely she was just loading up on more ammo to shoot in his direction.

"I talked to your teacher today."

"Which one. I've got seven. But then you wouldn't know that, would you. Because you haven't been home for almost a year."

"I get it, Nicole." His hands tightened on the back of the chair. "I've been a bad brother. I haven't been home for almost a year and you hate me. The problem is, none of that negative energy is going to help your grades or help you graduate with the rest of your class. So how about we save the I-hate-my-brother venom for later and move the discussion to why it is you don't do your assignments? Or better yet, let's talk about why you choose to put the effort into whatever the hell you want to write about instead of what everyone else is doing?"

"Because everyone else is doing the same boring thing."

"And you don't want to be like everybody else?"

She gave him a look that silently screamed, *Duh*.

"But in order to pass the class you have to do what's expected of you."

"And in order to be a part of the family . . . ditto."

God, he needed a drink. Preferably something ninety proof with an extra kick in the afterburn. For whatever reason, Nicole was looking for attention. He didn't know from whom, but she was sending a message loud and clear.

"Didn't we just have this conversation?" he asked. "I get it. You hate me. Can we just talk about *you* for a minute?"

"Why did you come back?" she asked, arms folded again, chin jutted. "For the money?"

"*Money?*" Was she serious? "Sorry to disappoint you, sis, but I don't need any of Mom and Dad's money. I've made more on my own than I'll ever be able to spend."

"Must be nice." Her lips curled in a sneer. Since he figured she wasn't about to burst into an Elvis impersonation, he took it for what it was—another wallop of attitude. "Hope it was a good replacement for your *family*."

This was going nowhere. Until she chose to cut him some slack he had to dish out the brotherly advice in small amounts. He stood and pushed the vanity chair back in place.

"Leaving so soon?" The bitterness in her tone scratched through his heart like a rusty nail.

"Just giving you a chance to pull yourself together so

we can talk in a more civil manner." He took the few steps that brought him right beside her bed, where she glared up at him, sneer firmly in place. "So don't get your hopes up. I'm not going any farther than downstairs. And I'll be back soon to make sure you start doing your school assignments so you can graduate."

"Good luck with that." She dismissed him by turning her back.

"Luck has always been on my side, little sister." Jordan closed the door behind him, and his shoulders dropped on a long sigh. He felt like he'd just been slammed into the boards by Andre the Giant. When he finally shook off the acid she'd spewed, he headed down the stairs and met Declan at the halfway point.

His twin looked him over. "I see you've still got your hide attached."

"Barely. She hates me, that's for sure."

"You tell her to get in line?"

The smile on his twin's face told Jordan the comment was in good humor, but at the moment not a damn thing seemed funny.

"I know everyone grieves in different ways," he said, "but Nicki sure seems a lot more angry than sad."

Dec's broad shoulders came up in a shrug. "Maybe she's having boyfriend problems."

"I think it's more likely she's having brother problems."

His brother glanced up the stairs. "I know you haven't been around much to know all her idiosyncrasies, but if you ask me she's needed a personality adjustment for a while."

"You have any idea why?"

Dec shrugged. "Guess I haven't been around as much as I should have either."

The answer gave Jordan no new insight, but the burn in the pit of his stomach led him to believe that something bad was lurking beneath the surface. His curiosity and concern deepened. He stuck his hands in his pockets and curled his fingers around the keys to his rented SUV. Before now the desire to run would have been too great to pass up. Instead he let go of the keys.

"How long are you sticking around?" Jordan asked.

"Ryan asked me to look over the accounts," Dec said. "So I'll be here about a week. You?"

His team was playing their first game without him tonight. The coach had given him only a week off and he'd already surpassed that. But he'd given his word to the family that he'd be all in and he tried to never break a promise. Although he was sure if you asked Lucinda Nutter, aka Ms. Diamond, she'd probably have a different opinion.

And why the hell had she popped into his head at a time like this?

"I told you," Jordan said, "I'm all in."

"Your team is heading toward the playoffs. How are you going to manage that?"

Jordan shrugged. "Like I said, I'll figure it out."

And he hoped to God he could.

Chapter 5

*I*n his younger years as a hockey player, Jordan had burned off excessive energy with partying, women, or both. He'd put in his time hanging with his teammates, playing darts, and tilting a longneck until the wee hours—even if they had a game the next day. He'd gone into more than one battle on the ice with a hangover pounding through his skull and twisting through his stomach.

Age had a way of putting your brain cells back to better use.

He entered Sunshine's twenty-four-hour gym prepared to burn off the frustration from his disastrous talk with Nicole. From his perspective their *chat* had been an epic fail. If Ryan weren't such a standup guy, Jordan would wonder if he'd been intentionally set up for the ass kicking his little sister had delivered. But revenge had never been Ryan's style.

The gym was small by Jordan's standards, but it had

the proper equipment to make him sweat out his irrita-
tion. An upbeat workout tune played from the overhead
sound system as he approached the compact and fit
guy at the reception desk. Judging by the patriotic tats
on his forearms, Jordan guessed the guy was former
military.

"Army?" Jordan asked.

"Yes, sir. Rangers."

"Thank you for your service."

"My pleasure. How can I help you?"

Jordan offered his hand as he introduced himself. "I
know it's late but I'd like to buy a membership."

"We're open 24/7, so there's no such thing as late
here." The guy offered a friendly smile. "You looking
for a month-to-month or long-term?"

Good question.

"How about we try a month-to-month for now."

"You moving into the area?"

Jordan glanced over at the row of elliptical ma-
chines. "Really not sure about that yet." The truth was
he'd set something in motion he wasn't even positive he
could live up to.

He wanted to.

His heart was in it.

But the logistics of his responsibilities elsewhere
were going to have to be dealt with before he could
make a permanent decision.

Maybe Nicole had been right after all.

God, he didn't want her to be right.

The guy went over the contract and Jordan handed
him a credit card. Minutes later he strolled toward the

back of the gym where they had the free weights lined up against a mirrored wall. The closer he got to the weights the more a secondary music thumped the walls. Initially he thought there might be a Zumba or aerobics class going on, but he didn't hear an instructor's voice over the music. Curious, he went to investigate.

Through the glass door he saw a woman going one-on-one with a traditional full-length training bag. With her pink gloves ready to strike and the line of sweat down the middle of the back of her sports bra, she balanced her weight in a boxing stance. Though he couldn't see her face he had to admit that not only was her body smokin', her poise and confidence were sexy as hell.

An amped-up version of "Welcome to the Jungle" pounded through the speakers as the woman took another step back. Her long ponytail swung across her back as she stepped into a vicious roundhouse kick. When she landed gracefully on her feet, she ended up facing him. Surprise vibrated through his blood.

Pink gloves lowered and dark brown eyes widened. *Holy hell.*

The last person he expected to see here beating the shit out of a punching bag and turning him on to the point of pain was Lucinda Nutter.

*T*he last person Lucy ever expected to see during her workout was the one standing on the other side of the glass door with his muscular arms folded across a massive chest barely covered by a loose navy tank.

Seeing his sexy self twice in one day was more than

her girl parts could take. The poor neglected things were dying to get his attention. While a smile played on his lips, she hoped he'd just continue on to wherever he'd been going.

He turned the brass knob and opened the door.

No such luck.

"Hello, Lucinda."

"Lucinda doesn't live here anymore. It's just Lucy now."

When his smile burst into a full-fledged grin, her girl parts began to swoon. To save herself, Lucy turned and delivered a forceful double kick to the bag, then followed up with several strikes of her gloves.

"Well then, hello, just Lucy now."

Gloves on hips, she turned to face him. "You knew it was me back in my classroom the whole time, didn't you."

"It took me a few minutes to recognize you," he admitted. "After all, it's been a long time."

"Has it?"

Chuckling, he closed the door behind him and came fully into the workout room as Kelly Clarkson's "Stronger" thumped through the sound system. "And in all those years, I never pictured you as the kickboxing type."

"Guess I'm just full of surprises."

He grinned. "I like surprises."

The grin undid her. She could totally do without all the flirting. Well, maybe she could handle it if it was genuine. But Jordan had a career-long reputation for charming the ladies.

"Was there something you needed?"

His eyes roamed her body. "I could make a list."

"I wouldn't bother if I were you." She turned back toward the bag and slammed her gloves into the solid surface.

"It's hard to flirt when you won't even look at me."

"Like I said, I wouldn't bother." Her comment was met with several long seconds of silence while she performed a series of jabs, crosses, and hooks. Apparently he didn't quite know what to do with someone who didn't flirt back.

"You need a sparring partner?" he finally asked.

"Yeah, see . . ." She looked down at her gloves, then back up at him. "I don't really condone beating on another person. Even if it's just for sport."

"Then you must hate football and hockey."

"I'm more of an ice dancing kind of girl. But it was nice of you to stop by and offer." Refocusing on her workout, she turned her back to him and planted her foot solidly into the bag.

After several uppercuts and sidekicks, the sensation of being watched tickled the back of her neck. She dared a peek over her shoulder and . . . yep, he was still standing there, head slightly tilted like he was trying to figure something out.

"Is there something else I can help you with?" she asked.

"Hopefully." He folded his arms and his biceps bulged. "How invested in my sister's situation are you?"

"Very." Hadn't she already made that point?

"I hate to ask, but I've hit a roadblock and I could

really use some extra help where she's concerned. Maybe we could go out for coffee."

"I'm not sure that would be a good idea." An understatement, to be sure.

"Because?"

"Because . . . I'm your sister's teacher and socializing with her relatives is frowned on."

"That's not really the reason why." He took a step closer, and she wondered how the man could smell so good all the time. "Is it?"

"You're right." She planted her gloves on the hips of her workout pants. "I don't like coffee."

"Then how about a drink?" The two steps he took brought him even closer, and she realized she'd have to be blindfolded not to be affected by his heart-stopping looks.

"After a workout it's best to consume electrolytes, not alcohol." She let her eyes roam his big, strong body. "But from the looks of you I'm sure you already know that."

"Is that a compliment?"

"If you need one, then yes, I guess it is."

"Then I'll say thank you."

"You're welcome. And as much as I'd like to stand here and chat, I really need to get this workout done."

"Yeah. Sorry about that."

"No problem. Have a nice night."

He turned to leave, then just as his hand reached the door, he stopped and came back.

"Lucy? I'm really in a bind. And, no bullshit, I could really use some help. I've tried to talk to my brothers but they seem to be as clueless as me when it comes to our baby sister. I spoke with my sister and I really need a woman's take." A hesitant smile tipped the corners of his sensuous masculine lips. "I know nothing about teenage girls. And as much as I hate to admit it, you're also right about me not knowing much about my sister. I'd like to change that. I really do want to help her. I'm afraid if I don't act now . . ."

He shook his head, leaving the unsaid lingering in the air.

Lucy didn't want to feel anything for this man. But the sincerity in his eyes and the crinkles of concern in his forehead told her he really was perplexed on how to handle the problem. She was sure even seasoned parents had issues with their troubled teens, so an unmarried brother who had no experience would be even more at a loss.

"It means a lot to me that you want to help her," he said. "That you recognized a problem prior to the loss of our parents. I respect your insight and your opinion."

His unnerving gaze cut right to the core of why she'd become a teacher. She wanted to help students, the same as she had when she'd been a student herself. Education was the lifeline people used to propel themselves out into the world. Without it, they'd be at a standstill. Along with that, a little kindness and understanding never hurt.

Lucy cared about Nicole Kincade. Beneath her recent obstinacy, she was a bright girl. With the sudden loss of her parents, she was going through a tough time. So even if Jordan Kincade rattled her in ways she never imagined, now wasn't the moment for Lucy to turn her back.

While Jordan continued to look at her with something akin to defeat in his eyes, she caved like a soufflé.

"All right," she said. "How about tomorrow? Four-thirty at The Muddy Cup? I can spare an hour before another appointment I have."

"I'd really appreciate that." With the sincerest of smiles, he turned and proved that some men looked good any way they chose to go.

That admission had Lucy slamming her gloves into the punching bag. She had no business looking at Jordan Kincade as anything other than a man she'd known from her past and the brother of a student in need.

So why were her girl parts suddenly dancing?

The day had gone from interesting to disastrous and back to interesting again when he'd run into Lucy at the gym. If you'd ever asked him what he thought the woman did in her spare time he'd have said jigsaw puzzles or volunteering at a hospital. He'd never have come up with kickboxing to heavy metal music.

This new Lucy surprised him.

In a good way.

Back in the day she'd been quiet and reserved. She'd dressed down instead of up. She'd hidden behind a pair of heavy framed glasses that did nothing to disguise her pretty face. She'd rarely smiled, and when she was deep in thought she'd snag her full bottom lip between her teeth. Talking with her brought back some good memories and somehow made him feel connected to her again. Like maybe down deep they had something more in common than being old schoolmates. He'd never been much of a talker, but with Lucy he couldn't seem to get his fill. He liked the way she gave as good as she got, as opposed to the old Lucy who'd never say a word in defense of herself.

Crazy that he remembered all that about her. But that was then and this was now. And finding the new Lucy all heated up in a skin-tight sports bra and work-out pants, kicking the shit out of a heavy bag, did something funny to his gut.

Or maybe he just needed a distraction.

It had been a hell of a week. Watching the urns that contained his parents' ashes being placed inside a marble vault for eternity had shaken him to the core and rocked the ground beneath his feet. His curiosity with Lucy really could be nothing more than a need for interference from all the emotional weight he'd been carrying. Or maybe he just needed to finally apologize to her for graduation night. Get it over with so the guilt no longer held his conscience in a stranglehold.

No.

It was more.

Something about Lucy intrigued the hell out of him. Maybe it was only because she didn't seem to respond to his flirting the way most women did. He didn't know what to do with that. Yes, she'd always been more of the serious type, but even old ladies responded to a wink and a compliment.

He wondered what she'd been doing all these years besides becoming a schoolteacher and changing her last name. Had the name come from a marriage? Once he'd recognized her, he'd immediately looked at her hand for a ring. But her long, feminine fingers, painted with some light blue nail polish, had been jewelry-free.

By tomorrow afternoon he'd have his answers to what she'd been doing and his curiosity would be sated. Hopefully. Then he needed to focus on the promises he'd made to his family while also trying to figure out a way to get back to his team.

No matter what, he couldn't let anybody down.

Struggling to find the keyhole in the darkness, Jordan finally unlocked the door to the Creekside Cottage— formerly known as his grandparents' house—and now a part of the three guest cottages that made up Sunshine Creek Vineyards Bed-and-Breakfast. Prior reservations on the cottages had been canceled upon the death of their parents. Currently he, Ethan, and Declan were in residence, while Aunt Pippy stayed up at the main house with Nicki. Parker had returned to his houseboat in Portland. Ryan and his daughter, Riley, remained at their farmhouse a couple miles away.

Stepping inside the old brick building, Jordan once again thought of the summers he'd spent right here in this house. His grandfather had been full of life and always game to try something new. His grandmother had been a patient woman who put up with his grandfather's practical jokes. Together they made quite a team and Jordan didn't need to guess where his father had learned the phrase *family first*.

He tossed the keys on a table near the door and walked through the living room, which had a dated yet comfortable feel, with a suite of leather furniture and a whitewashed brick fireplace. He continued into the kitchen and dining area, where he set the grocery bags down on the counter and began pulling out the contents. After fifteen years of basically eating and sleeping alone, he wasn't looking forward to adding one more night of solitude. Not when the memories of his parents and the cause of their deaths continued to haunt him.

And not when he knew his team would be playing without him.

With the groceries put away, he popped the top off a Naked Blonde microbrew and grabbed the Styrofoam container of take-out brisket from Cranky Hank's Smokehouse. Instead of sitting out back on the deck that overlooked the creek, he turned on the TV to watch his team go against Pittsburgh—the first game in three years in which he had not played.

Come rain or shine, broken bones, or mild concussion, he'd been ready to score goals and make the crowd cheer. The only thing that had prevented him from hitting the ice three years ago was a spilt above his eye that caused so much swelling he couldn't see to play.

Tonight he sat on a worn leather sofa all the way across the country from where his teammates were gearing up in the locker room. While the announcers gave a rundown on what they believed would happen in tonight's game, Jordan thought about his conversation with his sister, and once more he felt the guilt twist around his windpipe. He tried to loosen its grip with another slug of brew, then he dug into the brisket and let the sweet, hot flavor roll over his taste buds.

The TV showed his boys skating onto the ice to the roar of the home crowd. The announcers wondered how the game strategy would fare without him—their hard-hitting power forward. He wondered too as he shoved a forkful of coleslaw into his mouth while the camera zoomed in for a close-up of goalie Jack Riley stretching out in front of the net. Then the shot widened to show the Penguins skating onto the ice.

Jordan's last forkful of the brisket disappeared as the teams lined up for the National Anthem. Tonight a class of third-graders were doing the honors. Jordan couldn't help smiling at their serious faces and squeaky voices as their teacher led them into the song. Closing the lid on the Styrofoam container, he grabbed the Naked Blonde and leaned back to watch the game.

A knock on the door interrupted him before the bottle reached his mouth. When he got up to answer he found his twin on the porch, dressed more casual than Jordan had seen him in years. Not that he saw him that often. But for Dec, it was Hugo Boss suits all day, every day. Jeans and a blue Henley went much better with his Southern California tan.

"Hey, dirtbag." Declan grinned. "What's up?"

Jordan laughed. "Good to know it only took you a couple of days before you started calling me names again." When he stepped back to let his brother in, he noticed the paper bag in Declan's hand. "What have you got in there?"

Dec opened the bag and pulled out a six-pack of Hair of the Dog microbrew.

"So I guess you're planning on staying more than five minutes?" Jordan asked.

"Brilliant guesswork."

No sooner had Dec put his brews in the refrigerator and sat down before another knock came on the door. Jordan opened it to find Parker standing on the porch holding a paper bag.

"Let me guess . . ." Jordan eyed his younger brother. "You've got microbrews in that bag."

"And they say hockey players are stupid."

Jordan stepped back and waved him in. Dec lifted his bottle in a hello salute. Parker put his beer in the fridge, then came out of the kitchen holding a bottle of Rock Bottom Red Ale. No sooner had Jordan closed the door than another knock came. This time it was Ethan holding up a pack of Foggy Noggin' Scotch Ale. Behind him, Ryan trailed in with a pack of HeadKnocker Amber Ale.

While his brothers drifted around the small room, talking, joking, and shoving each other over on the sofa to make room, Jordan's chest tightened. "Not that I don't appreciate the company, but what are you guys doing here?"

Declan gave him a *duh* look. "Came to watch the game."

"You didn't think we'd let you watch your team play all alone, did you?" Ryan asked.

"Yeah." Parker grinned. "Just in case you need a shoulder to cry on."

Jordan knew his brother was joking, but he wasn't so sure he wouldn't have done exactly that had he been alone.

"We've got your back, brother." Ethan held up his brew and they all clinked bottles.

Jordan looked at the four men cramped together in the small living room and was overwhelmed by their love and support.

They knew he'd have a hard time watching his team play without him. They knew he'd made a promise he planned to work like hell to keep. They were being good brothers even when he hadn't bothered to be the same.

Things were different now.

They might be willing to freely give him their trust, but Jordan knew it had to be earned.

And he intended to do just that.

"Hey guys," he said over the thundering volume of the game. All his brothers looked up. He raised his bottle and choked back the emotion jammed in his throat. "Thanks."

Chapter 6

$\mathcal{H}$is team hadn't just lost; they'd had their asses handed to them in a 4–1 battle on the ice caused by too many reckless Viper penalties and too many opportunities for the Penguins. Guilt tightened another notch around his neck as Jordan walked into The Muddy Cup Café the following afternoon. He couldn't imagine how he'd ever get a cup of coffee past the regret tangled up in his chest.

As soon as he opened the door of the brightly lit café, he zeroed in on Lucy sitting with her back to him in a booth at the rear of the room. Head down, she studied the headline of the newest edition of *Talk of the Town*.

HOLLYWOOD'S BEATERS, CHEATERS, AND DIRTY DIVORCE SECRETS

Looked like the local newspaper was on top of important things in the news.

Today Lucy's hair was pulled up off her long grace-ful neck in one of those messy buns Jordan always thought gave a woman that sexy just-out-of-bed look. Lucy unwittingly had that look about her. Anyone could tell she wasn't the type who spent hours primp-ing in front of the mirror. But with a thick, dark sweep of lashes accenting her dark chocolate eyes, a smooth and lightly tanned complexion, and full lips with a nat-ural blush, she had a whole lot of sexy going on. Even if she didn't realize it.

He slid into the booth opposite her.

"You're late." She looked up, pressed the bridge of her glasses up with one finger.

"Only by five minutes."

"Well, now we only have fifty-five minutes to talk."

"I didn't know we'd be on a timer."

"I think I mentioned I have a prior commitment at five-thirty." She lifted her cup, took a sip of what he guessed was tea, not coffee, then set it back down in the saucer. "So the clock is ticking."

Leaning in, he smiled. "If I buy you a cookie, will you forgive me?"

One pretty arched brown lifted. "Make it two and I'll consider it."

"Done."

"On second thought . . ." The corners of her luscious lips quirked. "Make them white chocolate chunk with macadamia nuts and I'll even consider being late for my next appointment."

"In that case I'm buying all they have." He settled back in the seat and winked. "I'll be happy to give you anything you want."

Humor clicked in her brown eyes. "Are you flirting with me again?"

"I'm trying. But apparently I'm out of practice."

Her expression said it all. Men didn't flirt with her. But he did.

And he would keep on flirting with her until she told him to stop.

"I . . . don't know how to respond to that," she admitted.

"Don't worry. You'll get used to it." He flagged down the server. After the young woman rattled off about fifty types of coffee flavors, he ordered a plain black coffee for himself, a refill on whatever Lucy was drinking, and the entire tray of white chocolate chunk with macadamia nuts cookies.

"You want those to go?" the waitress named Tammy asked with a laugh. "Or do you plan on eating them all here?"

"Two for now, the rest you can box up."

As soon as the server walked away Lucy said, "I was kidding about the cookies."

"But I wasn't kidding about giving you anything you wanted."

She sighed, but the smile on her face said she might be open to a little flirtatiousness.

"Can we please get down to business?" she asked.

"It's what I do best."

"And now we've moved on to innuendos?"

"Sorry, teacher." He flashed her a guilty-as-sin smile. "I'll try to behave myself."

"I'm sure it would be a first. So . . . you spoke with your sister?"

He nodded and leaned his forearms on the table. The muscles in his neck tensed. "I went to her with all the intentions of discussing the class assignments and finding out why she wasn't doing them. But I hit a wall. I understand she—as we all—have suffered the sudden loss of our parents. But what I saw in her wasn't grief."

Lucy's head slightly tilted and concern darkened her eyes. "What then?"

"Anger."

At that moment the server appeared with their drinks and the huge box of cookies. Jordan paused until she was out of earshot.

"It was as if she was a balloon ready to explode." He sipped his coffee and found it too hot to drink. Then he looked up at Lucy. "Why would Nicki be so angry? Does she have social problems at school that you know of? Any major issues other than not turning in her work?"

"I asked the school counselor that very question today. She told me Nicole hasn't been in her office all year." Lucy folded her hands together on the table. "I do know your sister has become much quieter over the past month or so. I used to have to reprimand her and a few of her girlfriends when I'd catch them chatting or texting during class. I haven't had to do that in a while. Maybe the problem has something to do with them."

"Is there any way we can find out?"

"I'll talk to the counselor again and see if she wants me to ask or if she wants to call the friends into her office."

"That would be great. At least it's a starting point.

And I'll talk to my brothers again. Ryan's around her the most. He'd probably be a good one to ask although he hasn't been very helpful this far."

"He probably has a lot on his mind."

"Don't we all?"

"Life does hold some interesting challenges."

"Agreed," he said. "Some days more than others."

"I guess it keeps us on our toes."

"I'd be happy with a lot less drama."

"Me too." She chuckled. "Some days I wish I could just stay in bed."

He wouldn't mind staying there with her.

"I get what you mean," he said. "At least a short break from the chaos would be nice."

"I'd gladly join you on that deserted tropical island."

He smiled. "Before I start imagining all the possibilities of that in my head, maybe we should stick to the problem."

"Good idea."

"So, before this problem with Nicki, did she seem to like the class? Or has she always been a challenge?"

"There's a huge difference between then and now." Back to business, Lucy pushed the small stack of papers toward him. "You've seen the work—or lack of—she's handing in now. But take a look at this assignment from the first week of class."

She waited patiently while he looked past the hearts and flowers doodled on the corners in pink pen to digest the words his sister had written.

The assignment had been to describe a well-loved object. Nicki had composed a humorous and entertaining short story about Taffy Tickles, the orange ragtag bear she'd had since birth. The lightheartedness in her storytelling touched him deeply. He couldn't connect the person who'd written this story with the enraged and snide young girl he'd tried to talk to yesterday.

"Seems like two different people."

"I agree." Lucy took the paper back and added it to the others. "So maybe we're dealing with something on a grander scale here. Something more than just a rebellious nature, a fight with friends, or a broken heart."

"Drugs?"

Lucy shook her head. "I've had plenty of students go down that path. Nicole doesn't show any signs of drug use. She's just very withdrawn."

"This is way out of my league." He leaned back in the seat and stretched his legs as far as they could go. "I've never dealt with anything like this before. And she's made it apparent that I'm not her favorite person."

"Then who is?" She considered him through the dark framed glasses with a bug-under-the-microscope intensity that did a number on his conscience. "Maybe they could help."

"I'm ashamed to say I have no idea. I haven't been around much but I've made a vow to change that. Still, a promise for the future doesn't change the past or what needs to be done today."

"No, it doesn't."

Jordan rarely, if ever, asked for help. He'd always been a do-it-yourself kind of guy. In this case he needed someone objective to show him the way. He didn't mind learning new things or letting someone else take the lead. In fact, when it came to furthering his knowledge he was always game. Rebuilding a relationship with his sister—his entire family, for that matter—meant everything.

"I do want to see Nicole succeed," she said. "Helping children become independent, successful adults is why I became a teacher."

"So you'll help me?"

"I'll help *her*."

She had a right to be hesitant about him after what he'd done to her on graduation night. "I appreciate it."

"That remains to be seen, Mr. Kincade."

At one time in his life he'd spent hours and hours with this woman. Formality should be a thing of the past.

"Since we've known each other for a long time and we're going to be working together, shouldn't you call me Jordan?"

The hesitation in her response kept him on edge, much like those times a teammate worked the puck down the ice and he had to wait to see if it would sail in his direction or not.

"It might be best for everyone concerned—especially Nicole—if we keep this on a completely professional level."

"Then how about around my sister you call me Mr. Kincade. And in private you call me Jordan."

"There won't be any private moments."

"Are you sure about that?"

Something flashed in her eyes before she glanced at

her watch and stuffed the papers back into her bag. "I have to go."

"So soon?"

"Why don't you try to speak with your sister again? In depth. Get to know her as much as possible." She scooted out of the booth. "Try to find out what's bothering her. Next week is spring break, but before then I'll discuss the situation further with the school counselor and try to find a way to keep her interested in her schoolwork."

"Sounds like a plan." He hated to let her go, but trying to get her to stay might make him look weak and whiny. And in his mind, that just didn't compute.

"I'll be in touch." She slung the bag over her shoulder and headed toward the door.

For a moment he watched her walk away, if only to get a good look at the way her straight black skirt hugged all those nice curves he'd noticed last night. On anyone else, the white Keds tennis shoes she wore would be far from sexy. But he couldn't deny the woman's veiled sensuality.

As soon as she reached the café door he tossed money to cover their bill on the table, grabbed the box of cookies, and followed her outside.

"Hold up." He caught her at the curb. "You forgot the cookies."

"You really don't expect me to eat all those, do you?"

He grinned. "I can come over and help you make them disappear."

"Flirting again, Mr. . . . Jordan?"

"Always, Lucy."

"Have a nice night." She opened the door of a white Honda and set the cookie box on the passenger seat, giving him a nice view of her behind. "Feel free to contact me through the school with any relevant information on the situation and I'll do likewise."

Wait.

That's not how he'd planned for this to go.

He wanted a chance to talk to her now and again. He liked her. Or at least he'd liked the girl she'd been. He wanted a chance to get to know the woman better.

"I have another idea."

She straightened and curled her hand over the top of the car door. "Oh goody."

Despite her sarcastic tone, he moved up beside her. "How about we get together a couple of times a week to compare notes?"

"A couple of times a week?"

He nodded.

"A note or a phone call would be sufficient."

"I'm not much of a phone guy. I always do my talking in person. That's why I'm so successful on the ice."

"Yes." Her gaze dropped down his body, then came back up to search his face. "I'm sure you are."

Did she just check him out?

"So we can get together?" He tried not to sound hopeful and needy. But at the moment, that's exactly what he was. He didn't know how to reach his sister any better than he knew how to break through Lucy's barrier.

"Will you continue to pester me if I refuse?" she asked.

"Yes."

"How did I already know that?"

"How about I call you tomorrow to set up a place and time to meet again?"

"Tomorrow? I don't see how much can change in just a day."

He smiled. "I like to remain optimistic."

"So do I. Just be careful you don't put too much pressure on Nicole. Optimism is often disguised by impatience."

"See, that's the kind of thinking I need right now. But all I've got are replays of past goal shots in my head."

"You were never a dumb jock, Jordan. You just need to take a breath before you deal with this. Teenage girls are complicated."

"Got news for you. So are grown women."

She gifted him with another chuckle. "Give me your phone."

He pulled it from his pocket and handed it to her. He waited while she tapped in her number, then handed it back.

"Give me a call. You'll find me in your contacts between Bambi and Portia."

"So you're saying you're into threesomes?"

With an eye roll she slid inside her car, closed the door, and started her engine.

Before she put the car in drive, he tapped on the window and waited till she rolled it down.

"Did you forget something?"

"Yes." He took a deep breath. "I forgot to say I'm sorry."

"For?"

"For not showing up on graduation night to take you to the dance."

Her silence confirmed that she'd not forgotten that night any more than he had.

"That was fifteen years ago," she said. "It hardly matters now."

"It matters to me. It always did. I tried to call you to apologize and explain that when my friends found out I was taking you to the dance, they waylaid me and got me shitfaced before I knew what was going on."

"I'm sure they thought they were doing you a favor."

"I didn't give a shit what they thought. The massive amount of alcohol they poured in my soda was what stopped me."

"Like I said, it doesn't matter now."

"You're wrong, Lucy. And I'll prove it."

"No need."

As her little white Honda disappeared down the street, Jordan wondered how the hell he was going to multitask everything when so far in his life he'd been one-dimensional. But he'd made promises and he meant to keep each and every one of them.

Even if it killed him.

A regular school day could melt a teacher's energy depending on whether the students behaved or whether they'd chosen the wild kingdom rule of the day. Today, Lucy's students had called upon their inner hyenas, and by the time she'd reached her car in the school parking lot, she'd felt like a zookeeper on her first day on the job.

The meeting with Jordan had stolen another dose of her usual oomph. She'd expected nothing to get resolved. But he'd fooled her and stolen a little bit of her heart because he really seemed concerned about his sister's well-being. It was hard not to like a man who wanted to put his own needs aside and champion a young girl. Lucy wished she'd had someone like that when she'd been growing up. Heck, she wouldn't have minded a champion when she got older either.

And then he'd pulled the ultimate surprise.

He'd apologized for graduation night.

Yes, it might have come fifteen years late. But the part that had made her heart melt had been that it seemed important to him to apologize and explain fifteen years later. If you had asked her a week ago if she'd ever see that apology, she'd have laughed. Jordan Kincade—badass to the bone—didn't appear to be the kind of man to apologize for anything. And that gave her no choice but to accept it and move forward.

The final kicker in her energy boost had been the PTA meeting to organize the school carnival. As usual, when they asked for committee volunteers Lucy's hand grew a helium balloon. Since she was a single woman, everyone thought she had more time on her hands than those with families. And while maybe she did, she didn't want to be the appointed loser who always volunteered because others felt she had nothing important going on in her life.

As she parked her car in the driveway, she knew she had one more mission before she could call it a day and kick off her Keds. With next week off for spring break, she planned to do some heavy relaxing, reading, and catnapping.

She walked across her next-door neighbor's lawn and knocked on the door of the pretty little Craftsman-style house. The large front porch displayed an array of potted flowers and hanging fuchsias. In the corner sat a white wicker rocking chair with a cute little side table large enough for a pitcher of lemonade and several glasses.

The door creaked open and Mrs. Benner stood in the opening wearing her quilted robe, one blue house slipper, and one purple.

"Hello, dear."

"Mrs. B, you're supposed to look through the peep-hole before you answer the door. Remember?"

"I am?" Her steel gray brows pulled together over a pair of hazel eyes that didn't focus as well as they used to.

"Yes. We need you to stay safe."

"Oh. Well, I've got that covered. Chuck Norris keeps an eye out for me."

Chuck Norris was Mrs. B's twenty-pound cat who snored and wouldn't lift his head off the sofa unless a can of cat food was involved.

"Yes, I'm sure Chuck has iron paws. But I still need you to look first. Just in case."

"Okey-dokey."

Lucy sighed, knowing the eighty-year-old would most likely forget. Her mind, like her eyesight, wasn't what it used to be. Though the memory lapses mostly came on bad days when her arthritis was—as Mrs. B called it—kicking up. And because Mrs. B wanted to maintain her independence for as long as possible, Lucy had promised the older woman's daughter and son that she'd keep an eye on her. A promise that often included shopping, errands, and doctor visits. But Lucy didn't mind. Mrs. B was a sweet woman and Lucy respected her desire to remain independent.

"I thought I'd check in with you before I turned in for the night," Lucy said. "Do you need anything?"

"I could stand to knock a couple of years off my life so I can go dancing again."

Lucy gave her a sympathetic smile. A few years ago Mrs. B had belonged to the Blue Hair Hoofers, a dance group made up of women over the age of seventy. They performed for charity events and private parties, and Lucy knew Mrs. B missed that part of her life a great deal.

"I wish I could," Lucy said. "In the meantime, do you have enough food in the refrigerator to get you through until we shop on Sunday?"

"Well, if I don't, I'm sure Chuck will share," she joked. Hopefully.

"I planned to make some homemade soup tomorrow. I'll bring you over some."

"Oh, that would be lovely, dear."

Lucy gave the woman a hug. She'd stop by in the morning before she went to school to double-check. Otherwise she'd worry all day. "Okay then. I'll see you tomorrow."

"Okey-dokey."

Mrs. B shut the door and Lucy waited for the lock to click. When it didn't she knocked on the door again. And again Mrs. B answered without looking through the peephole.

"Hello, dear."

"Mrs. B, you need to lock your door when you close it."

"Okey-dokey."

"Go ahead. I'll wait here until I hear the deadbolt."

Mrs. B closed the door and Lucy sighed with relief when she heard the bolt slam home. It was only a matter of time before her neighbor would need professional assistance. In the meantime, Lucy planned to help out as much as possible.

She crossed the lawn and opened the door to her little Victorian cottage. In the distance she heard the click-click-click of nails on the hardwood floor. Without thought, she knelt down for the onslaught of poochie smooches from Ziggy. Her golden retriever didn't disappoint as he came around the corner of the kitchen, tail sweeping side-to-side.

Ziggy had come into her life at a time when great changes had been taking place. And though he'd never know, he'd saved her from herself more than once.

After she'd picked him out at the animal shelter three years ago, David Bowie's "Changes" had come on the radio. She hadn't missed a beat in the irony and immediately named him after Bowie's alter ego. Because of the surname she'd taken for a fresh start after her divorce, her students called her "Lucy in the Sky with Diamonds." Adding "Ziggy Stardust" to her life had been like having a friend sent down from heaven at a time when she'd really needed one.

Ziggy's job was to protect her against the spiders from Mars. Aka mean, scary people. Her job was to protect Ziggy from ending up in another animal shelter and giving him all the love he deserved. They had an understanding and a loyal relationship.

Perhaps the first in Lucy's entire life.

Ziggy just had one little problem.

He tooted.

A lot.

She'd changed his food and treats several times but it hadn't helped. The vet said his digestive system just created a lot of gas.

Whew. She'd say.

"Hey, Zigmeister." She rubbed his large head between the ears, then wrapped her arms around him for a hug. "How'd your day go? Find any squirrels to chase?"

Ziggy gave a quick bark, then moved his big body closer. Lucy ended up on her butt while her dog smothered her in canine worship.

Coming home now was so peaceful. Her little cottage was the one—the only—place she felt safe. And it was all hers. Not only did she not have to share it, she didn't have to ask permission for anything. She didn't need to seek approval on how to decorate or what to cook for dinner. She didn't need to ask for authorization to go into another room so she could focus on her studies, watch her favorite TV show, read a book for leisure, or work on the romance novels she'd begun to write in search of at least some kind of happily-ever-after.

During her marriage she'd had to tread lightly in fear of setting off her ex-husband's volatile temper. Somehow she'd survived.

Barely.

She pulled herself up off the floor, dusted off the dog hair, and dropped her bag into the chair by the door. Next, the deadbolt slammed shut and she took a deep breath.

"Who wants a treat before dinner?"

Ziggy's tail wagged in quick response and Lucy went to the kitchen cupboard for a Beggin' Strip. She broke the treat into four pieces and fed each one to him after he performed his tricks of rolling over, shaking hands, lying down, and covering his nose with his paws.

"Good boy."

He rewarded her by passing gas.

"Whew! What have you been eating?"

He gave a silly bark and got down on his front paws like, *Yeah, I reek, but aren't I cute?*

He was. Which was the only reason she forgave him for the constant stinkage.

After a thorough wash of her hands, Lucy rummaged through the freezer and pulled out the small tub of Dove Unconditional Chocolate ice cream. The best part of living alone was you didn't have to share, hide, or explain the reason you were munching on your guilty pleasure before dinner. She grabbed a spoon from the drawer, flipped off the top of the ice cream, and dug in.

"Mmmmmmm."

The smooth chocolate rolled over her tongue while Ziggy cocked his head.

"This is sinful, Zig. Be glad you're a dog and you don't have to try to refrain from stuff like this when your day goes from bad to haywire. Lord knows you don't need anything else to stink up your insides."

Studying the vintage enamelware on her reclaimed wood shelves, she snuck another bite and wished the sweet deliciousness could rewind her greeting to Jordan Kincade at The Muddy Cup. She hadn't meant to sound so snippy when he'd sat down five minutes late for their meeting. She hadn't meant to make herself look like a snob. Had it not been for her heart pounding like a captured rabbit, she could have handled the encounter much easier.

Clearly the man had an effect on her.

For several years after graduation, she'd hated him. Carried a grudge so big she'd needed a U-Haul truck to tow it around. Then she'd realized she'd had no one but herself to blame for the heartache. People couldn't hurt you unless you let them. She'd let her guard down and he'd seized the opportunity. Which was why she never thought she'd hear a word of remorse come from his sensuous lips. But he'd surprised her by doing exactly that.

She should have forgiven him even without an apology. She knew how teenagers were. Most didn't think about anything except what happened in their own little world. But when she'd found out the real reason he'd left her waiting that night, she couldn't stop the hurt.

Yes, she knew how the popular crowd Jordan had belonged to thought of her back then. She'd never be one of them. She wouldn't want to. She accepted who she was, and she was perfectly okay with the fact that it wasn't her lot to be glamorous or live a glamorous life.

After her marriage ended she'd had to learn to like herself again. To trust herself and her instincts. She'd always depended on being smart, yet it had totally let her down when she'd needed it most. Trusting herself and her instincts didn't come easy. Which was only one reason why she wondered how she'd proceed with this project to salvage Nicole Kincade's education and find out what was bothering the girl, when Lucy knew she might very well be distracted by Jordan.

Where he was concerned her instincts jumped up and down and waved a red flag. How could she go one-on-one, face-to-face with him in a matter that might take days, weeks, or even months? She didn't know if she had the kind of moxie she'd need to deal with him. Yes, she'd been strong enough to pull herself from the depths of hell once. But this was different.

Jordan Kincade was a different kind of trouble.

Call her shallow, but when confronted with a man who looked like a dark, sexy, sinful fallen angel, she couldn't stop her fantasies from taking flight. She imagined he'd fill a woman's head with pretty words, then touch her body with skillful hands.

She'd never known a man like that.

No one could deny he was good-looking. And probably more than a little self-centered. Not that she'd cyberstalked him, but in the photos she'd seen posted in celebrity news or sports Web sites he'd never down-played his wild behavior. With a different voluptuous female on his arm in almost every shot, his expressive eyes and wide grin flaunted the fact that he devoured every single moment of his fortune and fame like a fine wine. Those he'd left back in the little town of Sunshine hadn't stood a chance.

Jordan was a dangerous man. He lived a dangerous life. Played a vicious and dangerous game. Even more hazardous was the charm he turned on like tap water. It oozed from every pore and had probably lured more than one woman to heartbreak and disappointment. But Lucy knew she had to suck it up and tighten the waistband on her big girl panties in order to help Nicole. She'd have to be careful around the man. Never let her guard down. She'd played with the devil before and lost. She was proud to have survived the ordeal and come out wiser. But that didn't mean she'd willingly put herself back in the devil's path.

True, Jordan had apologized for something he'd done fifteen years ago. Her ex had *never* apologized. And he'd had a million reasons why he should have. The difference between the two was that Jordan at least had a conscience. Her ex had not.

After one more gigantic bite of ice cream, Lucy put the top back on the container. She fed Ziggy his supposedly flatulence-reducing kibble and went upstairs to change into something more comfortable. Her agenda for the rest of the night was to figure out a way to help Nicole with the least amount of exposure to the troubled girl's sexy big brother.

As Jordan turned the SUV onto the winding gravel road that led to his family vineyards, the sun sat low in the western sky. Beams of orange and gold shot out from its core while the puffy white clouds turned a picturesque pink.

Relief flowed through his veins that Lucy was onboard to help him with Nicole. Between the two of them they should be able to get things figured out and get his sister back on track.

That was if he could keep from being distracted by Lucy.

Tonight he still had business to handle. And for this mission he probably needed fireproof gloves.

Though the hand-painted Sunshine Creek Vineyards sign in front of the big stone pillars and iron gate had faded, the rows of grapevines on either side of the road made for an impressive entry. Once the vines turned a vibrant green and became laden with deep purple or golden fruit, the vineyard would look like a showplace. Unless you dug a little deeper, it was easy to miss the dated appearance of the buildings that dotted the property.

Before the funeral, he'd barely noticed, because he'd been too overwhelmed with shock and grief. Now it seemed like all he could see were the flaws. The condition of the place surprised him. He knew his father and Ryan had been working hard to develop new blends of wine for a more competitive brand. Maybe that's where all their focus had gone instead of on the bed-and-breakfast or the event center.

In recent years, his father had commented that the wine business in Washington State had exploded. Properties that were once open wilderness and rolling hills had been sold off to those who'd learned that their winemaking hobby could be profitable. Plus the lifestyle in the area had become very desirable. Other than a domestic call here and there or a group of beer-drinking teens causing a little trouble down at the river, Sunshine had virtually no crime.

The brochures set up in the tourist information center at the edge of town boasted the area to be a great place to raise wine and kids. But as Jordan turned the SUV up the winding road to the main house on the hill, he realized their corner of paradise needed some TLC. The big question for him was, why hadn't anyone else noticed? Surely his mother could have seen the deterioration. Why wouldn't she have done something about it, or at least said something?

He parked in the driveway, then, feeling like a guest instead of a family member, he knocked on the front door of the large two-story home. Footsteps could be heard on the hardwood floor from inside before the door swung open.

The amber light above Aunt Pippy's head intensified the fireball glow of her hair. Today's outfit was a yellow and orange mini dress with a wide white vinyl belt that buckled at her hips. Earrings that looked like melon balls topped with Shriners' fez hats swung from her ears. White vinyl ankle boots finished off the look that might have been better suited for *American Bandstand* in the 1960s than a home in a conventional wine town.

"Jordy!" Aunt Pippy's eyes, under bright blue eye shadow, popped wide with her surprise. "What are you doing knocking on the door?"

Good question. He should feel free to come and go in the house as he pleased.

He didn't.

And that was his own damn fault.

"Is Nicole home?"

"She sure is." She waved him inside, where the aroma of spaghetti sauce tickled his nose and made his stomach growl. "She's in the kitchen helping Riley with a school project."

"That's a good sign."

"Oh, sweetums." She patted his arm. "Don't get too excited. It's a third-grade diorama. Come on in. We were just about to eat. You can join us."

He glanced around the living room that now seemed cold. The eerie absence of his parents balled his stomach up in knots. "Where's Ryan?"

"Working late. He's got Declan locked up in the office with him. I think they're going over the financial reports."

Sounded like a ton of fun.

"You doing okay?" he asked her. After all, she'd lost her sister, and everything had to be as hard on her as it was on the rest of them.

"Just trying to get through one day at a time. Your mom and I went through a whole lot of sister stuff together. Being the oldest I always thought I'd go first." Her chest lifted with a long stuttered sigh. "Guess you just never know."

"I'm so sorry." He drew his aunt into his arms. "And I apologize. It's easy to get wrapped up in your own grief and forget that others are suffering too."

She patted his back and leaned her head against his shoulder. In that moment he didn't care if her makeup smeared all over his shirt, all he wanted to do was offer comfort.

"Jordy? You can't walk around your whole life apologizing for everything. At some point in time you just have to get on with getting on. We're all here for each other and we'll need each other in the coming days, weeks, and months. Don't forget that." She looked up, stroked his cheek with her long orange fingernails. "You're home now. And if you need to leave, *I* know you'll come back. When you do, we'll all be here for you."

"I appreciate that, Aunt Pippy. But I'm not planning on going anywhere."

"Never say never. Some things in life you learn quick. Some things you learn slow. Doesn't matter how long it takes, just that you're open to interpretation. As this great loss just taught us all, make sure you always grab hold of life with both hands and hang on tight."

"I'll try."

"I know you will." She patted his cheek. "Now how about some of that spaghetti before it gets all gummy? The rest of the boys went into town for dinner. Seems they weren't too keen on the idea of chicken going into the spaghetti. Parker especially had a problem. Told me I was breaking the rules."

"Everyone knows I don't follow the rules so chicken spaghetti sounds great to me. If you can spare a bowl I'm game." Jordan had never pictured his aunt as a domestic goddess. Hell, he didn't even know the woman could cook. All she'd ever made him when he'd been growing up were peanut butter, jelly, and potato chip sandwiches.

"You're such a sweet boy."

"I'd appreciate it if you wouldn't say that in front of my brothers."

"Wouldn't dream of it." His aunt laughed. "Although seeing you boys all wrestling might be more fun than watching the distance that's grown between you."

The truth hit him like a wicked cross-check. The reminder that he had a lot of work to do to make things up to his family stung. But he acknowledged it and intended to keep the promise he'd made as he followed his aunt toward the kitchen. The heartbreak that had stolen his breath moments ago moved aside for an onslaught of nerves. Spaghetti that clucked was nothing compared to the baby dragon that roared.

The murmurings and giggles stopped as soon as he entered the room, and Nicki's head snapped up. The smile on her face dissolved into a scowl.

Great.

Looked like he was in for another fun evening.

Yippee.

"What are you girls up to?" He headed toward the long farm table where they sat, heads together, concentrating on the task at hand. Well, except for the why-do-you-care? glare Nicki shot his way.

"Hi, Uncle Jordy." Riley's bright blue eyes sparkled as she smiled. "Nicki's helping me with my diorama."

At least Riley knew his name. That was a start. He smiled as he leaned over their heads to get a better look.

The shoebox had been covered in blue paper. On the

front of the box a sign read "Ocean Habitat." Inside, the girls had carefully positioned seashells and colored cutouts of fish and coral.

"That's pretty clever to hang the fish from the top with string," he said. "It looks like they're swimming."

"That was Nicki's idea," Riley said, scrunching up her little button nose. "She's a genius."

Nicki remained silent as she glued a tiger shark onto the string.

"I think she's pretty smart too." For that comment he received a scoff that came out sounding more like a snort. "In fact," he said, "I think she's brilliant. Did you ever hear her story about Taffy Tickles?"

Nicki's head came up so fast he heard her neck crack. Her eyes narrowed as she shot another death glare in his direction.

Oh good. At least now he had her attention.

"How do you know about that?" she asked.

"I read it."

Somehow she spoke through a clenched jaw. "Ms. Diamond isn't supposed to share students' work with anyone but a parent."

Losing your parents when you were a thirty-three-year-old adult was hard enough. Losing your parents when you were only seventeen and vulnerable to the world had to be ten times worse. Jordan settled his hand over Nicki's shoulder. "We don't have that luxury anymore, sis."

"Don't call me that." Nicole jumped up and dashed from the room.

Aunt Pippy and Riley gave him sympathetic puppy eyes.

Wise beyond her years, Riley said, "Give her some time, Uncle Jordy. She's sad and she feels all alone. It took me a while after my mama left to figure things out, but I'm okay now. Nicki will be too."

A million emotions flooded Jordan's heart. With the exception of Ryan, he and his brothers liked to poke fun at the former Laura Kincade—now Laura Landau—toilet paper commercial queen. The one thing they often forgot was how Laura's abandoning her family for Hollywood affected little Riley.

Jordan leaned down and kissed the top of Riley's silky hair. "Thank you, sweetheart. I'll keep that in mind." He tossed a look to his aunt. "Can you hold off dishing up that spaghetti for a few more minutes?"

"Take as long as you need."

"Might take a while." He pushed a breath of clogged air from his lungs. "I don't have all this figured out. But I'm working on it."

"Don't forget," Pippy said. "You've got four brothers who are all pretty smart. So don't go thinking you have to do everything on your own."

His brothers already had their hands full. And lucky for him, Lucy would be by his side.

"I know you believe you've got some making up to do," Aunt Pippy said. "But that's only from your side of seeing things."

He glanced up the stairs. "Pretty sure it's the way Nicki sees things too."

"Just give her some time. Like Riley said, she'll come around."

He hoped so, but he wasn't willing to bet on it.

With a nod, he curled his fingers around the bag in his hand, and went up to the baby dragon's lair. Not surprisingly her door was closed. He'd expected her to slam it when she'd rushed up the stairs, but somehow she'd refrained.

He knocked. Of course, she didn't respond. He knocked again. And again. And again. Until finally she yanked the door open.

"What's it going to take for you to go away?" she ground out between clenched teeth. "I know you're dying to."

He held out the white paper bag. "This is for you."

She eyed the bag curiously, somehow maintaining the stink-eye in the process. Talent. Pure talent to do that. It had taken him years to perfect the stink-eye on the ice. For him it had been no easy task—like patting himself on the head and rubbing his stomach in circles at the same time.

"What's that?" she asked.

"It's a surprise." He jiggled the bag. "For you."

She continued to eye him suspiciously.

"Just some stuff I picked up that I thought you might like," he explained. "I promise nothing will jump out and bite you."

While she continued to glare at him, he pushed past her and moved into her room.

"You can't just barge your way in here."

"Too late." He set the bag down on her bed. On his way out the door he stopped where she stood in the center of her room with her arms crossed, tapping the toe of one pink Converse high-top.

"Keep it. Toss it. Doesn't matter," he said. "What does matter is that I'm not going anywhere. And I'll be back tomorrow to piss you off some more." As he made his way toward the stairs he heard her sputter an obscenity. Then her door closed and he heard the distinct rattle of the paper bag.

A smile crossed his lips.

He hoped the pink floral journal and set of colored gel pens would give her the inspiration to start writing down what was on her mind. The king-sized Snickers bar had just been pure bribery. Whatever she chose to do with the contents of the bag tonight didn't have any weight on his plans for tomorrow.

He'd be back.

Chapter 7

Standing on the front porch of Lucy Diamond's little two-story Victorian cottage, Jordan realized he might be overstepping his bounds. Well, there was really no *might* in it. He was definitely breaking boundaries. She'd given him her phone number, not her address. He'd taken it upon himself to find out where she lived. He hoped she wouldn't see him as a stalker. Then again, that's exactly what he'd think, so he could hardly fault her if she did.

The soft glow of the porch light provided enough illumination to see the surrounding rosebushes and the blue trim on the door frame and windowsills. A clean white picket fence bordered the yard. And from the large tree, an old wooden swing swayed in the gentle breeze, which made him wonder if Lucy had kids.

He hadn't thought of that.

The house was the kind of place one would picture in a fairy tale, and it didn't exactly fit Lucy's straitlaced-teacher, kickboxing-tough-girl image at all.

Night had fallen hours ago and the air was crisp and cool as he knocked on the door. It took a minute, but then from behind the barrier, he heard the sound of scuffing footsteps approach. A long pause hinted that she might be peering at him through the peephole. Finally the door opened.

"Jordan. What are you doing here?"

The response tangled on his tongue as he looked her up and down.

Lucy was dressed in a pair of baggy plaid pajama bottoms and a white tank top with straps so thin they looked like spaghetti noodles. By the sheerness of the fabric and the dusky hint of her nipples showing through, he knew she didn't have on a bra.

Not that he minded.

Her hair was still pulled up in that sexy, messy bun on top of her head. Her dark framed glasses had slipped partway down her straight nose. And she wore a pair of fuzzy slippers on her feet. She held an open paperback book in her hand, and from somewhere in the house the sultry beat of JT's "What Goes Around" played.

"Hel-lo?"

He dragged his gaze up from her black and yellow bumblebee slippers. "Huh?"

"I asked what you're doing here." The book in her hand snapped shut—a romance judging by the couple kissing on the front cover—and yanked his attention back to where it should be. "And how did you know where I live anyway?"

"Which one do you want me to answer first?"

She sighed, and he realized that for the most part, the females in his life seemed to constantly be frustrated with him.

"Curiosity begs to know all of the above," she said.

Before she could close the door on him, he made the quickest, most ridiculous, and most desperate move of all time. He stuck his foot in the door. "I have something really important to tell you. And Google."

"People were so much safer before the age of the Internet." She shook her head. "And this 'something really important' is . . . ?"

"You're trying not to smile." He pointed at her luscious lips. "I can tell."

"Yes, well, we all have our moments."

"Mind if I come in?"

"It's late. This can't wait until tomorrow?"

"Yes, it's late. Yes, I shouldn't have just appeared on your doorstep. Yes, you should slam the door in my face." He took a breath. "But I hope you won't."

At that moment the gods of mercy took pity on him when a golden retriever ambled to the door. Jordan grabbed the opportunity.

"Hey. Nice dog." He moved past Lucy into the house, where the dog swept his tail from side to side. Jordan leaned down and gave the dog a nice rub over the top of his large head. "What's his name?"

"Ziggy. I'm thinking of getting a second dog." Lucy closed the front door. "Probably a German shepherd or something with sharp teeth and a lot of *bite*."

Jordan looked up. "Wouldn't do you any good where

I'm concerned. Dogs love me." He continued to pet the dog, who now wore a goofy doggy grin.

"Apparently." She crossed her arms. "And I don't remember inviting you in."

"Oops." He gave her a sheepish look.

"Word to the wise, that look doesn't work for you."

"I gave it my best effort."

"You might try to be more convincing."

He grinned. "If you let me stay, I promise I'll work on it."

"Please don't trouble yourself on my behalf. I try not to put myself in the gullible category."

"Teasing, Lucy? That's so unlike you."

"You don't know the half of it. And if you'll excuse me I have to go upstairs to get my twelve-gauge." She started toward the stairs and then turned back around to face him. The hint of a smile playing at her lips sent a tickle through his heart. "Don't steal anything while I'm gone."

That smile convinced him she wasn't all that mad he'd popped up on her doorstep.

"No worries. I left my cat burglar bag at home," he said.

When Lucy disappeared up the stairs, her dog flopped down at his feet. Jordan took the opportunity to check out the nearly all white living space. Small pops of color came in the form of pale blue, pink, and yellow and made him feel like he'd stepped inside an Easter egg. The good news was that the ultra feminine décor told him a man didn't live here. He hadn't been one hundred percent sure before. He was now. Any man worth his weight in testosterone would destroy a place this immaculate within minutes.

He had to laugh because everything he'd bought for his own apartment either came in leather so it could be wiped down, or in some kind of dark fabric that didn't show the dirt. When the boys decided to come over for a night of poker he didn't need to worry about the mess they'd leave behind.

Yes, he had a housekeeper who took care of the cleaning and stocking his refrigerator. But when he'd brought in a local designer to make the place livable, he'd requested the place be a typical guy's paradise—big TV, ear-splitting surround sound, and plenty of beer in the fridge.

Lucy's cozy house felt like a home.

Minutes later when she came back downstairs she'd covered up with a fuzzy white robe she'd probably put on for protection against his wandering eyes. Too bad her efforts came a little too late. He had a great imagination. And because he'd already seen her in the skimpy top, all he could picture was what was under that robe and how he'd like to peel it off.

As a teen back in high school he'd liked Lucy. Enjoyed her company. Appreciated the way her mind worked. But he'd never looked at her like he wanted to strip her down and mess her up.

But he sure was looking now.

*N*othing seemed crazier than Jordan Kincade standing in the middle of her living room looking both incredibly out of place and amazingly hot in jeans that fit like a lover's hand, a snug black T-shirt, and his black leather jacket. Wickedness dripped off him like tempting dark chocolate.

For the past few years Lucy had tried to put away those kinds of feelings toward the opposite sex. She'd been fooled once by a pretty boy exterior; she didn't need a second go-round.

On second thought, Jordan wasn't pretty. He was manly and gorgeous. With his dark, wavy hair casually pushed off his forehead, those thick almost black brows lowered over a pair of striking blue eyes, and at least two days of beard scruff on his chiseled jaw, he looked intense, powerful, and passionate.

He played a violent game for a living, one that drew thousands to pump their fists in the air when blood was drawn. She'd seen a few of his games on TV and she'd been astonished at the level of brutality. Knowing what he was capable of and the way those intense blue eyes looked at her now, she should feel threatened. At the very least, tense.

Incredibly, she felt something very different.

On a weird, illogical, purely core level, Jordan made her feel . . . safe.

The idea almost made her laugh out loud.

"I'll make some tea," she said, breaking the spell. "Then you can fill me in on your 'something really important.'"

"I'm not really a tea kind of guy." He followed her into the kitchen.

Tail wagging, Ziggy brought up the rear, completely

demolishing his part of the whole I'll-protect-you-and-you-protect-me deal.

"In that case"—she reached into the cupboard for her jar of green tea—"I guess you can say whatever you have to say and then be on your way."

"On second thought . . ." He sat down at her antique whitewashed table and Ziggy lay at his feet with a groan. "Tea sounds great."

"You don't seem very sure."

"I'm totally onboard. I . . . Ummm." He waved a hand in front of his face. "I think your dog just—"

"Oh. Yes. He does that." Lucy held back a laugh. "A lot."

"You probably buy a lot of air freshener."

"As a matter of fact I do." The conversation was odd and it did nothing to alleviate the awareness wrapped around her spine like a boa constrictor.

He pointed to the bench on the opposite side of the table. "Is that a church pew?"

"It is. I found it at a flea market in Oregon last summer."

While she put the kettle on the stove and dropped the teabags into mugs, he studied her kitchen from a chair that seemed two sizes too small.

"A chandelier of Mason jars. A vintage hotel sign. And cupboards filled with milk glass. You sure like old and white stuff."

"I'm fond of the simplicity."

"I'll say. Is there something specific that prompts that?"

"What do you mean?"

He shrugged. "Usually when someone cuts clutter from their lives there's a reason behind it."

Yikes. Nail on the head. "So I can't just like clean and simple?"

"You can like anything you want. You've made a really nice home here. Maybe all this white just makes me think of the trips I've taken to an ER to stitch something up or put it back in place."

The idea turned her stomach. "I'm sure you get injured a lot in your job."

"More than I'd like."

"Judging by your tone I'm guessing it's not the injuries themselves that you're opposed to so much as losing the battle."

"I definitely don't like to lose."

The wistfulness in his voice made her wonder if for him, losing the battle could also mean losing loved ones.

There was nothing harder to see than a gladiator brought to his knees by something he couldn't control. Sympathy unexpectedly tugged at her heart. Before she got too buried in it, like a saving grace, the teakettle whistled. She pulled it from the burner, poured the hot liquid into mugs, and set one in front of him.

"I like sugar."

"I'm sure in your line of business you can use all the sweetening you can get." She handed him the sugar bowl, then she sat on the church pew and set her mug on the white linen placemat in front of her. "So, Mr. Kincade, tell me . . . exactly what is your 'something really important.'"

"Ah, ah, ah. Private moment, Lucy." He dropped two spoonfuls of sugar into his mug, and stirred. "Aren't you supposed to call me Jordan?"

She smiled. "Aren't you supposed to quench my curiosity?"

"Cagey." He grinned. "I like that."

"Don't get used to it. Spill."

"Something came up tonight."

"And it couldn't wait until tomorrow?"

"Sometimes things can't wait." A frown crinkled the smooth skin between his eyes as he sipped the hot tea. "The one thing I've learned in the past couple of weeks is that *nothing* can wait. If something needs to be said, now is better than later. You never know when your time is up. And if I'm going to help Nicki get past this trouble she's going through, it has to be now. No one ever knows if they'll get another tomorrow."

"I'm sorry." Unable to meet the dark emotion in his eyes, Lucy briefly glanced away. "Of course. I completely understand your urgency. So how can I help?"

"I bought her a journal. You know, one of those fancy ones with flowers all over it. And I got her a set of colorful gel pens too. I thought maybe if she had something pretty to look at she might be inspired to write things down and get them out of her system."

His thoughtfulness and sincerity touched her deeply. Lucy didn't know why it surprised her that he'd gone the extra mile for his sister with no prompting from anyone, but it definitely made her take an extra look. The man sitting at her little kitchen table appeared to be nothing like the person she'd imagined all those years.

"That's a great idea."

He shrugged. "I was just walking down the aisle of some artsy store in town and—"

"Punkydoodles?"

"That's the place." He set his mug down. "I saw all the bright, colored stuff in the window and figured it couldn't hurt to check it out. Then I saw the journal and pens in an aisle full of total girly stuff. It just looked like Nicole."

"Did you give it to her already?"

Expression solemn, he nodded.

"And it wasn't well received?"

"I don't know. She was so busy hating me I only got the chance to put the bag on her bed and get out of there before she threw an all-out hissy fit." He shook his head. "She reminds me of a kitten. You know, one of those tiny ones who gets all fired up and starts hissing and spitting like they're ready to take on the world?"

Lucy nodded. That was exactly how she saw Nicole too.

"I threw in a king-sized Snickers bar for good measure," he said. "Figured if I couldn't win her over with the journal and pens, chocolate might do the trick."

After the fiasco on their graduation night, Lucy had imagined many things about Jordan Kincade, starting with wrapping her hands around his throat and squeezing until his eyes bulged. Before tonight she would have sworn he was a man with a gigantic ego. Instead he appeared to be a man with a gigantic heart. Of course, time would tell. Not everyone revealed his or her true self in the beginning.

She'd learned that the hard way.

"Chocolate is always a good choice," she agreed, feeling herself melt a little at his thoughtfulness.

"If it helps, I'll buy her a whole damn store full of the stuff."

"So, besides being willing to buy massive quantities of white chocolate chunk with macadamia nuts cookies and Snickers bars . . ." Lucy fidgeted with the antique lace doily beneath the Mason jar that held a small bouquet of daisies. "I take it you'd like me to encourage her to write down her thoughts and feelings?"

"Do you think that might give us some insight to what's going on with her?"

"I doubt we'd ever be able to read what she's written."

"True. Unless I played secret agent, snuck into her room, and stole it."

Laughter bubbled from her chest. "You don't really fit the part."

"What? You don't find me debonair like 007?"

She found him hot, sexy, and even a little sweet. "I think you might lean a little more toward the Hulk."

He tossed his hands up and smiled. "Well, there goes all the money I spent on spy school."

For the second time in as many minutes, she laughed. For her, laughter didn't happen very often. She'd always been the serious sort. Tonight, she was learning that laughing felt pretty darned good.

"There's a good chance Nicole had a bonfire with the stuff after I left," he said.

"I doubt it."

He shook his head, and the light from the overhead chandelier made his dark hair shine. "I wouldn't be so sure."

"Maybe all she really wants is your attention."

"Hell of a way to get it."

"She's a teenager." Lucy leaned back, feeling more at ease than she had in a while. "Don't you remember what it was like?"

"I remember being a jerk." His eyes searched her face. "I'm sure you can attest to that."

Lucky for him she was rethinking that very thing. "We're not talking about me."

"We should."

Her silence verified she didn't feel comfortable being the topic of discussion.

"So why the name change?" he asked.

"What?"

"Your last name used to be Nutter."

"And I hardly ever got any crap about that."

"So you changed it for professional reasons?"

"No." She pressed her lips together. She didn't want to go there. Not with Jordan. Not with anyone. She'd blocked out that part of her life and she liked the deep, dark grave in which she'd buried it. "I was married."

"And you're not now?"

"It ended several years ago."

"Yet you kept his name? Why? Do you have kids?"

"No kids." Thank God. Not that she didn't want any. She did. She loved children, but she was thankful that she'd been very careful about birth control during that time in her life. No child needed to grow up in an abusive environment. She had firsthand knowledge of that, growing up with verbally abusive alcoholic parents. "And I didn't keep his name. After my divorce I wanted a fresh start. So I took the name from one of my favorite Beatles songs. Although now some of my students sing the song to tease me. So maybe I should have just picked a last name out of the hat."

"Yeah." His dark eyes brightened. "You could have gotten real creative . . . Lucy Lovelace, Lucy Luscious . . ."

The names were so ridiculous she laughed. Again.

"You have a beautiful smile." His expression turned serious. "You should do it more often."

Compliments had rarely been a part of her life. Maybe that was the only reason his observation made her feel like lightning bugs were waltzing with butterflies in her stomach. Completely unsure of how to respond, she sipped her tea.

"You're not used to compliments, are you?" He leaned back in the chair, folded his arms, and studied her.

She shook her head.

"I can't imagine why not."

When she threw him a skeptical look he said, "I can't imagine why you aren't told daily what a beautiful smile you have, or how pretty you are, or that when you bite your bottom lip like you're doing now, what it can do to a man."

If he'd smiled when he said those words she'd have known he was having a laugh at her expense. No smile crossed his lips. He appeared to be dead serious. Lucy didn't quite know what to do with that.

"What happened to your marriage?"

The question wasn't out of line. But that didn't make it any easier to answer.

"That's personal." She lifted her mug that was too small to hide behind.

"It *is* personal." He leaned forward, stretched his long, muscular arms out on the table. "But we were friends once. And as a long-ago friend who's trying to get reacquainted, I'm interested in what's happened in your life."

"There's not much to tell." She lied. There was a lot. "He presented himself as someone other than he really was."

"Such as?"

Her hesitation to respond spilled over into an awkward silence. Jordan touched her arm with enough leverage to pull the mug of tea down and away from her face. "It was bad?"

She nodded. "I can't talk about it. I swore I'd never relive it all. And that's what talking about it does."

"Seems to me like you might feel better if you did."

"No." Hating the bite of the old terror sneaking up, she shook her head and looked away. "I can't."

"Okay."

He withdrew his strong hand and she watched it slide back across the table. The memory of other strong hands flashed like a bad nightmare. Oddly, while Jordan had large hands, he didn't appear to be the type who'd use them on a defenseless woman. But she pitied the men he faced on the ice.

"If you ever do feel like talking, I'm the last person on earth who'd ever judge anyone," he said. "Just give me a call."

"Thank you, but that day will never come."

He shrugged. "Never say never."

"Is that your philosophy on life?"

He laughed. "I've never had a philosophy. I never thought I'd have regrets. I even thought of having 'No Regrets' tattooed somewhere. Glad I didn't."

"Because they aren't created with erasable ink?"

"Yep."

"So you have other tattoos?"

"A few."

Lucy swallowed. Tattoos on a man were sexy. She didn't like when men were so covered you couldn't see their skin or you couldn't figure out the design, but she did appreciate a few well-placed pieces of art on a strong, hot body.

"You?" he asked.

"No ink for me."

"You don't like it?"

"I'm too chicken."

"It only hurts a little."

"Says the man who throws punches for a living."

He laughed. "That's inaccurate. I hit a puck for a living."

He took the last sip of his tea, then stood. "Come on. Walk me to the door."

"As opposed to kicking you out the door?"

When he reached for the handle on the front door, he stopped and turned toward her. "I'm hoping you'll never do that."

"It all depends on how I grade your behavior. You know, I grade my students on more than academics."

"Then how about you grade me on this." He cupped her face in one hand, leaned in, and pressed his mouth to hers.

Caught off guard, Lucy froze. The warmth and softness of his lips melted her surprise. When his other hand came up to cup her face, a low moan rumbled from her throat.

Jordan Kincade was kissing her.

Wow.

She slid her hands up beneath the back of his leather jacket, and his warmth seeped through the cotton of his T-shirt. Her palms settled on firm muscle. His delicious scent rolled over her like an intoxicating wave. His tongue teased the crease of her lips, and she didn't even think about pushing him away. The kiss deepened as he pulled her closer. Bodies pressed together, Lucy got the message that given time and circumstance, Jordan could rock her boat like it had never been rocked before.

Too soon he ended the kiss with two smaller presses of his lips to hers.

"How'd I do?" he asked. "Did I pass?"

"I don't know. I might have to have you come in after class to make sure."

"If you promise to wear garters under your skirt, I promise to bring you a shiny red apple."

Maybe she should still be surprised he'd kissed her, but she figured she'd enjoyed it too much to complain. "Oh, the shameless flirting, Mr. Kincade."

"Do I get extra credit for that?"

"A wise man once told me, never say never."

Chapter 8

"Rumor has it that the superstar of the Kincade brothers has come home to stay."

Lucy walked the hall of Sunshine Valley High next to Claudia Locke, a woman who could be considered her best friend on a good day and her pain-in-the-ass friend on a day when she was trying to pry Lucy from her comfort zone. Lucy had a sneaky suspicion that was going on right now.

"And where did you hear this earth-shattering bit of info?" she asked as they approached their classrooms.

Claudia shoved a thin newspaper in Lucy's hands. "This morning's edition of *Talk of the Town*."

CAROLINA VIPERS STRUGGLE AS
HOCKEY HUNK COMES HOME TO STAY

Lucy stopped. "Seriously? *That* made the newspaper?"

"Of course." Claudia juggled books as she reached

for her classroom door. "Don't give me that look. First of all you have to consider that the Kincade brothers *are* hot and hunky. Then you have to consider that the brother in question is a rich and famous hockey player who has left his team in the lurch while they head toward the playoffs."

Lucy didn't have to ask how Claudia knew that. Her friend followed sports. She'd had no choice, growing up in a household with three brothers, and now she was married to the king of watching sports on TV all weekend, every weekend. Where Lucy didn't know the difference between offsides and a false start, Claudia could recite exactly who the Seattle Seahawks had taken in the NFL draft and how much they'd been paid.

"He didn't leave his team in the lurch. In case you've forgotten, his parents were killed." Not that Lucy felt the need to defend him—even after the hot kiss they'd shared—but as she glanced toward her own classroom door, she saw Nicole walk inside and some kind of weird protectiveness thing emerged.

Jordan had been so nice last night. So caring and considerate. He genuinely seemed concerned about his little sister. Call it compassion or whatever you wanted, right now Lucy didn't want anyone using him or anyone else in his family for that matter, as a source of gossip.

"The woman that runs that paper is nasty," Lucy said. "All she wants to do is cause trouble. Jordan Kincade stayed to help out his family. But that doesn't mean he's giving up hockey or that he's blowing off his commitment to his team."

"Doesn't mean he's not either." Claudia opened the

door, leaned against it to hold it open as her students piled in, and grinned. "He's been away from the team for two weeks. They're barely hanging on by a skate's edge."

"Surely one man can't be the savior for an entire team."

"Sometimes it's more than just what they do on the ice, or the field, or the court, depending on what sport they play. Sometimes that one person offers leadership to a team and invokes the confidence the players need before they step into the arena."

"That's a whole lot of pressure for one person."

Claudia shrugged. "It's all part of what they do. That's why you won't find any sissy men in contact sports. They have to be tough in both mind and body."

Well, Jordan did have a perfect body. That was for sure. And he definitely knew how to kiss.

"Now, as for the unfamiliar SUV being parked in front of your house last night?" Claudia grinned. "Loooocie, you got some splainin' to do."

Before Lucy could respond, Claudia winked, then disappeared into her classroom.

Thank God.

She didn't know what she would have said. It wasn't anybody's business anyway.

A number of problems existed when you lived in a small town. Any one of them could prevent a person who craved privacy from moving in. When you added in a busybody who ran the small local newspaper, you doubled the dilemma. Until the past couple of nights Lucy's life had been too boring to pop up on anyone's radar. She minded her own business and always hoped everyone else would do the same.

Yes, she had skeletons deep in her closet, but no one who'd known her before she'd left for college would have had a clue of what she'd been through. When her father died six months after Lucy had gone off to college, her mother had moved to Oklahoma to live with Lucy's aunt, who also had alcoholic tendencies. She hadn't spoken to her mother in a long time. Maybe she should feel guilty about that. But for her own peace of mind, she didn't.

No one in Sunshine knew Lucy had gotten married except Jordan. No one even remembered her when she came back. So no one was the wiser and she planned to keep it that way. She'd worked way too hard to put the past behind her to allow anyone drag it out into the open.

As she entered her own classroom, the bell rang and Cody Christianson slipped into his seat just in time to receive her death glare.

"You're pushing your luck, Mr. Christianson."

"Made it before the bell ended."

Lucy set the box in her hands down on her desk without giving the handsome young man another look. She already knew she'd find his endearing smirk and matching flash of mischief in his green eyes. Cody was one of those students who pushed the envelope just far enough to make him feel like he was spreading his wings, but never too far to get himself in actual trouble. He reminded her a little bit of what Jordan had been like back in their school days—a hell-raiser in training and so charming no one had a clue.

Finally she turned to face her class. She flashed Cody a look and waited until he took out his notebook. Then she scanned the roomful of students. Toward the middle of the class she found Nicole deep in thought as she read something inside a very pink and flowery journal. Lucy bit back a smile, because Nicole also held a bright purple gel pen in her hand.

Looked like Jordan's thoughtful gift hadn't gone up in smoke after all.

For a few minutes, Lucy discussed that in creative writing, the ability to look deeper than what the eyes immediately registered was key. As an example, she pulled out a clear clamshell package that contained a small plastic toy bear wearing a Hawaiian shirt and sunglasses. The class twittered with laughter.

"Pretty obvious, right?" she asked the class. "Bear on a vacation. Anyone see anything different?"

Cody raised his hand. "Bear undercover for Miami vice."

She smiled. "Good one, Cody. Anyone else?" When she received no further responses, she continued with the assignment. "When I look at this bear I see that after twenty years of working without a vacation, he's finally enjoying some time off. But since he's not smiling, I see him as on that vacation alone. The sunglasses hide his tears and the Hawaiian shirt hides his broken heart."

In the classroom of twenty-four students, you could hear crickets.

Lucy knew that, for the moment, she'd made them stop and think. Hopefully. Which had been her plan. Even Nicole appeared to be paying attention.

"Your assignment—which will be handed in before you leave the classroom today—is to look deeply at the next object I pull out of the box and write its story." She glanced about the room and saw frowns, blank stares, and very few encouraging nods.

Nicole's expression gave away nothing.

"Ready?" Lucy reached inside the cardboard and pulled out a bedraggled stuffed bunny she'd once seen at a thrift store and hadn't been able to leave it behind. So she'd taken it home and given it a place to live on a shelf in her living room. After propping the bunny up on her desk so all the students could see, she said, "You only have until the end of the hour to tell me his or her story. So get started."

After five minutes, the quiet in the room stunned her. Usually there were whispers, note passing, under-desk texting, or a giggle here and there. Today every student appeared to be working—even Nicole. A sense of accomplishment floated over Lucy. Maybe she'd finally found the key to what worked for this class. Then again, she wouldn't be surprised if a few of them wrote line after line of "I can't think of anything." She'd seen that happen before.

The minutes dragged on in silence and when the bell rang, a few students flinched like they'd been caught off guard.

"Please turn in your papers on your way to the door. No sneaking out. If you don't pass by my desk and hand in the assignment you get a big fat zero for the day." She hated threats, which was why she usually saved them for the end of class.

As the class filed out and each student passed her desk and dropped a paper on the surface, Lucy beamed. Some had written only a paragraph, others a full page. When it came Nicole's turn, she dropped a paper that appeared to be full of delicate handwriting on both sides of the pink floral paper with purple pen. A completed assignment. Lucy's heart raced.

"Nicole, could you stay after class for a few minutes?"

From beneath her heavy brown eye shadow, Nicole rolled her eyes. "Whatever." Bad attitude dripping like toxic waste, she went back to her desk, clearly expecting to be reprimanded.

When the classroom emptied out, Lucy motioned Nicole to come forward. With a huff, the teen got up and approached Lucy's desk, accompanied by irritated stomps of her Ugg boots.

"I'm proud of you," Lucy said. The lift of delicately arched brows said she'd obviously shocked the girl.

"Why?"

Lucy lifted the paper. "Not only did you finish an assignment, but you handed it in."

"Whatever." Nicole glanced away as if she was either embarrassed or waiting for the other shoe to drop.

"How about we celebrate?"

Nicole's head snapped around. "What?"

"Come on, Nicole. You know you've got talent. I know you've got talent. You accomplished something today that matters. I say that calls for a couple of warm cookies and a cup of hot tea. You game?"

"I have talent?" She pressed a hand to her chest, and moisture sparkled in her eyes.

"Loads." Lucy stood, fighting the urge to pull this poor—now parentless girl—in for a hug. "And aside from being your teacher, I'd love to talk to you about the ways you can use that talent and creativity all the way into your future. So come on, it's the last class of the day, what do you say? I'll even spring for cheesecake."

"I'd . . ." The girl hesitated, then let go of the first genuine smile Lucy had seen all semester. "I think I'd like that."

Sometimes accomplishments came easy. Most times you had to work hard for them. Nicole's smile and willingness had been like a ray of sunshine on this gloomy day. Lucy would not call it a complete success until they had a chance to talk. Maybe she'd gain some insight, or maybe all Nicole really wanted was a sugar rush and a chance to get away from school and home. Whatever the reason, Lucy planned to make the best of it.

*L*ight rain drizzled down from a bank of low, steely gray clouds while Jordan waited in front of Lucy's cottage for her to come home. She'd called him little more than an hour ago and asked him to meet her. He didn't know the reason she wanted to meet. He didn't ask. She'd called, and that's all he cared about.

Last night after he'd left her house, he realized he'd probably drilled her pretty hard about her marriage. Maybe too hard. Her past wasn't any of his business. And yet he wanted—needed—to know.

What made Lucy tick?

What did she love? Hate? What was her favorite flavor of ice cream? Did she like her steak rare or well done? Or since—aside from an obvious passion for cookies—she seemed so health conscious, was she vegan? Did she like to make slow, sweet love on rainy days? And why had the man she married not seen her value when *he* had seen it all the way back in their senior year?

Yeah, his plate was already full and he didn't have the time or capacity for this sudden attraction to her. He'd always liked her, but now it was like seeing her in a completely different light.

Lucy had substance.

Digging emotionally deeper with a woman wasn't his usual thing. Yet now with Lucy, it became something he craved.

And she had heart.

Made obvious by her willingness to help his sister.

When he'd figured out she didn't seem to smile as much as she should, he wanted to be the one to put a smile on her face. He wasn't quite sure how to make that happen but he wanted to know. He wanted to spend more time with her. Figure things out. See what Lucy was all about.

The only thing he was damn sure about was that after kissing her he wanted to go back for more.

Moments later when her little white Honda pulled into the driveway, he was out of his SUV and at her car by the time she parked. He helped her from the car, then rolled her bag into the house just as the rain began to fall harder.

As soon as she unlocked her front door, Ziggy started doing a doggy version of the happy dance. Jordan stepped back as Lucy dropped the rest of her things to the floor, sank to her knees, and proceeded to engage in the hugs and baby talk that told Ziggy what a good boy he'd been and what a handsome boy he was.

Jordan appreciated seeing the straitlaced school-teacher let a happy bubble of laughter take flight. Knowing how much love and devotion she put into her pet gave Jordan an inkling of how much love she probably had to share.

Not that he was looking for love.

Since he'd left home at the age of eighteen, he'd never had a dog, a cat, or even a goldfish. There had barely been enough time in his life to date the same woman from the same town twice.

Okay, maybe that one had been on purpose.

"I'm sorry," she said to Jordan as she got up off the floor and dusted herself off. "Ziggy and I have a ritual and I need to get his Beggin' Strip before you and I talk. Is that okay?"

Jordan often had selective hearing. Lucy on her knees, making a little sweet talk and mentioning something about begging, jumped out like bullet points on an important document.

"I'm in no hurry." He jammed his hands deep into the pockets of his leather jacket. Well, maybe he was in a hurry to find out what she had to tell him. But as soon as she walked away from him in that hip-embracing skirt, he lost his train of thought.

It wasn't like the damn material was see-through,

or short, or anything special at all, really. It just gently hugged her hips and her perfectly rounded rear end. That's all.

Ordering himself to pull it together, he followed her into the kitchen and watched while she had Ziggy perform a short series of tricks before he sat like a "good boy" to receive his treat. While Ziggy chomped down the snack and Lucy wrapped her arms around the retriever's neck, Jordan thought he might do tricks too for one of those hugs.

Yeah. Totally not why he'd come here.

He shook his head to clear it, then waited until she washed and dried her hands.

"Would you like some tea?" she asked him, setting the kettle on the burner. "Besides green, I have orange spice, mango sunrise, and Earl Grey."

"I'm good." He'd like a beer or something stronger, but since Lucy seemed like a healthy food and drink kind of girl, alcoholic beverages were probably out of the question.

"Is it okay if I make a cup for myself? I just indulged in a lemon bar and hot chocolate from Sugarbuns. I think my body is going into shock."

He scanned the body in question up and down.

Looked pretty damn good to him.

"An after-school meeting?" he asked.

"As a matter of fact, yes. With Nicole. And while she didn't offer any answers to her behavior, she was very friendly and open to discussion about school." A smile brightened her face and showed off the rarely seen dimple in her right cheek. "Have a seat and we can discuss."

Last time he'd sat in her kitchen chair his butt had gone numb. Apparently his hesitation prompted an alternative.

"Better yet, how about we use the living room?" She poured her tea and, cup in hand, led the way.

Watching the woman leave a room was as fascinating as watching her enter. Lusting after a woman like a sex-craved teenager hadn't been on his agenda for a long damn time. Yet here he was, needing to roll his tongue back up in his mouth.

"Thanks for coming by," she said. "I'd have picked somewhere else to meet you but it's been a long day and I didn't want to have to wait to share this news."

"Judging by the smile you're wearing I'll guess it's a good thing?"

"Indeed." Her smile shone all the way up into her eyes. "Today I handed out an assignment specifically with Nicole in mind." Lucy sat on the edge of the white sofa and pulled a pale blue pillow onto her lap. "Something I hoped would spark her interest and maybe give her an outlet to release some of that anger."

Her long, delicate fingers played nervously across the pillow's lace-trimmed edge. He hoped it wasn't him making her nervous, then he realized that making others uneasy was what he was paid to do.

Though there were two comfortable-looking armchairs, he sat beside her and took pleasure in her sugary scent, no doubt left over from the bakery.

"I gave the students until the end of class time to complete the project."

"How'd that go?"

"Better than I imagined." She lifted her hand, then

dropped it to her knee with a slap. "Every student handed in their papers at the end of class. Even Nicole."

"Yeah? But did she do the actual assignment?" He forced a smile that hid the fear that while the rest of the class wrote a story about bugs, his sister wrote a story about grizzly bears eating tourists who hiked in the woods.

"She did." With a grin, Lucy reached into her bag and removed a folder. She pulled out a stack of papers and handed one to him.

The pink paper had flowers, and the feminine handwriting had been written with a purple pen. He recognized the paper immediately as being from the journal he'd bought his sister. His chest tightened and his heart gave a hard, out-of-tempo thump.

"She used the journal."

"She did." She squeezed his forearm. "*And* she used the pen."

He didn't know why the hell something so simple felt so damn good. It just did. "But I probably shouldn't read this. Right?"

"You're her guardian." Her head tilted slightly and her long ponytail slid across her back. "Of course you should read it."

"But I'm not her *only* guardian. My brothers and I all share equal custody."

"Doesn't matter how many there are. And because you obviously care a great deal about Nicole's welfare, I think you have every right to read it." A smile softened her face. "Of course, you might not want to let her know you've done so. Give her the privilege of at least believing she has *some* privacy. I say that only know-ing how it feels to be a teen who's trying to stretch her wings."

He remembered Lucy as a teen. But he didn't re-member her as the type to try and spread her wings. In fact, she'd seemed like the type who'd put herself in a box and tried to live quietly within those tight, confin-ing walls.

"I can keep a secret," he said.

"Then don't feel guilty. Believe me, if you had an ulterior motive for wanting to butt into her life, I'd stop you in your tracks. But I know your heart is in the right place."

She might think she knew his heart; it was just a good thing she didn't know his mind, because it was wandering all over the damn place. "I wish Nicki trusted me as much as you do."

"Who said anything about trusting you?" She smiled to take the burn off the remark. "If you don't mind, I'm going to run upstairs for a minute and give you a little privacy while you read."

"Works for me." What didn't work half as well was trying to focus on the task at hand and not wonder where Lucy slept. Or where she bathed. Did she sleep beneath soft cotton or silky sheets? Was she a long hot bubble bath or a quick shower kind of woman?

Mind swirling in all the wrong directions, he watched her disappear up the stairs. Ziggy came over and lay down at his feet with a long groan. Jordan hoped that didn't mean he'd passed gas. When the air remained clear, Jordan gave the top of the retriever's head a couple of long strokes before he read the words his baby sister had written.

Chester Rabbit had seen better days. His long ears, which had once proudly stood erect, now flopped like old wet rags on either side of his head. During the move from the house where his Misty Marie had been born, to the new home where she would finish growing up, Chester had been left behind. In the chaos of the move, Chester had fallen from an overfilled cardboard box while the movers cleared out Misty Marie's pink and yellow butterfly room.

Out in the cold, hard rain, Chester lay on the big front porch until the sun began to set behind a wall of dark, ominous clouds. The storm continued while Chester lay there waiting for his Misty Marie to come back and take him to their new home.

She would come soon. He just knew it. She would dry him off and then they would snuggle.

Night turned to day but the storm raged on. By mid-afternoon when the mail lady came by he wanted to jump up and shout, "Help me! I've been forgotten!" Because the alternative that his Misty Marie didn't love him anymore was too difficult to imagine.

As the mail lady climbed the steps to place a note behind the screen door, she looked down and discovered Chester lying there, sad, wet, and bedraggled.

"Oh!" she exclaimed as she reached down, picked him up, and brushed some of the water from his face. "There you are, Chester."

Hooray! She knew his name!

Chester's happy rabbit heart nearly pounded from his once fluffy chest.

"Misty Marie has been crying all night because she thought you were gone forever," said the mail lady. "I'm so glad her mommy called me and asked me to come looking for you."

Chester wanted to cry with relief, but he was already a soggy bunny.

"Let's get you home and all dried off so when Misty Marie comes to pick you up, you'll look good as new."

Chester wanted to thank the mail lady, but he was too relieved to speak through his little heart-shaped embroidered mouth.

"No worries, little bunny. We'll get you back in the arms of the one who loves you the most."

And as good as her word, she did.

A few hours later, Chester was snug in the arms of his Misty Marie, where he lived happily ever after.

Jordan held the pink paper tightly in his hands. He blinked fast and hard so the moisture in his eyes couldn't escape. The story was short but beautifully written deep from within Nicki's heart.

A heart that for whatever reason, she'd turned cold against him.

At first glance, nothing in her story indicated anything of a personal nature. But Jordan couldn't help wondering if his baby sister wasn't feeling a bit like Chester, a little lost and lonely, and a whole lot forgotten. He wondered if after the tragedy she'd suffered, she was worried about finding her way or her own happy ending.

At that moment Lucy came down the stairs dressed in a pair of jeans, a soft white sweater, and bare feet with light blue painted toes.

"Well?" Those light blue toes came to a stop right near the edge of the sofa where he sat. "What did you think?"

Jordan didn't think.

He couldn't.

Not with all the hope and gratitude lifting up his heavy heart.

Unable to speak, he stood and pulled Lucy into his arms.

$\mathcal{G}$od only knew how Jordan Kincade's lips had ended up locked on to hers again. As soon as Lucy regained some use of the gray matter in her head, the sensation zapped her body like a ten-million-watt circuit. Once again his lips were surprisingly soft and warm and she found herself melting into his embrace and parting her lips when his tongue teased the seam, seeking entrance. She wrapped her arms around his neck, lifted to her toes, and kissed him back with everything she had.

He gave even more.

Someone moaned and Ziggy let go a growling bark. Breathless, she pulled back. "Wow."

"Wow is right."

"That probably shouldn't have happened again."

"But it did. And if you give me another chance I'll come back for more."

So would she. Heck, if Jordan's kisses were a hint of the passion he was capable of, sign her up for the whole shebang.

"And I'm not going to apologize," he said.

"I wouldn't ask you to."

"Good." His broad shoulders lifted in a shrug. "Because I think that kiss is something we should have done a long time ago."

"Back then I probably wouldn't have allowed it," she lied.

The big bad hockey player closed the gap she'd put between them and stepped right into her personal bubble. She tried to hold her ground even though her knees wobbled like gelatin.

A corner of his mouth kicked upward. "Are you sure about that?"

"What I'm sure of is that we've gotten way off track. Again. And I want to hear your thoughts on Nicole's story." Flustered, Lucy escaped to the kitchen and set her mug of tea in the sink. To heck with herbal tea, she needed a glass of wine. A large glass. Preferably a Big Gulp size.

Opening the refrigerator door, she grabbed the bottle of Sunshine Creek Vineyards Chardonnay left over from her book club group last week.

"Nice to know you're supporting my family's business."

Of course he'd followed her into the kitchen. Where else would an alpha male go when he'd been left behind? Alphas didn't like to be left behind any more than they liked to be led. And there was no doubt in Lucy's mind that Jordan was one hundred and fifty percent alpha.

"I support as many local businesses as I can." She grabbed a wine goblet from the cupboard, uncorked the bottle, and poured the glass half full. "And your family makes delicious wine."

"Aren't you going to offer me a glass?" The lift to his dark brow suggested he might be amused.

"Don't you have plenty at home?" Of course she should offer him a glass. But that kiss had thrown her off-kilter.

Way off.

"Probably." He opened her cupboard door, took out a goblet, and poured himself a glass. "But it's a lot more fun sharing with you."

Golden liquid splashed up inside the globe as she watched him pour. He tapped his glass against hers, then took a sip. For a brief moment he remained blessedly silent while the wine settled on his taste buds.

"Nice blend. Ryan's doing a good job."

"Your brother is good at many things. I would guess his job is one of them."

The frown on his face said he didn't like her comment. When he leaned closer, the frown deepened even as something in his eyes sparked. "Let me ask you straight up. Are you interested in my brother?"

Jealousy?

No way.

"If you mean am I interested in him because he's now one of Nicole's guardians, then yes, I'm interested." She didn't know why she felt the need to reassure him. Jordan wasn't the type of man who needed to be reassured about anything. "If you meant something different, then you'd be mistaken."

"Are you sure about that?" He backed her toward the counter and trapped her efficiently with only the presence of his powerful body. Then he dipped his head and ran his nose up the length of her neck.

Chills drifted down her back and reawakened the girls in the basement, who were suddenly standing at attention. She said, "Positively certain," even though she wasn't positive of anything other than she wanted her hands all over his hard muscles.

He lifted his head and smiled. "Good."

Good?

There had been times in her life, when Lucy questioned a man's words and the meaning behind them. "You stupid bitch" had been one she'd never had to clarify. "Good," in this case, perplexed her enough to step into the big pile of doo to which they were most likely headed.

"I'm not quite sure I understand what you mean by 'good.'"

"Then let me make this real simple." The sparkle in his eyes spelled trouble. "Because I like to be clear about things. Especially if it comes down to being in competition with my own brother."

"Apparently you're not making it simple enough," she said. "Competition for what?"

"For you, Lucy."

*S*omething turned over inside Jordan when Lucy blushed. And that something wasn't quite what he'd expected.

"Don't be ridiculous." She grabbed the bottle of wine and headed into the living room. Ziggy followed close on the heels of her bare feet.

Jordan followed too.

"I'm not the kind of girl men fight over," she said as she made her way toward the sofa. "It's okay. Believe me, I'm fine with that. And please don't tease me."

Her clenched jaw and wide eyes made something tighten in his chest. Someone had done a number on her. Or maybe a lot of someones. Including him. God, he could kick his seventeen-year-old self's ass right now.

"Tease you?" He held up his hands, careful not to slosh wine onto the floor. "Only in a good way. But if you think you're not the kind of woman men would fight over, we need to have a serious talk. Because you are definitely that kind of woman."

Expression now passive as though she didn't believe him, she sat down on the sofa, tucked her legs up, and pulled Nicole's paper onto her lap. "As much as I'd like to continue this exchange—please note the sarcasm in my tone—I'd much prefer to get back to the reason I called you here. Your sister's future. You do remember that was my original intent, don't you? And not all these deviations in subject matter?"

"What I remember is how good your lips felt on mine and how good you feel in my arms." Intrigued, Jordan sat beside her, sipped his wine, and wondered what it would take to get Lucy to let down her hair. Literally and figuratively. "But I can assure you that my sister's welfare is never far from my mind."

"Then let's discuss the next steps toward helping guide her toward a bright future."

"You mean so we don't have to talk about you?"

Her dark eyes turned even darker. "As much as I appreciate the compliment—"

"You'd prefer to keep the conversation about my sister."

"Yes. So if staying on task is something you feel unable to do, please say so now. I can always contact one of Nicole's other guardians for help in this matter."

"Not an option." And only because he didn't want it to be. Any one of his brothers could handle this issue. But rediscovering Lucy after all these years was like finding the diamond in a stack of coal. And there was no way in hell he intended to share.

The realization rattled him.

Even though his friends called him cynical when it came to relationships, he'd been happy with the way his life had been going. He thought of himself as a realist—frugal of the heart and lifestyle. By choice he lived in an apartment near Charlotte instead of an expensive house on Lake Norman. He drove a Range Rover instead of a Maserati. And most nights he cooked at home instead of dining at five-star restaurants. He'd been brought up in a pennywise environment and he still tended to live that way. Not that he was cheap by any means; he had the money and could splurge at any given moment. He just had a healthy respect for the hard-hitting way he earned a living.

At the age of thirty-three, he realized his days on the ice were numbered. Most likely he had a couple more years, and then he'd have to find something else to do. He'd like to live out the rest of his life comfortably without worrying whether he'd have enough to pay the rent. In the future he wanted to invest in a business. And at some point, he'd like to come home to a wife and family.

Yes. He admired the woman Lucy had become. But was he ready for *that*? Was he ready to get *involved* with someone? And why the hell was the thought even entering his mind?

"Why isn't it an option to call on your brothers?" she asked him.

"They're all too busy." Sometimes a lie was the best way to handle something. Especially when you weren't quite sure what you were doing.

"And you're not?"

Lucy knocked him off balance. And for a guy whose career depended on his stability, it was an unnerving place to be. "*I* need to do this," he said, understanding that this, at least, was the truth. "Me. And nobody else except the help you're so generously giving me."

When she didn't question his motive, they discussed the possibility of a deeper motivation behind Nicole's assignment story. In the end, Lucy agreed with him that something bigger might be at hand and that questioning a few of Nicki's friends would be the best place to start.

"I'm not sure me approaching a group of young girls would be wise," he said. "I wouldn't want anyone to get the wrong idea."

"You're probably right. I'll handle it as soon as we get back from spring break."

"Next week is spring break?"

She nodded.

"So we have to wait an entire week to find out?" He jammed his fingers into his hair and groaned. "I can't just let my sister's situation sit on idle. I'm worried about her."

If he at least knew what he was dealing with, he could get Nicki the professional help she needed. "Her anger and her constant expectation that I'll leave are unreasonable."

"Then it's important for you to stick around," Lucy said. "Can you do that? Can you put your life on hold for another week?"

Jordan knew where his heart wanted to be. He knew where his dedication lay. But he also had a professional contract and things in that direction could turn real ugly, real fast. He didn't even want to acknowledge the part of him that missed lacing up his skates and hitting the ice.

It had been weeks since he'd played. He missed the roar of the crowd. The camaraderie with his team. The rush through his blood. He loved what he did for a living. Without it, he really had no idea who he was or who he could be.

It didn't surprise him that he defined himself by his career. It was all he'd ever had. Changing that now would take time and focus—two things he currently didn't have stockpiled in his favor.

"I'll figure it out," he said. "I need to do what's best for Nicole."

Lucy smiled. "You're a good brother."

"I'm a shitty brother who's trying to make up for practically ignoring her her whole life."

"Well, hopefully her friends will have some insight. I'll see what I can do to speed up the possibility of speaking with them."

"I'd appreciate that."

Jordan took a drink of his wine and his mind wandered for a minute. When he refocused Lucy was talking about Nicole's group of friends. Her expressions became more animated. Or maybe that was just cause and effect of the wine she'd been sipping. He'd refilled her glass twice, and since he didn't know her well enough, he figured he'd best keep an eye on how much more she drank. Not that he was opposed to her loosening up a little.

Nope.

Not opposed at all.

"It's crazy," she said, waving her half-empty glass.

Uh-oh. What did he miss?

"Did you know there are girls at Sunshine High who spend over a thousand dollars on prom?" she asked him, then continued because obviously he had no answer. "Whatever happened to just buying a dress and a corsage and borrowing Dad's car? I mean, now these kids rent stretch limos and have *after* parties that go till dawn. And they dress like movie stars. They guzzle champagne in the back of the limos with fresh strawberries dropped into their crystal flutes even though they aren't legally old enough to drink."

Jordan frowned. How the hell did they get on the subject of prom?

"Oh come on. Isn't that what prom was like for you?" he teased.

"Me? Pfft. I didn't go to prom."

"Why?"

"Didn't have a date."

"If I hadn't been such an idiot, I would have asked you."

The wineglass halted halfway to her lips before she returned it to the table. With her fingertips she edged the glass farther away. "I'm sorry. I've been talking too much. This isn't about me. It isn't about prom or spoiled teenagers. We're here to talk about Nicole."

Maybe, but he definitely noted something in her words and tone. Although she'd never admit it, she felt left out having missed one of the traditions of the high school years.

"If I remember right, prom is just around the corner," he said. "So maybe that fits into all of this with Nicki."

"I never thought of that."

"Mind if I ask you something?"

Her head tilted back a little, like she didn't quite trust where he was going. "Sure."

"When a conversation becomes about you, why do you always turn it around to something else?"

An uneasy laugh bubbled from her lips. "I don't do that."

"Yeah. You do. It's like you think you're not important enough to talk about. Well, I think you are." Frustrated, he sipped the last of his wine, then grabbed her half-empty glass from the table and carried them into the kitchen.

While rinsing the glasses he tried to clear his mind of all the unpleasant things Lucy must have gone through in her life. The moment he turned off the faucet, he wasn't at all surprised by what thought surfaced to the top. A plan, really. And one she probably was going to fight like a bad hair day.

When he came back into the living room, she stood by the front door while Ziggy remained stretched out with his big brown eyes watching every move she made.

"Thanks for coming by," she said, opening the door and averting her eyes anywhere but on him. "I hope you're feeling more encouraged about your sister."

Behind her back she kept her grip on the doorknob that left the door partially open. Still, he received the message.

We're done here.

He'd put her in an uncomfortable place when all he really wanted was to find out more about her.

"I promise to see what I can do about talking to her friends, but the soonest I'll be able to contact anyone probably won't be until Monday," she said. "And that's only if I can get in touch with anyone. A lot of people go on spring break vacation. I'll call you as soon as I know anything."

Though Jordan played a game for a living, he didn't play games in real life. He was a man who usually knew what he wanted and always did his best to get it. For the first time he was unsure. But right now, he thought maybe he wanted Lucy.

He walked up to her, placed his hand on the open door beside her head, and pushed the door closed. She shuffled backward until she became trapped between two unmovable objects—him and the door.

"Not good enough." With his skates on, he was the epitome of in control. With Lucy he was ready to throw caution into the fire.

"What do you mean, 'not good enough'?" Annoyance puffed from between her moist, rosy lips. Fists slammed down on her shapely hips, and a furrow tightened the skin between her rich, brown eyes. "That's all there is. I'll find out and I'll call you."

"Don't you see, Lucy? I don't want just a call." He touched the side of her face. Trailed the backs of his fingers down her cheek. "I want more."

When her eyes widened he was tempted to just lean in and give her another toe-curling kiss. "Go out with me tomorrow night."

"What?"

"You know . . . you, me, a movie, a box of popcorn. A date."

"You're asking me out on a date."

A statement, he noticed. Not a question. As if she couldn't comprehend the meaning. And that pissed him off. Lucy should be taken out often, shown off, and treated well.

"I believe that's what I just asked. So are you game? Or do I have to start clucking?"

"Clucking?"

"Because you're too chicken to say yes."

"I'm not chicken."

"Perfect." Fighting a smile, he eased his way into the open space and stepped out onto her porch. "Then I'll pick you up at seven o'clock tomorrow night."

"Seven?"

"Seven." It didn't take much to pull her against him. She didn't fight it or the brief kiss he gave her to erase the confusion from her face. "Good night, Lucy." Then he closed the door and said from the other side, "Lock the door so I don't come back in there."

Behind him the deadbolt slammed into place.

He didn't know if she'd take him seriously. Didn't know if she'd actually be ready at seven, or if she'd dodge him and wouldn't even be home. Even with all those negatives hanging over his head, as he strolled to the SUV, he found himself whistling because he had a good feeling she'd be there. And when he felt this good he knew there was always a chance the evening would turn out to be everything he wanted.

Then again, there was every chance it would be a complete disaster.

Lucy threw the deadbolt. Then, unable to stop herself, she marched over to the window, pulled back the curtain, and watched Jordan walk toward the black SUV. When he opened the driver's door, it was as if he sensed her watching. He turned, caught her red-handed, and flashed her a smile. She let go of the curtain and huffed out a growl.

Ziggy lifted his big head and looked at her like she'd gone off the deep end.

"He drives me crazy, Zigs."

Her dog responded with a little whine.

"Seriously over-the-edge crazy." She peeked out the window again but he was gone. "I don't know what he expects from me."

Throughout her entire life she'd left spontaneity at the door. With the exception of her rotten marriage, everything in her control had been planned to within an inch of her life.

Jordan knocked her carefully laid plans and her logical thinking askew.

She'd always made valiant efforts to blend into the background and remain as invisible as she could. To keep her head on straight and move forward through life as quietly and as unassumingly as possible. She didn't live with high expectations. And she no longer dared to dream.

Big, flashy dreams were dangerous. For her, happy and content were enough.

Jordan, on the other hand, didn't ask. He took. He didn't back off. Didn't blink. He just forged ahead like a steamroller. Granted, his forcefulness was nonthreatening. But still, like those dreams, he was dangerous.

When he'd had her trapped between him and the

door, heat had radiated off him that had nothing to do with the temperature in the room. It had been pure sexual masculinity and she'd wanted to lose herself in him. Wrap herself around him and climb him like a tree. Unwrap him like a present and touch all those hard, sexy muscles with her hands and, dear God, her tongue. For the first time in longer than she could remember, she desired a man.

Sweet baby Jesus.

One thing was certain.

Locking the deadbolt and securing herself inside her home was going to be a lot easier than securing her heart against Jordan Kincade.

On the way home, Jordan put his cell phone to good use. By the time he was driving up the hill toward his parents' house he'd put things for his date with Lucy in motion. She might be expecting popcorn and a movie, but Jordan wanted to give her much more. And if all went according to plan, she'd be completely surprised.

He knew it was late, but he'd spotted Nicole's little Sonata in the driveway and he didn't want to miss an opportunity to let her know that, despite her ambivalence or wishful thinking, he was still here.

A light drizzle beaded on the sleeves of his jacket as he tested the front door to the house and found it unlocked. For the first time in years he let himself in without feeling like he needed an invitation.

With the exception of the glow from the big-screen TV in the family room, the house was dark and quiet.

Before he headed in that direction, he glanced toward the stairs and wondered why his teenage sister would be locked up in her room on a Friday night.

Or maybe she wasn't.

Maybe she'd gone out with friends and had left her car there. He hadn't considered that before he'd come inside.

Trying to cope with the eerie absence of his mom and dad, he kept walking. In the family room he found Declan stretched out on the sofa, legs crossed at the ankles, with a huge bowl of popcorn balanced on his flat stomach. Surprisingly Mr. GQ was dressed in a T-shirt and cargo shorts. On the big-screen TV, Joe Fox—aka Tom Hanks—was writing an e-mail to Shopgirl.

"I always knew you were a sentimental sap."

Declan jerked upright and popcorn flew from the bowl. He turned to Jordan with a murderous glare. "What the hell are you doing here?"

Jordan chuckled. "Hoping to stay hidden long enough to see you weep into your hankie. Guess my cover's blown now."

"Great." Dec started picking up the popcorn kernels and tossing them back in the bowl. "Now I'll have to make a new batch."

"Dude. I just caught you watching *You've Got Mail* without a girl in the room and you're worried about the popcorn?"

"I had a girl on the phone while I was watching. Does that count?"

"Depends on the girl."

"Brooke Hastings."

"Your assistant?"

Dec nodded.

"Were you having phone sex?"

"With *Brooke*?"

"No, with the neighbor down the road." Jordan sighed. "Yes with Brooke."

"She's my assistant."

"And hot as hell."

The brief silence told Jordan that his brother hadn't considered his assistant in that way. But he damn well should. The long-legged blonde had a beach bod, brains that went on all day, and a bubbly personality that said she could easily be a kid sister, best friend, mom of the year, or the hottest thing between the sheets ever. She was every man's dream. Except apparently Declan's.

Stupid ass.

"Jesus, Dec." Jordan planted himself in the recliner. "Don't tell me you're one of those all work and no play kind of guys."

"I've been building a business."

"Brother, it's built. You're a success. Time to have a little fun. When was the last time you went out and had a good time?"

"Mmmm . . ." In deep thought, his brother studied the ceiling. "Maybe a charity event to fund a new hospital wing or something."

"You don't know?"

"I know I banged a hot redhead that night when I went home."

"Well, at least you're getting laid."

"Yeah."

Thanks to his twin, Jordan felt a headache coming on. "Exactly how the hell long ago was this charity event?"

"October?"

"You asking or telling?"

"No." Dec snapped his fingers. "November."

"So what you're saying is you haven't gotten laid for at least six months, you're not having phone sex with your hot assistant, and you're watching a rom-com. *Alone*."

"You make it sound so bad."

Jordan laughed because there was nothing else to do in the situation. "Brother? We've got to take care of this situation pronto."

"I can find my own women."

"Prove it." Jordan scooted to the edge of the recliner. "Pick up your phone right now and call Brooke back."

"Haven't you ever heard mixing business and pleasure is a bad idea?" Declan set the popcorn bowl on the coffee table.

"Then if you have to choose, take pleasure. Unless you like going to bed alone and your morning wood becomes a sad little man because he knows he's going to be lonely again."

"Watch how you use the word *little*, jackass." Declan glared. "And if you're such hot stuff, when was the last time you got laid?"

Jordan didn't hesitate. "Two weeks ago."

"Dry spell huh?" His brother leaned back on the sofa. "Guess everything going on kind of takes away the mood."

"I didn't say I wasn't in the mood." Hell, if Lucy gave him a green light he'd be all over that in a matter of seconds.

"Spare me the details."

Jordan laughed. God it was fun joking around and giving his brothers hell again.

Dec ran a hand through his short dark hair. "When are you heading back to North Carolina?"

"No plans to go back."

"Seriously? Your team is working their way toward the playoffs and you have no plans to go back? Are you fucking crazy?"

"No crazier than you for not noticing your hot assistant."

"Touché."

"I made a promise to the family." Jordan shrugged. "I intend to keep it."

"Everyone understands you have a career and responsibilities that go with it." Declan hit the MUTE button on the remote when a commercial for toilet bowl cleaner came on. "I'm dedicated to working things out here too. Hasn't your coach or your agent been wondering when you're coming back?"

"So far they've been polite and understanding. But Coach left a voice mail tonight and he doesn't sound so patient anymore. Guess the team lost again."

"You haven't been watching the games?"

"They're not all televised."

"They want you back so they must think you're the man to save the team."

"I'm no savior. I just have a hell of a right hook and a mean slap shot."

"And don't forget you're an expert at warming the bench in the penalty box." Dec's smile vanished. "I'm serious, Jordy. The family will understand."

"Our sister won't." He glanced over his shoulder at the darkened staircase. "Which reminds me, is the baby dragon home?"

Dec nodded. "Upstairs with her headphones on and texting so fast I'm sure her fingertips are raw."

"Gotcha." Jordan stood. "I'll be back."

"Okay, Arnold." Dec hit the MUTE button again, and the room filled with the fiesta party sounds of a cruise line commercial.

Rebuilding camaraderie with his twin felt good, Jordan noted as he climbed the stairs. They still had some awkward moments, but things were definitely better.

Upstairs, he knocked on Nicki's door even though he didn't expect her to respond. The music raging through her headphones could be heard all the way through the solid wood barrier. Damn. The girl was going to be deaf before she hit legal drinking age.

Caught off guard, he brought his head up as her door swung open. The instant narrowing of her eyes told him she'd expected Declan or anyone other than him.

"You don't hate me," he said.

She yanked the headphones off and tossed them behind her. Luckily they landed on the bed. "What?"

"I said, you don't hate me."

Both hands, accented by goth purple nail polish, slammed down on her hips. "Who told you that lie?"

"I just know, Nicki. And I wanted to stop by and say . . ." He opened his arms and gave her a cheesy grin. "See, I'm still here."

"Did you come bearing bribery gifts again?"

"Nope. I just brought this." His open arms surrounded her as he pulled her in for a hug. As expected, she froze like a Popsicle. Then he kissed the top of her head and whispered, "I love you, Nicki. You can be as mad at me as you want, but I'm still going to love you. Never doubt that."

He kissed the top of her head again, let her go, then stepped away. "Night, baby sister. See you tomorrow."

Before his feet hit the top step, she slammed her bedroom door. He paused. When he heard her let go of a huge sob, everything inside him told him to go back in there and console her.

Baby steps.

In order to gain her trust, he couldn't overwhelm her. He just needed to continue to reassure her that he loved her and he was here to stay.

God and the NHL willing.

Chapter 9

Family meetings were never fun. Especially when they were called at the crack of dawn and you'd had only a few hours of restless sleep.

Surrounded by aging casks of Merlot and Cabernet, Jordan grabbed one of the big wooden chairs at the center of the extra long farm table in the barrel room. In the past, the room had been part of the event center. Small weddings and private parties could be held here. Though a bit on the cool side, the oak walls and barrels made for an attractive rustic décor, and the fragrance of aging wine added a nice touch.

He hadn't even had time to make a pot of coffee this morning before Ryan sounded the alarm. Sipping the slightly bitter brew made from the heavy-duty office coffeemaker, he glanced around the table. His brothers looked to be in no better condition than he. On the other hand, Aunt Pippy, an important member of the family though not an official member of the new board of directors, looked bright-eyed and ready to take on the world in her gold and orange dress, blue plastic headband, and red suede ankle boots. Then again, if she was really that bright-eyed, wouldn't she have noticed that nothing she had on matched?

Stifling a yawn, Jordan took a long drink and prayed the java gods would do their wakey-wakey dance in a hurry.

He'd spent half the night finalizing things for tonight's date with Lucy. While he worried his plan wouldn't come together, he now had to focus on the reason they'd been summoned to the vineyards on such short notice.

Ryan came into the room with a frown and a cardboard box he set down at the head of the table. As he settled his palms on the surface, his broad shoulders visibly slumped. "I didn't ask Nicki or Riley to join us today because, well, I just don't think they need to be involved. Since they're both under eighteen, it's up to us to take care of things."

"Good thinking," Aunt Pippy said, then took a slug of coffee.

"As much as I'd like to be standing here telling you that everything is great," Ryan said, "I can't."

Jordan hated starting out the day on a sour note. But it didn't look like any of them had a choice.

"Declan and I spent all day yesterday going through the ledgers and bank accounts and . . ." Ryan folded his arms across his chest. "Well, there's just no other way to say it except someone's been stealing money from the company. A lot of money."

"Define *a lot*," Parker said.

Ryan lifted the lid off the cardboard box and withdrew a folder. And even though Jordan was sure the specific amount had kept Ryan up all night, his brother read the figures printed on a stack of papers.

"Somewhere to the tune of a hundred and fifty grand."

Obscenities flew.

Parker wanted to know, "Was the money taken in large or small amounts?"

Ryan shrugged and Declan took over. "The paper trail is hard to follow. There's no direct path. It's going to take further investigation with someone more skilled at this kind of thing than any of us."

"Did Mom and Dad make investments that weren't properly documented?" Ethan asked.

"There's no sign of that." Declan lifted his mug of coffee and took a drink. "It looks like someone knew the system and figured out how to work it."

Jordan glanced at those gathered around the table. "Who had access to the accounts?"

Eyes dark and troubled, Ryan looked up. "Only Dad and I had access. Each night Dad locked the files up in the safe."

"What about the computer files?"

"We have a well-protected system."

"Well, there's nobody on earth more honest than you, Ryan." No way did his brother have anything to do with the missing money. Jordan knew by the pained look on his face that Ryan was deeply troubled by this discovery. "And since Dad's not here to speak for himself, I say we hire an investigator."

"I'll second that," Declan said.

"I appreciate the vote of confidence. Anyone else have an opinion or maybe have a clue where that money might be?" Ryan glanced around the table. "Or where Aunt Pippy ran off to?"

They all looked around and were surprised to find no sign of her except her nearly full coffee cup abandoned on the table.

"Looks like she slipped out while we were in deep discussion," Ethan said.

Seemed she did that a lot. Jordan frowned before Parker pulled his attention back into the conversation.

"Maybe we should start looking into the workers," Parker suggested. "I know they don't have access to the accounts, but money can be pilfered in many ways."

"A hundred and fifty grand worth?" Jordan asked.

Parker shrugged. "Happens all the time. Someone hires a nanny or an assistant and the next thing you know your hard-earned cash is gone with the wind. Or the hacker."

"Unfortunately, until we have an answer, everyone is suspect." Ryan scanned the room. "Even me. That's not all the news I have. But believe me, this isn't any better."

"When it rains, it pours," Ethan murmured.

"We finished the fiscal tax year in the red." Ryan let the other shoe drop. "Not deep, but in the red nonetheless."

"Fuck." Parker scratched his head. "So how do we fix that?"

"We find ways to make the company more profitable."

Declan got up, poured another cup of coffee, then returned to the table.

"Such as?" Jordan wanted to help in any way he could but he had no idea what it took to turn around a flagging family winery.

"At this point we need to consider everything." Declan shrugged. "All ideas are welcome and necessary."

"How about some Sunday wine festivals?" Ethan asked. "Maybe with some local bands. Local restaurants could do the catering with a portion of their profits going to the winery as an operator's fee."

"*Or* the area's food trucks," Parker added, knowing he had one of the best. "Maybe we could create an onsite trattoria in the building next to the event center."

"What about a wine club?" Jordan suggested. "With an annual membership fee that would include special wine deals. Maybe they could also receive VIP tickets to the Sunday festivals."

"These are all great concepts." Ryan seemed relieved that everyone had put a positive spin on such a negative situation. "Maybe everyone could make a list of their ideas so when we come back together we can vote on each project."

"Just so you know," Jordan said. "I'm more than willing to financially invest in the business."

"Me too," Dec said.

"I'll put up the cash for a trattoria," Parker amended. "I've been saving to open my own restaurant. Might as well put it here."

"I'm no millionaire," Ethan said, "but I'll gladly

invest what I've got. And I can put in some sweat equity too."

"Yeah, but will you shave that beard before things start growing in there?" Jordan joked.

"Consider it done." Ethan chuckled. "Although don't you hockey players have some superstition thing and start growing *Duck Dynasty* beards as soon as the playoffs get going?"

"Not me. The ladies don't like them."

A groan of consensus passed around the table.

"Maybe this was all part of Mom and Dad's plan— bringing us back together," Ethan said.

"I don't know." Ryan shrugged. "But it sure as hell beats wondering what everyone else is doing when we're spread throughout the country."

Jordan couldn't agree more.

When his cell phone vibrated on the table in front of him, he glanced down at the incoming number. Coach Reiner. For the fourth time in less than twenty-four hours.

Shit.

He let the call go to voice mail.

Again.

Tomorrow he'd deal with the situation.

Today was all about family.

And Lucy.

As everyone got up from the table and clustered around the coffeemaker for refills, Jordan caught Ryan off to the side of the room.

"Don't sweat this," he said. "I can tell by the ready-to-keel-over look on your face that you've lost sleep trying to figure it all out."

Ryan nodded. "Haven't really slept much since the call came in about Mom and Dad."

"I'm right there with you." Jordan clamped his hand on his big brother's shoulder. "Just remember, we're all in this together. You don't need to bear the burden alone."

"I appreciate that. I haven't been able to spend much time with Riley lately. It's starting to feel more like she's the parent and I'm the kid."

"What do you mean?"

"She's lost so much. Yet she constantly worries about *me*. She's always trying to take care of me. Make sure I eat right. Hell, because of the circumstances she's been thrown into, she's growing up too fast. It's not fair. I want her to be a little girl for as long as she can."

"Sometimes life just hands a kid a tough road. But she'll come out of it okay. Because she has you. Never fear that."

"I do. I just wish her mom wasn't so . . ."

"Wrapped up in toilet paper?"

Ryan groaned. "I can't begin to tell you what it does to a man's ego when he knows he can't compete with something you flush down the shitter."

"I'm sure there are women lined up to take her place."

"Don't know. Haven't dated since she left."

"Dated." Jordan's eyebrows jacked up his forehead. "As in you haven't—"

"Nope. Haven't done that either."

"Jesus. You and Dec are giving the Kincade men a bad name."

"Pretty sure I don't want to know what's going on—or not going on—with him."

"Let's just say the two of you could start a celibacy club."

"Not the kind of club I'm interested in."

"I would imagine not." Jordan patted his brother's broad shoulder. "So, change of subject?"

"Yes please."

"Thank God." Jordan sipped his coffee. "I thought I'd give you an update on Nicki."

"I appreciate that you're really taking this situation to heart," Ryan said. "I've got—"

"Your hands are full." Jordan acknowledged the cold, hard facts. "I totally get that. And while I don't have all the answers yet, I am making progress with the help of her creative writing teacher."

His brother smiled. "Lucy's a nice woman."

Nice. Complicated. Smart. Sexy. And Jordan knew there was a whole lot more he'd yet to discover.

"Yeah. She's great," he said. "She plans to talk to the school counselor to make sure we're taking the proper steps to help Nicki."

"What?" Ryan's head went back. "Wait a minute. You? Following rules?"

"I don't break them all, you know."

"Well, I appreciate the extra effort," Ryan said. "And especially for your patience with our sister. I know she's not always the easiest firecracker in the box to handle."

"The baby dragon?" Jordan chuckled. "She's not as tough as she thinks she is. Besides, I'm wearing her down."

"Oh really?"

"Yeah. I'm sticking around. She swears I'm going to run out on her. I have to prove I'm not."

"That's a big order to fill, little brother. What about your career? The team? The playoffs?"

Jordan shrugged. "I'll figure it out."

Famous last words.

"Well, whatever you do . . ." Ryan clamped his hand over Jordan's shoulder. "It's really good to have you around for a change."

"Thanks. It's good to be here. Does that mean I can borrow the keys to the event center tonight?"

"What have you got planned?"

"I could tell you but then I'd have to kill you."

"Sounds serious." Ryan's brows came together over a piercing glare.

"Just the opposite."

"Then yes, you may have the keys." Ryan grinned. "Just make sure you don't break anything."

"No worries." The last thing he had in mind was a brawl. Then again, he wasn't exactly sure how much Lucy liked surprises.

At eleven minutes to seven Lucy felt like she was about to break down. Or throw up. She paced across her bedroom floor, holding this skirt or that blouse up to her body so she could inspect her clothing choices.

She realized too late that she didn't have the appropriate clothes to wear on a *date* and it was too late to go shopping.

Not that she had a clue where they were going.

She had work clothes, casual clothes, workout clothes, and sleeping clothes. Everything in her closet consisted of black, white, or blue, if you counted the jeans she owned that were not going-out-appropriate attire. Nothing she had sparkled, shimmered, or glowed. She didn't own pearls or even fun costume jewelry like her friend Claudia wore, so she couldn't even dress up a boring outfit.

Not for the first time in her life did she regret her nonexistent fashion sense.

In eleven minutes, Jordan Kincade would arrive at her door, expecting her to be ready to go out.

With *him*.

Mr. Hotness.

Whatever possessed the man was beyond her. And even though she'd never really agreed to let him pick her up, he'd be on her doorstep in exactly . . . ten minutes and thirty seconds.

Holy cow.

From the foot of her bed Ziggy watched as she fluttered by, cursed under her breath, and attempted to find a good excuse not to go when he showed up. Maybe . . .

That was it!

Like a red light had suddenly appeared in the middle of her room, she stopped.

She'd feign illness.

No one would be the wiser if she answered her front

door dressed in her robe with her hair a mess and a blotchy face that proved sometime in the past twenty-four hours she'd developed a deadly disease that made it impossible for her to go anywhere.

She was contagious.

Yes!

And it would be cruel to subject him to something that would obviously make him feel as horrible as she looked.

Brilliant!

Trying not to cackle with devious laughter, she reached for her robe. In that moment conscience caught up with genius and pounded the idea down with a hammer. A wave of regret poured over her.

At the sound of her overly dramatic moan, Ziggy cocked his head, lifted his little doggy brows, and tooted.

"Don't look at me like that. I'm not crazy. And I'm not going to get you a treat just because you're cute either. Especially when you smell like *that*." Accustomed to her dog's stinky winds, Lucy patted him on the head, then shoved her arms into the robe. Anxiety tumbled through her stomach. "I'm just . . . disappointed in myself. No need to go into an explanation, I'm sure. You've seen the routine before."

Ziggy whined, then put his head down between his paws. His big brown eyes continued to watch her every move.

"Good thing you don't judge me or we'd be in a heap of trouble."

With no other option than to go through with the ruse,

she grabbed her hair up into the messiest knot she could assemble. When the doorbell rang, she pinched her nose and her cheeks hard, shoved her feet into her house slippers, then shuffled off to answer the door. Hand on the knob, she did a few extra pinches, took a steadying breath, gave an Oscar-worthy cough, and opened the door.

"Cinderella?"

Lucy stared at the trio of strangers on her doorstep. Tightly put together in a deep purple suit with a black and white striped shirt and a hot pink tie, the small-statured man smiled and his head wobbled as if he was tipsy. The two women beside him appeared a little less dramatic in spring dresses and high heels that had to be at least five painful inches tall.

"I'm sorry," Lucy said, clutching the neck of her robe with one hand while she prepared to close the door with the other. "You must have the wrong house."

The man leaned back to check out the metal address numbers beside her mailbox near the door. "This is 173 Daffodil Lane, correct?"

"Yes."

"And you're Lucy Diamond, correct?"

"Yes. But who are you?"

"Why . . . we're you're fairy godmothers, sweetie." The man waved his hand like a wand. "Bibbidi-bobbidi . . . oh, fussbudget. Step aside, my darling, we're on a mission."

Panic reared its head as he pushed past her.

"Stop." Lucy tried to restrain her alarm. "You can't just barge in here. I don't know you. And you could be . . . a mass murderer for all I know."

"Sweetie. Do I look like Charlie Manson?" He waved a hand over his loud outfit. "No. I do not. The closest I come to a Charlie is via the Chocolate Factory because Johnny Depp is so delicious in that movie I can barely control myself. But I digress."

Not buying it, Lucy dug her cell out of the robe pocket to dial 911.

At that moment Ziggy rushed down the stairs barking. When he hit the landing he did a doggy dance as if he wanted to be a part of the party too.

"Put away your phone, my darling. We aren't here to rob you or steal your life. We're here to make you beautiful." The man stepped back and gave her a good once-over. "And I must say, not a minute too soon."

The two women held up black carrying cases as proof, then they shrugged as if this was routine.

It wasn't.

More confused than ever, Lucy had to admit that the man seemed a lot more the type to flitter and fuss than stab or maim.

"This is the last time I'm asking before I call the cops. Who. Are. You?"

"*I* am Rashard. These lovely ladies are Gloria and Beatrice. They work with me at Stardust Creations in Vancouver. We're here to make you presentable for your date."

"You're what?" She blinked.

"Are you sick?" Rashard leaned in for a better look. "Your nose is quite red and though I always enjoy a good robe for relaxing, yours looks a bit like . . . well, frankly, it's seen better days."

"I'm not sick."

"Ah. I see. Faking it then? Was that your plan to get out of the date? Believe me, faking *anything* simply isn't worth the time." The man turned to Gloria and flicked his wrist. Gloria set down her black case, then slipped out the front door. Moments later she came back with an armful of beautiful, sparkly, lavish gowns.

"Have no fear. We'll have you looking marvelous and feeling like a beauty queen in just a short time." Rashard clapped his hands and the two women sprang into action. "Now, my darling, let's get you somewhere a little more private so we can begin the transformation."

"*Transformation?*" Overwhelmed, Lucy stood there, gaping like a fish. "Wait. I'm . . . confused. Exactly *who* asked you to come here?"

"Hired us, my darling. Rashard does nothing for free."

"Who *hired* you to do this?"

"I'm not quite certain," he answered as he hooked his manicured hand around her forearm and began to lead her up the stairs. "The request came from several different directions. And while we were already booked for another special occasion and usually only work on bridal parties, we were offered a handsome sum to make sure *you* looked like a princess."

"I don't need to look like a princess."

Ignoring her, Rashard said, "Quite a beauty you are too, hiding behind those pinched cheeks and the paranoid look in your eye." When they reached the top step he turned to look at her. "Why don't you just relax a little? Because we can't wait to work our magic on you. Am I right, girls?"

Gloria and Beatrice uh-huh'd as they came up the stairs, lugging the black cases and beautiful dresses with them. Barking and bringing up the rear was Ziggy, who was still in tail-wagging party mode.

"You don't happen to have a vanity, do you?" Rashard asked.

Lucy wrinkled her nose. "A vanity?"

"I'll take that as a no."

When they reached her bedroom, a flurry of activity took place that told Lucy two things. One: Rashard, Gloria, and Beatrice knew what they were doing. And two: *she* had no clue. Her paranoia, however, was sliding into the amused category as she watched the trio buzz around her room.

"Quickly." Rashard clapped his hands again. "Let's take off the robe so we can decide which dress you'll wear. It matters, you know, to choose the dress first so we can apply the proper makeup and nail polish."

Lucy clutched the robe tighter. "Ummm . . . I'm not wearing anything under here."

"Well then, by all means put on your prettiest underthings. I'm sure your handsome prince will appreciate it. In the meantime, we promise not to peek."

All three of them turned their backs.

What. Like she was going to strip down to her birthday suit right here with perfect strangers in the room?

"Make it snappy, Cindy."

"Lucy."

"Whatever. We haven't got all day."

Lucy opened the top drawer of her shabby chic dresser. She might not have spiffy outerwear, but she did have nice bras and panties. Splurging on something that made her feel a little prettier even though no one else could see was the one thing she did for herself that she refused to feel guilty about.

"Strapless bra, please."

Lucy turned to look at Rashard. "Strapless?"

"You don't have one?"

"Yes, but I never—"

"—wear it in public?" Rashard sighed. "You do now, my darling. Don't you worry. Rashard will have you not only looking but feeling like a princess before you step out that door. Your man will never know what hit him."

Her man?

Dear God. She needed a drink.

An hour and a half later, with her eyes closed as Rashard had requested, Lucy stood in front of the only full-length mirror she owned, which happened to be attached to the back of her bedroom door with double-stick tape. For the past ninety minutes she'd been buffed, puffed, powdered, fluffed, and schooled on not only how to look like a princess, but also how to actually act like one.

Apparently time for the big reveal had come.

Lucy still didn't know why these people had showed up at her door, didn't know why they'd come prepared with all the fixings to turn a toad into . . . well, not a toad. She didn't know what to expect but she was both excited and scared half to death.

"Now. Take a deep breath." Rashard demonstrated. "And once you've pushed all the air from your lungs, open your eyes."

Lucy gave up the fight.

Heart pounding, she did as instructed.

When her eyes managed to flutter open past the weight of the false eyelashes, she had no option but to gasp.

"Is that . . . me?"

On a daily basis Lucy knew she looked average, not dreadful. But for the first time in her life she looked . . .

"Gorgeous," Rashard confirmed.

"Stunning," Gloria clarified.

"Magical," Beatrice corroborated. "Cinderella has nothing on you."

Glasses gone, contacts in place, Lucy blinked. "You weren't kidding about being my fairy godmothers."

"My darling." Rashard took her now beautifully manicured hands in his. "It's impossible for a woman to look as dazzling as you do right now, every day. The trick is to do whatever it takes to *feel* dazzling. This proves you've got what it takes to look like royalty on the outside. You need to feel and believe that you are beautiful on the inside as well."

Guilty as charged. Lucy never gave herself much thought. The only time she'd ever really focused on herself had been when she was battling for her life.

"Now. I want you to step out that door feeling like a princess, because you certainly look like one. Let your heart be light and step into the arms of the man who wanted you to have this experience."

The man who wanted her to have this experience.

Gloria handed Rashard a sealed envelope, which he then handed to Lucy, then gave her an air kiss to each cheek. "Make us proud, my darling."

Lucy looked down at the envelope in her hands and the short bold strokes that spelled out her name. When she glanced up to thank her fairy godmothers, they were gone.

She spun around but they were no longer in the room. If it hadn't been for the sound of the front door closing, Lucy would question her sanity.

Slipping her finger beneath the flap, she withdrew the card inside.

Lucy,

Please come downstairs and join me for Wishes, Dreams, and Happily-Ever-After.

Jordan

Lucy's heart skipped.
Wishes, Dreams, and Happily-Ever-After?
What was going on?
Lifting the skirt of her floor-length Cinderella ball gown, she sighed and looked at Ziggy, who lay stretched out on the foot of her bed. "If I'm not home before midnight, either promise I won't turn into a pumpkin or you'll call the cops."

Ziggy barked.

"Good enough."

When the doorbell rang Lucy nearly forgot everything she'd just been taught. Her heart sprang into action. While she wanted to rush off, she instead wiggled her toes in the sparkling high heels and carefully made her way down the stairs. With her hand on the knob she took a breath to quell her racing heart and opened the door.

Had she not had to admit that Rashard and the girls had done an amazing job of turning her into Cinderella for a night, the look on Jordan's face said it all.

And because of that, for the first time in her life, she really did feel beautiful.

"*Y*ou're wearing a . . . tux," Lucy said as soon as she opened the door. "I don't know what to say."

For a moment, he didn't know what to say either. Because she simply stole his breath.

"No worries. I've got that covered." He took her hand and gave her a little twirl. "You look gorgeous."

When she blushed Jordan realized that he might not always say or do the right thing, but when he got it right, he nailed it.

The strapless lavender gown fit at the top in a sparkling cut that formed a heart-shaped neckline at her lush cleavage, and the bottom of the gown floated out in an array of lilac ruffles. The gown fit her perfectly. But it was Lucy herself who made the gown spectacular.

Her silky hair had been left down in a carefree tangle of soft curls he wanted to wrap around his hands. Her makeup had been artfully applied not to mask her beauty, but to accent it. And her full, kissable lips were highlighted only by a swipe of shiny gloss instead of a dark color to hide them.

"You take my breath away, Lucy."

Her shoulders lifted on an intake of air. "You don't have to say that."

He leaned in and inhaled the sweet scent that drifted up from her warm skin. "Get used to it." Noticing her uneasiness, he smiled. "Because the way I see it, whether you're dressed like you're ready for a ball or walking the corridor of school, you're a stunning woman."

"Not that I don't appreciate it, but I'm wondering why you sent three strangers to my house. Other than the obvious."

"I might say I overstepped. But clearly, I sent the right people."

"They scared me to death. I thought they were here to rob me."

He grinned. "Someone named Rashard from a place called Stardust Creations scared you to death?"

"Well, maybe not after he told me his name and why he was here."

"Scaring you was never my intent." He realized he was still holding her hand, and he gave her cool, soft fingers a little squeeze. "Surprising you with something I doubt you'd ever do for yourself was my only objective."

Her pillowy breasts lifted above the sparkling neckline on an intake of air that she let go with a little sigh. "You make it very hard to be mad at you."

"Good. I'd hate to waste the entire evening with you angry. I have more surprises in store."

"Thank you." She leaned in and kissed his cheek. "No one's ever done anything this nice for me before."

"You're welcome." He smiled. "And I'm glad it makes you feel good."

"I feel . . . fancy." Her laughter brought forth the dimple in her cheek. "And I certainly hope you didn't reserve a table at Cranky Hank's, because this dress really is too fabulous to worry about soiling it with sweet and sticky barbecue sauce."

"I agree." Even though the mention of sweet and sticky did not bring barbecue sauce to his mind. "And no, I didn't make plans to take you to any of the restaurants in Sunshine."

"Where then? Your note was a little cryptic."

"There are more surprises in store." He offered her his arm. "Shall we?"

"I'll admit"—she settled her hand on his forearm—"you do have me curious."

With a laugh and a wink to Ziggy, who'd stretched out beside the coffee table, Jordan pulled the front door closed. Then he led her down the walkway to where the limo driver stood with the door open and waiting.

"Where you going all gussied up?"

Jordan looked up as an elderly woman next door came out onto her porch.

"Hi, Mrs. B." Lucy gave the woman a little wave.

"You sure look pretty."

Even in the dark Jordan caught the blush on Lucy's cheeks.

"Thank you, Mrs. B."

"Hot date, huh?"

Jordan chuckled. "I promise I'll take good care of her."

"Nonsense," Mrs. B said. "What that girl needs is to

get her feathers all ruffled. In a good way, if you know what I mean."

"Mrs. B!"

"I'll see what I can do," Jordan reassured the woman. He turned to Lucy. "Looks like your neighbor thinks you should be going out more."

"Yes, well, dementia makes people say all kinds of crazy things."

"I don't have it and I agree with her."

Lucy looked up into his eyes and before she could protest, he lifted her hand and kissed the backs of her fingers. "How about we get in the limo and see if you might agree too."

For a long, silent moment Lucy looked at him. Then she turned toward her neighbor. "I'll be by tomorrow to take you grocery shopping, Mrs. B."

"Okey-dokey." Mrs. B waved from her porch. "You enjoy yourself tonight. Who knows what tomorrow will bring."

"Wise woman," Jordan said as Lucy watched her go back into her house."

"I worry about her. I don't think she should be living alone anymore."

"Nice of you to take her shopping."

"She's like the grandma I never had. So I look after her when her son and daughter are too busy."

"Does that happen a lot?"

"Unfortunately."

Jordan noted that Lucy seemed to be a caretaker. An admirable quality he was sure those she chose to care for appreciated. "Your chariot awaits, my lady."

"I've never been in one of these before," she said, sliding onto the long leather seat.

"Stick with me, kid, I'll show you all kinds of things." He waited until she moved aside the ruffles on her dress, then he slid in beside her. "Why should the teenagers have all the fun?"

"Good point." She spread her fingers across the seat and caressed the buttery leather.

While Jordan imagined how those long, dainty fingers would feel on his skin, he lifted the bottle of Moët that had been chilling in the stainless ice bucket. He poured the bubbly into crystal flutes and watched her eyes widen when he dropped a ripe strawberry into each glass.

Yes. He'd tried to remember every detail she'd mentioned last night. He handed her the drink. "I hope this will be a night of many firsts for you."

"It's certainly off to a good start."

When Lucy let her guard down and looked at him like she was right now, he felt like a completely different man.

A better man.

Now all he had to do was figure out how to keep her looking at him like that for longer than a few minutes.

Guilt had played into his initial reason for planning this night. He owed it to her since he'd taken that long-ago night away. But the more he was around her, the more she intrigued him. For him, Lucy was like that special gold foil–wrapped chocolate in a box of assorted treats. You didn't know exactly what you were going to get until you unwrapped it and took a bite.

Lucy had many interesting places he'd like to taste.

He lifted his glass to hers and they toasted. As Lucy pursed her luscious lips and sipped her champagne, the only thing Jordan thought could possibly make this night even better was if he could sip the champagne from her naked body. As a bonus he could think of plenty of ways to use the ripe strawberries. And heaven help him if a can of whipped cream came into play.

Imagining Lucy spread out on a big bed with soft sheets made his tuxedo pants tighten. As difficult as it was to keep his mind where it should be, not even a raging hard-on would get him to break the promise he'd made to give Lucy a night she'd never forget.

She deserved to have a night just for her. It seemed she was great at helping others. Jordan wanted her to have a night where she could hopefully have a little fun and break free from any chains from the past that had bound her and stopped her from seeing herself as a brilliant, beautiful, desirable woman.

That's how he saw her.

"So if not Cranky Hank's, where are we going?" She sipped her champagne, then dipped her fingers into the glass, brought the strawberry to her lips, and took a bite.

The move wasn't calculated, Lucy didn't play that way. But he wondered if she had any idea at all how incredibly sexy she was. Whether she was in her kitchen wearing a big fluffy robe and pouring a cup of tea or wearing a ball gown and plucking a strawberry from a glass, she fascinated the hell out of him.

He didn't even want to think about the dream he'd

had of her in the few hours he'd actually slept last night. The zipper of his pants was already tight enough.

"Maybe you missed the part about all this being a surprise?"

She wrinkled her nose. "I'm not a very patient person."

"Good to know, and too bad." He refilled her glass. "Because in about two minutes I'm going to have you close your eyes."

"What if I don't trust you enough to close them?" The upward tilt of her lips let him know her words were just a tease.

Heaven help him. He did like a playful woman.

He grinned. "What do I have to do to win you over?"

The heat of her gaze warmed him as those dark chocolate eyes looked him up and down, then searched his face. His fingertips tingled to touch her.

"Between the dress and the limo I think you've probably already proven yourself."

"Then how about you close those gorgeous eyes now?"

Her lashes fluttered, then her eyes closed in a display of trust.

And damned if he wasn't about to break it.

He leaned in and touched his lips to hers.

Briefly.

Because he had to.

To her credit, she didn't open her eyes as he lifted his head. Instead a sexy little hum vibrated in her throat.

"Careful, Mr. Kincade."

She looked so delicious sitting there with her long,

curly hair, her pretty lips, and her luscious cleavage teasing him from behind that sparkly fabric. Everything male inside him wanted to lay her back on that buttery leather seat and feast on her in the privacy of the darkened limo. He wanted to lift all those lavender ruffles and run his hand up her long legs until he discovered whether she wore silk panties or nothing at all. But he'd gone to a great extent to make sure she had something she'd never been able to enjoy before.

Tonight wasn't about him and what *he* wanted. Tonight was about putting a smile on her face for reasons other than what he'd fantasized in his head. Tonight was about making up for the ass he'd been back in high school. And tonight was probably about a whole lot more he wasn't yet willing to consider.

"Ms. Diamond, I should probably let you know *careful* isn't in my vocabulary."

When the limo stopped, Jordan peered through the window, hoping everything was in place. If so, it would be a miracle. "Keep your eyes closed, Lucy."

"I am."

"Do you trust me?"

"No."

"Not even a little?"

"Maybe a smidge."

The driver opened the door, and Jordan slid out onto the cobblestone path. He gave a nod and a handsome tip to the man, knowing he'd provide his own transportation to get Lucy either back home or to his Creekside Cottage should she choose to extend the party after hours.

He reached inside the limo, took Lucy's hand, and helped her from the car. When she stood beside him she tilted her head slightly as if listening for clues to their location. But the only sound was that of the creek bubbling over rocks and the distant call of a western bluebird.

"I hear water," she said. "But I can't imagine dressed like this we're going for a swim."

"There's a place nearby. But that's not on the menu unless it's something you feel strongly about."

Eyes still closed, she shivered a little. "Still a little too early in the season for that."

"I agree." Although if she wanted to skinny-dip, he'd bend over backward to make it happen. He took her hand, placed it in the crook of his arm, and led her to the big double doors.

Jordan had never been the type to get excited over much except shooting a perfect goal, winning a game, or inching ever closer to winning the Cup. For the first time, his heart gave a funny jump as he guided Lucy inside the building and found everything exactly as he'd imagined it. When the door closed behind them, he turned her to face the room.

"You can open your eyes now."

Lucy's fingers flew to her mouth to cover her surprise. "Oh . . . my . . . what is this?"

An enormous teardrop chandelier shot prisms of colored light onto the walls and wood floor of a large ballroom. Beneath the chandelier sat a single table covered with black and white linens, white pillar candles, and an artfully designed stargazer lily centerpiece. On the table was a sterling ice bucket that held yet another bottle of champagne. A stage at the end of the room displayed blue castle walls with a golden carriage at the center. And twinkling fairy lights danced from behind panels of sheer white curtains. From overhead, a sound system softly played "I'll Be."

Jordan reached for her hand. "Hopefully the prom you never had."

Wonder filtered through her every pore as she turned to him. He looked unbelievably debonair in his black tuxedo with his dark hair all sleek and combed back. And although she preferred his sexy five o'clock scruff, he'd shaved his strong jaw and chiseled cheeks. "Prom?"

"I know it might seem kind of corny. But it could have been worse the way I first imagined it," he explained with a wary look in his eyes. "When I contacted Principal Brown on his day off, he wasn't impressed by my NHL stats and refused to give me carte blanche to use the high school gym. The best I could do was talk the drama teacher into letting me use the cardboard props from the Cinderella play they did last fall. We're in the event center at Sunshine Creek Vineyards."

"You . . ." She turned to look at the room again. "I . . ."

"Is speechless a good sign, Lucy?"

She inhaled a breath she hoped would calm her nerves and nodded. "It's a very good sign."

"That's what I was hoping for."

"So . . . your note . . . wishes, dreams, and happily-ever-afters?"

"I dug my old yearbook out of the closet to find the theme for the prom in our senior year."

"I never knew."

"I figured as much. Too hokey?"

"Not at all. You went to a lot of trouble."

"It was my pleasure. I liked you back in high school, Lucy. Had I not been such a stupid, self-centered ass, I would have asked you to prom." His broad shoulders shrugged. "I'm just trying to make up for errors and lost time."

"You really need to let that go."

"I will. After tonight."

"I . . . really don't know what to say."

"Say you'll dance with me." He held out his hand. "I probably haven't improved any since high school, but I'm willing to give it a shot if you are."

She placed her hand in his. "Can I tell you a secret?"

"You can tell me anything."

For maybe the first time in her life, she found she'd like to tell someone all her confidences. But she'd long ago buried them and she wouldn't let the thought of them resurfacing now put a damper on this wonderful moment. "I don't know how to dance," she whispered.

"Then we'll figure it out together."

When he swept her into his arms and across the floor, Lucy knew he was a big fat liar. The man danced like he'd taken lessons from Fred Astaire.

Of course he was sure-footed and full of male grace. The man did his job and had spent most of his life on thin steel blades whooshing across slippery ice. To his credit, he made following his steps easy. Maybe it was because he held her close enough that the rich, woodsy scent of his cologne wrapped her up in a web that made it impossible to do otherwise. Or maybe it was the look he gave her that said, *Trust me*.

They danced for several slow, romantic songs before he led her to the table in the center of the room, pulled out her chair, then pushed it back in after she was seated. Standing next to her, he lifted the bottle from the ice bucket and uncorked the champagne with a flair that said he'd done the task before. Then he filled their glasses and they clinked crystal.

He moved his chair next to hers before he sat down.

"You're very good at all this," she said.

"*This?*"

"Dancing. Pouring champagne. Making fairy tales come true." She sipped her champagne and smiled when the bubbles tickled her nose. "If you're not careful, you'll shatter the beer-drinking, belly-scratching, Neanderthal image of hockey players I've been harboring all these years."

He laughed, and the sound that came from deep in his chest called out to something at the very core of her foundation. She'd never known a man to go to such extremes without expecting something in return. At least, that had always been her past experience. Still, tonight she was determined to keep that past where it belonged.

"I can guarantee your image might not be far off base. There are several guys on my team who'd probably admit they're barely above knuckle dragging."

"You're kidding."

He shook his head, and that dark hair and smile gleamed beneath the chandelier light. "The Rock grunts at everything. It's his favorite form of communication."

"The *Rock*? I thought he was a movie star who got paid for talking."

"Different guy. The one on my team got the nickname for how many times his head has hit the boards, yet he always comes up smiling."

"Sounds brutal."

"It can be. No one plans it. But there's so much aggression to get to the puck it sometimes ends up that way. If a guy keeps getting in your face or plays dirty, you can't help but want to check him and let your fists do the talking."

"*Check* him?"

"Slam him into the boards to stop his forward motion or try to steal the puck."

"There's so much I don't know about this game." She grimaced. "And I'm not exactly sure I'd want to learn."

"Have you ever been to a hockey game?"

"No." And she didn't want to admit that she'd seen him play a few games on TV either. "But my best friend and her husband are sports nuts. I've caught a few minutes of a playoff game on TV once or twice."

"It's different when you're actually in the arena."

She finished her glass of bubbly. Interested in the conversation, she leaned in while he poured them both another glass. "Different how?"

"You get caught up in the energy of the crowd. The fast pace of the game. You ever watch football?"

"A few times." And only when she'd been forced to because she'd been invited to a Super Bowl party.

"It's a lot like when the running back has the ball and he's racing toward the goalposts and the crowd is sure he'll score. That kind of thrill happens constantly in hockey."

"Did you know your eyes light up when you talk about it?" They really did. And as crazy as it seemed, that wondrous glow made him even more handsome.

"I'm not surprised. It's all I've ever known and for a reason. I love the game."

"I feel like that about teaching." Although they didn't need it, she smoothed the ruffles on her dress. She wasn't used to talking about herself. But she guessed talking about her job was safe enough. "Sometimes I'll get a student who not only has talent but is enthusiastic about learning. I get a crazy burst of adrenaline and I can't wait to get back to school the following day to help guide them some more. I always dream that I may have the next Ernest Hemingway or even the next generation's J.K. Rowling in my class."

"Do you write?" he asked, refilling the glass she didn't even know she'd emptied.

"I dabble," she admitted, figuring it was a safe enough answer and that he really wouldn't be interested in asking more. "But my main focus is teaching."

"What do you write?" He leaned both tux-covered forearms on the table and gave her his full attention.

Okay, so she'd underestimated him.

Lucy bit her lip—literally—trying to decide whether to answer him truthfully or to stretch the truth in another direction. Then again, she could always divert the conversation with . . .

"I love this song. Bruno Mars is my favorite." Not that she didn't really love Bruno, but right now he was her only way out of this conversation. She stood and held out her hand. "Dance with me?"

"Sure. And if you like it that much I'll be happy to play the song again." He captured her hand so she couldn't escape, then gave her a little tug so she'd sit down again. "Right now I'm more interested in what you write about."

Deep breath, Lucy. You can do this.

"I write . . . don't laugh . . . love stories."

"Really?"

She nodded. When he didn't laugh, she gathered the courage to continue. "Actually, I've written several stories about two characters who meet during an adventure. They're both after the same treasure, so throughout the books each is trying to outsmart the other. Of course, all the while they're falling in love. Sort of like Indiana Jones meets Katniss Everdeen."

For a moment he just looked at her, like he couldn't figure out whether she was serious or had seriously lost her mind.

"What inspired you to write?"

How did she explain that because her own life had been so miserable, the only way to find happiness was to write characters and help them find their own.

"There's a really long explanation, but for the most part I got the idea one day while I was"—*wrapping a bruised rib*—"waiting for my class to hand in their work. The whole story unfolded in my head in about five minutes. Of course, it took me much longer to actually write the work."

"I'd love to read them."

"Oh. No, you wouldn't." She scoffed and looked away, suddenly finding the castle backdrop on the stage riveting. "But it's kind of you to say so."

He tucked two fingers beneath her chin and turned her head so she'd look at him. "I'm not really the kind of guy who bullshits about things, Lucy. So unless you're trying to insult me by saying you don't think I'm smart enough to read because I'm a dumb jock—"

"I would never say that!"

"Then why is it so hard to believe that I'd want to read your stories?"

The sincerity in his eyes knocked her over. How was it that this man kept surprising her?

"Okay. It's not you. It's me. I've never let anyone read my work. To be honest, I just don't have that much . . . confidence."

"You're one of the smartest people I know."

Apparently not smart enough.

Once upon a time she'd thought being smart was her ticket out of a miserable life and into something wonderful. But even with her high IQ, she hadn't been smart enough to trust her instincts and she'd walked right into a nightmare.

"I'm sure what you've written is wonderful," Jordan said. "But no one will ever discover that until you take a chance. That's what life is all about." He leaned back. "Hell. I'm taking so many chances these days I can barely keep up with myself."

"You mean with your sister."

"My sister. My entire family, for that matter. My career." He sipped his champagne, watching her over the glass. When he was done he tilted the flute in her direction. "And you."

"Me?" She pointed to herself like there was some-one else in the room he could be referring to.

A slow nod came with a smile. "In case you haven't noticed, I've been chasing you all over town. I took a chance you wouldn't shut the door in my face after the way I treated you on graduation night."

His honesty took her aback, and only one response would do. "Why?"

"You intrigue me. You challenge me. And to be honest, I just flat-out like you."

"I've . . . never had anyone say that before."

"You're kidding."

She shook her head in beat with her pounding heart.

"Well, then I'll have to remember to say it more." He leaned in. "I like you, Lucy."

"I . . . like you too."

"Great." He stood and held out his hand. "Then how about we make some more memories."

She put her hand in his. "Where to now?"

"The corner."

"Like a make-out corner?"

"Nope. Saving that for later." He led her to a small, curtained-off area, pulled back the black drape, and gave her a playful push inside. "Right now we're going to make complete asses of ourselves in this photo booth."

"A photo booth?" She looked at the window and

camera light in front of them and immediately felt intimidated. She'd never done anything like this before.

"Stay here," he said. "I'll be right back."

He was gone only a minute. When he came back his arms were full of props—a colorful zebra print hat, a bright boa, a pink jeweled tiara, a huge mustache on a stick, and glitter-framed glasses.

"Oh. You are so wearing the boa." She laughed. Since he'd gone to all this trouble she could hardly say no to a little fun. Even if she looked silly doing it. "And the glitter glasses."

"No problem." He plopped the tiara on his head. "I'm perfectly comfortable enough in my masculinity."

Another giggle bubbled from her throat as they piled on the props, then posed like complete fools just before the camera flashed. Lucy had never done anything so crazy and she was surprised at how good it felt. Being with Jordan made her feel good, almost like she was a different person. And for the most part, that wasn't such a bad thing.

As the camera counted down for another shot, she tilted her bright yellow zebra fedora, held up the red paper mustache, and pursed her lips. Jordan caught her around the waist and pulled her in for a mustache kiss.

The kiss lasted long enough for several flashes, and wrapping her arms around the boa circling his neck, Lucy forgot all about the camera until he lifted his head.

"Ready to see how crazy we look?"

She nodded and he tugged her hand, and they pushed

aside the curtain to wait for the developed pictures to drop into the slot.

"Oh my God." She pressed her fingers to her lips to hold back a laugh. Tux-wearing Jordan Kincade wrapped in a hot pink feather boa, a tiara, and silver glitter glasses was a sight to behold. "Those are total blackmail worthy."

"Yeah." He chuckled. "I'm sure my teammates would love to get their gloves on these."

Lucy snatched them from his hand and dropped them down the front of her dress. "Which is why you should be nice to me." She grinned and backed away when he reached for her. "Be afraid, Jordan. Be very afraid."

When he caught her it was mid-laugh. But that didn't stop him from kissing her again and making her toes curl inside her very sparkly high heels.

He removed the tiara and settled it on top of her head. "I officially dub you Prom Queen."

She touched the plastic crown. "I've never been queen of anything before."

"Honey, you can order me around all you want." He gave her a quick kiss. "Now, how about we get you something to go with the bubbly? Something to keep your energy up for the rest of the night." He swept his hand in the direction of a table she hadn't noticed.

"Holy . . ." She gasped. His attention to detail touched her deeply. "A chocolate fountain?"

"Uh-oh. Too much?"

"Too delicious." She grabbed his hand and tugged him toward the table. "Strawberries, pineapple, marshmallows, and . . . oh my God, Rice Krispies treats."

"I assume you like chocolate?"

"As much as I try to eat healthy, I adore it. I swear, if chocolate was a church I'd pray there every day." She picked up the silver tongs and dropped several delicacies onto a white china plate before she stuck them under the Willy Wonka fountain of rich, dark chocolate.

"The French believe it's an aphrodisiac," he said, holding a giant marshmallow beneath the chocolaty ripples.

"I can understand why." Lucy took a bite of a chocolate-coated pineapple spear, closed her eyes, and moaned. "Oh. My. God. So good."

When she opened her eyes he was looking at her. Watching her with lust in the depths of those dark sapphire eyes.

She didn't know if the French were right about chocolate, but the desire she saw in his eyes tickled her in the center of her chest before it moved down toward her pink lace panties.

For her the sensation was rare. Not that she didn't ever have those kinds of feelings, but they'd been buried so deep beneath a layer of mistrust and displeasure she'd almost forgotten they existed.

Jordan had no problem helping her remember.

Before she knew what she was doing—or could stop herself—she grabbed the lapel of his tux and tugged him down until she could reach his lips.

And then . . . she kissed him.

*I*f he never did anything like this again in his life, every moment Jordan had spent putting this faux prom together exploded like a flash fire when Lucy pressed her lips to his and moaned like she was in the throes of passion.

Dancing with her so close had been sweet torture. Laughing with her had been even better. The sweetness of her scent bloomed around him like summer roses. The heat of her body, the softness of her skin, enticed him like nothing he'd ever experienced in his life. And in his life he'd experienced a lot.

Lucy was magic.

With her lips on his he could barely control his passion. A rarity for him because he was all about control. Which did not bode well for his fantasy of laying her out on that table, spreading chocolate all over her luscious body, and licking it off.

Hungry for more than just a light press of their lips, Jordan blindly set their plates on the table, drew her into his arms, and took possession of her mouth. She parted her lips, and the sweet taste of chocolate swept across his tongue. The intensity of the kiss deepened, burning him with the need for more. He filled his hands with her backside, pulling her in tighter to ease the ache behind his zipper. Her moaned response took him to a higher level of need. It clawed inside him, forcing past common sense and headed into dangerous territory.

He wanted her.

It was then he realized her moans didn't seem quite real. Like she was timing them or inserting them into a blank space.

What the hell?

He eased out of the kiss and her eyes popped open.

"Should we take this to the back of the limo?" she asked in a tone meant to sound seductive but instead came off sounding anxious.

And not in a good way.

Her actions and her comment were very *un*-Lucy-like.

"I let the limo go. Figured I'd take you home in the SUV."

A combination of relief and embarrassment darkened her eyes.

"Lucy. I didn't set all this up with the expectations of anything more than giving you something you missed fifteen years ago."

"Oh." She glanced away as if she couldn't look him in the eye anymore. "Well . . . it's been a lovely evening and I sincerely appreciate all your efforts although it wasn't necessary. The past is the past."

"Hey." He didn't give her the opportunity to do otherwise when he captured her face between his hands. "What's going on?"

"I don't know what you mean. I've had a lovely time. I've thanked you. And I expect now you'll want to take me home."

"Is that what you want me to do?" He didn't understand the sudden disconnect. He thought they'd been having a good time. Now she'd flipped a switch and seemed ready to run like a rabbit back to her hidey-hole. "Talk to me, Lucy. What's going on inside that head of yours?"

"It's been a long day for me. I'm not used to all . . .

this." She waved her arm at the room. "I think it would probably be a good idea for you to take me home. Or I can call a cab."

"Do we even have cabs in Sunshine?" He was joking, but clearly she wasn't in the mood.

"I can find a ride," she insisted.

"If that's what you really want, I'll take you."

"That's what I really want."

"Why?"

She looked up at him, obviously confused. "Why what?"

"Why do you want to run? Weren't you having a good time?"

"Yes, but . . . if you must know, because I'm quite sure you've never dealt with it in your entire life, rejection is a hard pill to swallow."

"Rejection?"

"See." She looked away again. "I knew you wouldn't understand the concept."

"Is that what you think I'm doing?"

"I offered to . . ."

He took her by the shoulders and forced her to look at him. "I don't want you to offer anything because you think you owe me something, Lucy. You owe me nothing. If you're going to kiss me, I want you to do it because you feel compelled to do so. Because you can't stand it another minute unless you make it happen."

He caught her by surprise when he wrapped his arm around her, brought her up hard against his body, and pressed his mouth to hers. Their tongues danced and tangled and she tasted just as sweet and enticing as she had moments before. He pressed her hand against his erection and her gasp ended the kiss.

She looked up at him, clearly surprised by his action.

He was surprised too.

He'd never had to try so hard to convince a woman he was interested and he couldn't understand why Lucy didn't get it. Usually all it took was a smile and a wink. Lucy was complicated. And for the life of him, he didn't know how else to get his point across.

"What you're feeling isn't a man who's rejecting you, Lucy. That's coming from a man who wants you but is trying his damnedest to behave like a gentleman. So if you want me to take you home, I will. But I'm hoping you'll stay."

Her dark eyes searched his face like she was looking for some hidden message. "You want me?"

"Yes. Why does that surprise you?"

"Because . . ." A harsh bark of laughter pushed through her lips. "I'm me."

Jordan had tried not to think too much about her past. Before he'd returned home, he never considered how much a person's past defined their present and future. He was quickly learning how much it mattered. With Lucy, the answers were becoming apparent. And he did not like what he saw.

"You were married," he said. "Surely you've had a man desire you so much he can't think of anything but you."

"Yes. I was married. But I can assure you, the last thing my ex ever thought of was me."

He grabbed their dessert-filled plates. "Come on.

Let's go sit down. I'd hate to waste all this. Unless you really would rather I take you home."

She eyed the chocolate-covered treats. "I didn't get to taste the Rice Krispies."

Relief washed over him and he smiled. He'd talked her into staying. Now hopefully he could get her to open up about what had gone wrong in her marriage. Not only because he wanted to know her better, but because he couldn't imagine a man not being obsessed with her body, mind, and soul.

*L*ucy bit into the chocolate-covered treat and knew that once she started devouring the sugary delights, she'd have a hard time stopping. Especially if it delayed her having to answer the questions she knew were on the tip of Jordan's tongue.

She'd never had a man blatantly admit that he wanted her.

Scratch that.

She'd never had a man tell her he wanted her, *period*.

It was new, uncharted territory. And as much as it intimidated her, it also delivered a powerful punch of yearning. It went without saying that Jordan Kincade was the most attractive man she'd ever met, but the closer she got, the more she realized it was the heart of the man that might very well be his most appealing quality.

To say she'd been shocked when he'd placed her hand on his sizable erection would be an understatement. It had been a blunt, bold move. It had also intrigued her and fed into the fantasies she'd had since he'd first walked through her classroom door. What would it be like to be made love to by a man like him?

"Which one is your favorite?" he asked, licking marshmallow and chocolate off his thumb.

Did watching him lick marshmallow and chocolate off his fingers count?

"It's a toss-up. The Krispies treats call to my inner child who never had such luxuries. But the strawberries are just so . . . decadent. What's your favorite?"

"Watching you eat the decadent strawberries."

"I don't know what to say to that, Mr. Kincade. You keep catching me off guard."

"Then my plan is working, Ms. Diamond." The genuine smile he gave her put her completely at ease. "I'd really like to get to know you better. To know what went wrong with your marriage."

At ease until he said *that*.

"Why is it so important to you?"

"Because you're important to me, Lucy. Don't you get that?"

As much as their past history said otherwise, she wanted to believe him.

"Never mind. I don't want to pressure you." He stood and held out his hand as if he understood how difficult the topic might be for her. "So how about we dance?"

Christina Aguilera's "Beautiful" played softly through the speakers, and Lucy had to wonder who'd put together this wonderfully romantic mix of music. Anxious to break the tension of the conversation, she wiped her hands with the cloth napkin, then placed her hand in his.

Instead of leading her out to the dance floor, he took her in his arms right there by the table. He held her close, and for maybe the very first time in her life she felt safe.

*J*ordan knew he'd pushed her too hard. He hadn't brought her here tonight, hadn't jumped through all the hoops to make tonight happen, just to interrogate her. If he could take back the last part of the conversation, he would. He liked the feel of her in his arms and he didn't want her running off anywhere because he'd opened his big mouth and stuck his entire size 13½ foot inside.

"We met during the last semester of college." She said the words so quietly he barely heard her over the music. "At first I didn't really notice him because I was focused on graduating at the top of my class. Next thing I knew he was in one of my study groups. Then he came into the bookstore where I worked."

Jordan tried to get her to look up at him, but she kept her cheek firmly planted on his chest as she continued.

"We met a couple of times after I got off work and he talked me into going out with him on an actual date. He was handsome, and charming, and his family was very wealthy from old money. In the town where they live they were like the Kennedys—almost royalty. I'd never had a man pay attention to me before and I'm ashamed to say he literally swept me off my feet."

"I don't know why you'd be ashamed."

"Because I only knew him for a short time before he asked me to move in with him after graduation."

"That's nothing to be ashamed of, Lucy."

"I'm ashamed of the string of bad decisions I made. I'm ashamed that I let my inexperience lead me instead of the intelligence I always depended on. I didn't really know him. Yet six weeks later we got married in a small ceremony. With my student loans I couldn't afford a lavish wedding and his family didn't want to shell out for it either. Later I found out that was because I was his second wife and they'd shelled out big bucks for a ceremony that included over five hundred guests."

"Five hundred? Wow."

"Imagine that. Married, divorced, and remarried before you were even twenty-five. I completely ignored the red flag waving in front of my face."

"Sometimes it's hard to see clearly when you're too close to the subject."

"Maybe. But I've always been proud of my intellect. I'd always done well in school. It was just real life I had trouble with."

"That's just being human."

"No. That's being blind and stupid. Three months after the wedding I realized why he wanted to marry me."

"Because you're a wonderful person?"

"Because I was easy prey. It was then I took to hiding a rescue card in my shoe."

His stomach tightened and turned. "A rescue card?"

"It has the name and number of someone you can call who will come rescue you if the abusive relationship you're in becomes life-threatening and you finally gather the courage to get out."

Jordan sucked in a breath. His feet stopped moving but he didn't let her go. He fought for a living with men who could hold their own. Striking a woman for any reason was just wrong.

"Fear and shame got the best of me." She leaned back and finally looked up at him. "It took me three years to finally make that call."

"I'm so glad you made it out." The desire to find this guy and beat him to a pulp lived and breathed like a flash fire in Jordan's soul. Instead, he drew Lucy back into his arms and hugged her tight.

She should have kept her mouth shut.

When Jordan took her home, she wrung her hands. Fiddled with her grandmother's ring. Straightened the layers and layers of dress ruffles like it mattered.

Now he knew.

Many people judged a woman who was or had been in an abusive relationship. They often thought she either was too stupid to get out or had asked for it. Lucy wondered about Jordan's take. Did he think she'd *asked for it* because she'd stayed? Or that she was stupid? Or weak? Her entire life flashed before her, and until recently it was a pathetic script. It might have taken her a while, but she'd finally taken control. And she was proud of her accomplishments.

"Stop fidgeting."

Jordan's tone held no censure. Instead his words

were delivered with a smile she could see even through the darkness of the SUV's interior.

"I can't help it. I always fidget when I'm nervous."

"It's the end of our date, what could you possibly have to be nervous about now?"

Duh should have been enough of an explanation. But no, Lucy just had to open her big yap . . . again.

"I know you did this whole prom thing because you thought you needed to make up for graduation night. But you didn't. I appreciate your efforts and it was wonderful. But somewhere during the night I forgot that the whole thing was just an apology. I had fun. But everyone knows on a first date you don't tell a person you're interested in all your deepest, darkest secrets. I should have kept my mouth shut."

The SUV rolled to a stop in front of her house. Mortified, she grabbed the door handle. His big hand reached across all those lavender ruffles and stopped her. His gorgeous face was inches from her own and she felt a blush of embarrassment creep up her cheeks.

"You're interested in me?" he asked.

"Is that all you heard?"

"No." He smiled. "I also heard you say you had fun."

"I did."

"Good to know. Stay right there." He got out of the SUV, came around to her side, opened the door, and held out his hand. "A date doesn't end until the gentleman walks the lady to her door."

"You don't have to do that."

"You're right. I don't have to. I *get* to." He waved his hand, encouraging her to take it.

When she finally did, he helped her from the car, tucked her hand in the crook of his arm, and walked her up the path that split her small front yard. Then he waited until she unlocked her door.

Key in hand, she turned to thank him. "It really was a wonderful night. And I'm sorry I—"

Gently he cupped her face between his large hands, then lowered his head and pressed his lips to hers. The kiss was slow and sweet. He tasted like rich chocolate and leashed passion as his tongue stroked hers in a sensuous rhythm that lit a fire down deep. As she clutched her hands in the lapels of his tux, she knew she wanted—needed—more.

Too soon he lifted his head and while he still framed her face between his hands, she licked the delicious taste of him from her lips.

"Never apologize, Lucy." His dark blue gaze looked right into her eyes. "Not for who you are, who you've been, or what you've been through."

He kissed her again. Briefly. "I think you're an incredible woman. And I'm damn happy you're interested in me. Because I sure as hell am interested in you."

"Jordan, I—"

His lips came down on hers again and he swept her up in another wave of want and need. She was just about to pull him inside the house when the kiss ended, his hands slipped from her face, and he took a step back.

"Sweet dreams, Lucy. Don't think about the bad stuff. It's all behind you now."

He gave her a smile before he turned and walked

back down her pathway. Before he got in the SUV, he stopped and said, "A woman like you deserves to be treated well because she matters. You matter to me, Lucy."

As he drove away, any remaining ice around her heart completely melted.

Chapter 10

*J*ordan parked the SUV at his grandfather's cabin. Instead of going inside, he walked behind the brick structure to the creek, which flowed at full capacity from the spring snowmelt and rains. Moonlight filtered through the trees and dotted the dirt pathway with dancing light. He reached up and undid his tie as he walked and listened to the water tumble over rocks and sand to clear his head. Before he knew it he found himself strolling up and down the rows of Chardonnay and Riesling grapevines.

When he'd been a kid he enjoyed this place because of the adventures he and his brothers had. But when his grandparents passed away and his family relocated here he'd felt no real connection. If he had to be honest, a part of that came from him not wanting to move from the East Coast, where hockey rated higher on the sports ladder than pro football. As a teenager he'd never been around long enough to get to know Sunshine Valley well. Maybe if he'd gotten his hands dirty in the soil that grew the grapes that made the wine, he would have found that bond. Hard to say.

Except for hockey he'd never really made a deep connection with anything other than his family before.

The events of the past few weeks had changed everything.

With his family he was trying to make up for lost time. With his sister he was trying to step up and be the good big brother he should have been all these years. With Lucy he'd started out trying to make up for the way he'd blown her off on their graduation night, but his feelings for her were transforming into something bigger than he'd ever imagined.

The dark situation Lucy had been in for so long haunted him to the core. Not only because of how horrible it must have been for her, but also because he couldn't ignore the part he might have played in her marrying such a mean son of a bitch. Maybe if he'd actually taken her out on graduation night like he should have, she would have believed she had more value than to ever get involved with someone like that.

The possibility weighed heavy in his chest. But it had nothing to do with the way he saw her now or the way she made him feel.

His sister had some serious issues he needed to figure the hell out. Fast. He worried about her. She seemed so miserable. So breakable. And because he didn't know her well enough, he worried she might do something to harm herself.

A shiver ran down his back at the horrible thought.

And then there was the fact that someone had been

stealing from his parents. Who would have done such a thing? And why? His parents had been warm, generous people. If someone had been in need, all they'd had to do was ask for help.

He wished they were here now. He could use a little parental advice. A little nudge in the back and a pat on the head that told him he was doing the right thing.

God, he missed them.

An ache filled his chest and his eyes watered. If he could just have a few minutes with them again to tell them he loved them.

"What the hell are you doing out here?"

Jordan wiped his eyes and looked up to find Ethan strolling toward him.

"Trying to work some shit out in my head. What are you doing?"

"I heard your SUV pull up but didn't hear the cabin door close." Ethan shrugged his broad shoulders. "I got worried."

His baby brother had always been the most sensitive of their motley crew. Ethan had been the one they all thought would set down roots, marry young, and have a bunch of kids running around. But the girl he'd loved had broken his heart and Ethan had gone in a direction opposite of settling down.

"No need to worry," Jordan said. "I've just got a bunch of stuff to figure out." Like the string of text messages he'd been receiving from his agent and coach.

"Yeah?" Ethan gave him a crooked grin. "Well, you're getting your shiny shoes muddy out here. So what's with the tux?"

Jordan started to walk again and Ethan was right there beside him. "I did something really shitty fifteen years ago to a girl who didn't deserve it and I was trying to make it up to her."

"You didn't succeed?"

"Maybe. But—"

"There's more to the story?"

"I wouldn't even know where to start."

"Sounds serious."

"Life has definitely taken some twists and turns in the past couple of weeks."

"I hear that." Ethan reached down and picked up a piece of vine cut during last year's harvest. "If you're worried about Nicki, I had a chat with her."

"At least she'll talk to you. All she does is yell at me."

"She's pretty damn good at that."

"Yeah." Jordan gave a harsh laugh. "She makes it no secret that she hates my guts."

"She doesn't hate *you*, but she's definitely pissed about something. I think you're just in her line of fire."

"Did she give you any insight as to what's going on?" Jordan asked as they came to the end of the row and headed toward the guest cabins. "I already asked Ryan, Dec, and Parker, but they had no clue."

Ethan shook his head. "It's like she talks in code. The only thing she said was that the rest of us had no idea what it was like to be her. And that the only possibility of a resolution was gone."

"Cryptic."

"Yeah." Ethan made a cynical sound. "I'm pretty sure that young or old, I'll never figure out women."

"They're definitely one of the great mysteries of life."

"Amen to that. So . . . this girl you were trying to apologize to . . . you've got feelings for her?"

"She's pretty special."

"But?"

"She's been through a lot." Without giving away details he said, "She needs someone to give her what she needs. What she deserves."

"And you're not that guy?"

As much as he wanted to be that guy, he wasn't sure he could be. "She deserves someone better than me. Someone who has their life all figured out. Not someone who has too many balls juggling in the air to be sure of anything."

Jordan never expected to have such strong feelings for her at all, let alone in such a short time. His instincts were to protect her. To show her that loving someone didn't have to be painful. That making love was supposed to be warm and fulfilling for both parties. He'd meant it when he'd told her he was interested in her. He meant it when he said she deserved to be treated well and that she mattered to him. And as much as he wanted to be *that* guy, he didn't really know what he was capable of. This was his first trip to the rodeo.

"The look on your face says you want to be that guy, regardless of the juggling."

"Yeah, but too many things are piling up," Jordan said. "And I'm probably not the guy who can make it all better."

"Such as?"

"I can't bring our parents back, or find the missing money, or fix Nicki's troubles in the blink of an eye. I've got the coach and my agent sending me text threats that I need to get my ass back to work ASAFP. And I can't focus on anything except that I've skated on my duties to this family for years. It's my turn to give."

"Yep." Ethan shook his head. "That's a load of shit all right. You ever think about letting go of stuff you have no control over?"

"No. I'm programmed to take care of business."

"Too bad real life isn't as easy as slamming some guy into the boards, right?"

"That's about the only thing I'm good at."

"Bullshit. Stop being so fucking hard on yourself. You're right. As much as I'd like you to be able to, you can't bring Mom and Dad back. Let that go. Mourn them. Miss them. Hold your memories close. It's okay to live your own life and still be respectful of the loss. As far as the missing money goes . . . Ryan and Dec will get it figured out. It might take a while, but they'll find out what happened and then we'll get this place updated so it starts making money again. When it comes to Nicki, the rest of us will help out wherever we're needed. We've just taken a step back because you seem so determined to do right by her. We don't want to take that away from you." He grimaced. "Plus she's scary as hell."

Jordan chuckled because it was the truth.

"So that leaves you only two things to focus on— your lady friend and your career." Ethan clapped his hand over Jordan's shoulder. "One you should be able to sweet talk, the other you can fast talk. Get it done and quit your bitching."

As his well-meaning brother walked away, Jordan knew the truth. He wasn't much good at anything except smack talk on the ice.

Only one thing in his life was certain; as soon as he returned the calls to his agent and coach, he'd become the guy who made promises he couldn't keep.

*T*he deep breath Jordan took didn't do much to calm the dread tightening in his chest as he knocked on Nicole's bedroom door early Sunday morning. According to Aunt Pippy, who'd met him downstairs with a cup of coffee and a warm cinnamon roll, Nicki was still asleep. Unfortunately what needed to be said couldn't wait for her to leisurely arise.

He'd been prepared to knock several times before she'd even consider answering, but she surprised him by opening the door almost immediately.

Hair mussed and wearing long-sleeved flannel pajamas with cats and polka dots on them, she squinted up at him from one bloodshot eye. "What do you want?" she muttered.

"We need to talk."

"About what? What did I do now?" She shifted her weight to one hip, which indicated a definite attitude was in play.

"I don't know that you did anything wrong unless you have something you want to admit."

"No," she answered suspiciously fast.

"Can I come in?"

"Whatever. Even if I tell you no you'll come in anyway." She turned and shuffled back to the bed, where she sat down, crossed her legs, and pulled a fuzzy purple blanket up over the top of her like she wanted to hide. Her blue eyes stared out at him from beneath her cocoon.

He followed her into the room and leaned his backside against her dresser. Without all the makeup and perfectly styled hair, she looked about ten years old. Which didn't help lessen his guilt for waking her early just to drop a bomb on top of her temperamental little head.

"Late night?" he asked.

"It wasn't a school night so don't get your tighty-whities in a wad."

"That wasn't an answer."

"That's because it's none of your business. You're not the boss of me."

"You have approximately, what, five months before you turn eighteen?" He folded his arms, and without giving her a chance to respond, he continued. "Until then everything you do is my business. You heard Mom and Dad's wishes. I *am* the boss of you, along with Ryan, Declan, Parker, and Ethan. So humor me. In the future when I ask you a question, please respond with an appropriate answer. Okay?"

She folded her arms and jerked her chin upward just enough to deliver a silent, rebellious *Screw you*.

"We need to talk about—"

"You're leaving." Her eyes narrowed and she scoffed. "I *knew* it."

"Nicki—"

"Don't *Nicki* me like you care!" She jumped up and paced the room, throwing her hands up in a barely controlled temper tantrum. "How dare you make promises you knew you wouldn't keep. You're just like everybody else."

"I'm only leaving for a few days. I'll be back."

"Bullshit!" She grabbed the pillows from her bed and threw them at him. "Get out."

"Nicki—"

"Get out. Get out. Get out!" Each *out* was accented by the hurling of whatever she could get her hands on—books, stuffed animals, a bottle of nail polish.

Fuck.

He couldn't handle this. He didn't know what the hell he'd been thinking trying to take on Nicole and her gargantuan attitude.

He wasn't equipped for this.

Failure slapped him in the heart as he escaped before the bottle of Juicy perfume conked him on the head.

As soon as he closed the door behind him he heard her sobs.

They broke him.

Crushed him.

Made him desperate to know what was going on in her head.

Yes, she'd just lost both of her parents, so tears and sadness were to be expected. But it was the bitter anger and inability for her to be even remotely reasonable that caused him such concern. He might not know teenage girls very well, but he knew his sister's outbursts weren't normal. Something very deep was going on that for some reason she didn't want to share with anyone.

Especially him.

As her sobs continued and concern strangled him, he took two steps toward the stairs and stopped.

Fuck.

What kind of an ass was he?

If he left her like this he'd be exactly the kind of selfish bastard she accused him of being.

The wheels in his head spun, searching for a resolution. Then he turned around and, without knocking, opened her door.

Face red, blotchy, and sniffling, she looked up, obviously surprised by his return.

"I know I'm not very good at this," he admitted. "I have no experience at being a parent, a guardian, or hell, even a big brother." He crossed the room, pulled her into his arms, and hugged her tight so she couldn't squirm away. "But I love you. And it kills me to see you like this. So get some clothes together. You're going with me. Be ready in two hours. No excuses. No bullshit. Be at the door waiting or I'll come up here and haul your ass down the stairs. Got it?"

Instead of arguing, she sniffed and nodded.

He shut the door, dropped his head back, closed his eyes, and prayed to whoever could help him out.

Forget a damn can of worms; he'd just opened up the gates to hell.

A typical Sunday morning for Lucy was to sleep in, make blueberry pancakes, and then take Ziggy for a walk down at the park by the river. He loved to catch a Frisbee, and her backyard was too small for him to be able to run far enough to make his huge running leaps.

This morning, however, was anything but typical.

Not only had she not slept in, she hadn't slept all night. She hadn't meant to unleash the demons of her past with Jordan, especially when he'd gone to so much trouble to set up such a wonderful evening. He hadn't needed to know all the trials and tribulations she'd been through. He hadn't needed to know that she'd allowed someone to treat her that way. Still, for some reason she'd opened up.

If you'd asked her two weeks ago if she'd ever trust Jordan Kincade enough to tell him her deepest, darkest secrets, she would have laughed. Amazing how things had changed in such a short time. While she'd told him—in part—of the emotional abuse, the torment, and the unforgivable way she'd been handled in a sexual sense, he'd held her tight, letting her have her say in a quiet, supportive manner she'd never expected.

By the time she'd finished telling him, the muscles in his jaw were clenched so tight she thought it would break. She understood most men didn't like to be dragged into a load of drama, so she'd made sure she delivered the information as matter-of-factly as she could, leaving her emotions at the door as much as possible. When she finished, he'd said, "I wish I could have been there to help you."

She wished he could have too.

At the time she'd wished anyone could have been there to help her. But it was a mess she'd gotten herself into and a mess she'd had to get out of on her own. Still, she appreciated his sentiment and understanding.

Of course, his consolation only made things worse on her conscience. He'd planned such an amazing evening and she'd ruined it all by spilling her guts. She wouldn't be surprised if he wished he could take back all the effort he put into the date. Even if that wasn't how he acted when he'd walked her to her front door and kissed her very gently on the lips.

Getting to know him proved one thing—you could never judge a book by its cover. Or in this case, a hockey player.

Then again, time would tell.

Though he'd said he was interested in her, he could have only meant he was interested in the way an ento-mologist studied bugs.

She'd just folded fresh blueberries into the pancake batter when her doorbell rang. Wiping her hands on a kitchen towel, she figured Mrs. B had shown up early for their grocery-shopping excursion. Unprepared for company in a pair of cutoff sweats, a ratty "Live Love Teach" T-shirt, and slippers, she scuffed her way to the door anyway. The last thing she needed was to make the sweet, fragile woman wait on her doorstep.

Instead of her neighbor, Jordan stood at her door. How someone managed to look tired, frazzled, and yet still as handsome as ever in a dark blue Henley shirt, jeans, boots, and that oh-so-sexy black leather jacket was a mystery.

"Good morning." She tried to hide her surprise and dismay that he'd caught her looking less than presentable.

"Did I wake you?" His dark blue gaze shifted down and up her body as a suggestive smile tilted his lips.

"No. I was just making blueberry pancakes. Come on in, I have plenty to share."

Having heard Jordan's voice, Ziggy dashed into the room, tail wagging and looking for some affection from the new arrival. Jordan complied, bending at the knees and giving her dog a rubdown before he followed her into the kitchen. The retriever rewarded him with an audible toot.

"Dude." Jordan chuckled.

Ziggy wagged his tail.

Her dog's habit could be embarrassing. Still, it must be nice not to give a rip when you had to let one rip.

"I'm surprised to see you up and about so early. Coffee?" When Lucy turned to get his response he was sitting at her little kitchen table looking dazed and confused. "Are you okay?"

He nodded and then shook his head. "I need to ask you a favor. And I know you don't owe me anything but . . . I need you to tell me yes."

She laughed before realizing he was serious. "That sounds dangerous."

"You're going to think I'm crazy. Hell, *I* think I'm crazy. But I'm going to ask anyway."

"Well, now I'm really curious." She leaned her

backside against the counter and folded her arms, hoping to hide some of the T-shirt stains.

"If I don't go back to North Carolina and play the next series of home games I'm in breach of my contract and it will cost me upward of four million."

"Wow. I can't even fathom that kind of money. But the bottom line is your team obviously needs you."

"My family needs me too. And I'd be willing to give up that kind of cash if it was just about me." He hesitated. "But right now the vineyard is in financial trouble and I might need that money to help bail it out."

"Financial trouble?" Stunned, her arms dropped to her sides. "But the wine is so good."

"It's not the wine." His long fingers nervously tapped the tabletop. "My dad and Ryan have worked really hard on getting the blends just right and several have won multiple awards at the Washington State and Seattle wine awards. Everything else at the winery is a little run-down and needs revitalizing. But the biggest problem is when Ryan and Declan went through the finances, they discovered someone has been stealing money."

"Stealing!"

He nodded. "As generous as my folks have always been, it's hard to imagine someone took advantage of them like that."

"Any idea who took it?"

"None yet. They're still trying to figure it out. Whoever took it was really smart about it. There's no paper trail to follow, and the winery is currently in the red. That's why I have to go back to North Carolina."

"I completely understand." Reality reared its head. Maybe *she* understood but she was sure someone else wouldn't. "Did you tell Nicole?"

"Yeah." He barked a harsh laugh. "And believe me, that did *not* go over well. Which brings me to my favor."

"Ask away." How could she refuse him a small favor after he'd gone to so much trouble to set up a prom for her?

"Remember . . ." He gave her a smile that turned her knees to water. "I need you to say yes."

"I'll do my best."

"After I told Nicole I had to leave for a couple of days she broke down. She cried so hard it killed me. There's no way in hell I can just walk away and leave her like that. I don't know what's going on with her but I can't just desert her. And since that's obviously a major issue, I'm taking her with me."

"And you want me to give her some extra credit work to take along?"

"Not exactly." He stood and gently clasped his hands around her arms. "I want you to come with us."

"You want me to what?" A quiver of disbelief mixed with fascination tingled at the back of her neck.

"I want you to get on a plane and go with us to North Carolina. Before the games I'll have practice. I'll be gone for hours each day and I can't just leave Nicki alone in a strange city. She's too unstable right now."

"Jordan, I can't just walk away from everything."

"It's spring break. You have a week off."

"But I have other responsibilities. I have to take

Mrs. B grocery shopping today. And tomorrow she has a doctor appointment and—"

"And you're wonderful for taking such good care of her. But she has children in the area who appear to be taking advantage of you."

"I don't think of it that way."

"I know." He kissed her forehead. "That's what makes you so wonderful."

"I can't leave Ziggy."

"Ziggy can come along." His warm hands slowly caressed her arms. "I know you don't owe me anything. And if I weren't so worried about Nicki, I wouldn't ask you to drop everything to help me out. But my sister means everything to me. And right now there's something going on with her that I can't figure out. It might help if she had a woman to talk to."

"You're a very hard person to say no to," she admitted.

"Then please don't." He flashed her a cheesy grin. "Pretty please? With chocolate-covered Rice Krispies treats on top?"

Want, need, guilt, and a dash of excitement warred within her heart. She agreed that taking Nicole with him was a good idea. Also, it might help the girl if she had someone objective to talk to. But if held at gunpoint, Lucy would have to admit those weren't the only reasons she was giving his request some consideration. "Give me a couple of hours to arrange things."

"So you'll go?" A hopeful smile tilted those masculine lips.

"I'll go."

Relief flashed through his eyes just before he lifted her off her feet and kissed her senseless.

*W*hat the hell was he doing?

Strapped in the seat of a charter jet across the aisle from Lucy and Nicole with Ziggy stretched out at their feet, Jordan questioned his decision to bring the whole gang with him back to North Carolina just so he could play a couple of games.

The awkward silence on the plane was deafening and he scrambled to figure out what to say, what to do, and how the hell to make this work.

The only thing in his favor was Lucy—a careful, brilliant woman who no longer made rash decisions despite the fact that she'd taken a leap of faith with him. Having her in his corner gave him a lot more confidence in the situation than he'd have if he was handling it alone.

For over an hour Nicki had sat silently with her arms folded and looking out the window. Lucy had kept herself busy reading a book about character traits. Maybe she was trying to find a way to figure him out.

He couldn't believe she'd agreed to come, but he was beyond grateful. Helping out with his sister while he was at practice would be a huge relief. And since he planned to have them both attend the games, he wouldn't worry about them.

But that wasn't his only reason for wanting Lucy along.

Last night they'd jumped a hurdle when she'd

opened up and talked to him about her marriage. He'd appreciated that she trusted him enough to share. That confidence had made him like her even more. He didn't want to be gone for a few days, weeks, or longer and put a dent in what could be developing between them.

As if she could feel him watching her, Lucy looked up. She pushed her glasses up her nose and smiled. A hot arrow of lust shot through him. Why he found that simple gesture so sexy he had no idea. But it made him realize he was probably in deeper than he'd initially thought.

She deserved to have a man treat her like a queen. A man who'd love her and make her his top priority.

Could he be that man?

He didn't know.

But the more time he spent with her, the more he wanted to be.

She smiled again, and, not that he didn't love his sister, but he suddenly wished he and Lucy were alone. He could teach her a hell of a lot about the art of seduction at thirty thousand feet.

"Are we almost there?" the baby dragon asked.

"Almost," he said. "Think by the time we land you can find a smile?"

She flashed him the most forced, scary-looking grin he'd ever seen.

"Well, that's a start."

Across from him Lucy took his cue, put her book aside, and leaned in to engage Nicki in a conversation about the upcoming prom. It took a few minutes before Nicki warmed up to the discussion. When she finally did, she amazingly still managed to flash him the death glare.

All he could do right now was close his eyes, wish the jet had booze on board, and pray all the way to North Carolina.

*L*ucy followed Jordan and Nicole into Jordan's high-rise apartment. While the place was nice, with everything in rich dark wood, black leather, and granite, it wasn't overly extravagant like she'd expected. She'd have thought he lived like a spoiled superstar in a huge house with useless rooms he never bothered to visit. He certainly portrayed that image when the paparazzi captured him leaving a celebrity event or fancy restaurant with a gorgeous blonde on his arm.

The furnishings were definitely masculine, so it seemed almost comical to imagine him standing in a Home Goods store selecting the delicate rose and lily centerpiece in the middle of the big black dining table or the modern pieces of art and mirrors on the walls. The fact that the place was spotless led her to believe he had help come in and clean.

"I only have two bedrooms," he announced as he parked Lucy's suitcase by the sofa. "Nicki, I'll put you in the one down here."

Lucy followed as he led his sister down the hall and into a nice-sized room with a queen-sized bed and a private bath. Again, the room had a masculine flair, but Lucy didn't think Nicole would mind. She might protest loudly, but Lucy couldn't help thinking the young girl was more than a little excited that her big brother had seen fit to bring her along.

"It has a smart TV with every cable channel you can think of." He tossed her bag on the bed. "If there's something specific you want to watch, just order it on Netflix."

"Whatever." Nicole rolled her eyes.

"Yeah." He sighed.

As Lucy followed him back out into the hall, she wished she could resolve the reason for Nicole's anger. No doubt the girl was complex. Alarmingly, it seemed the girl couldn't push past her anger enough to be able to grieve the loss of her parents. Maybe Jordan was right. Maybe with a little time together, Lucy could at least begin to understand.

"I'll put you in my room," Jordan said to Lucy, grabbing her bag from the living room floor.

"But where would you sleep?"

"On the sofa."

"Don't be silly. I can't push you out of your bed. You have to be at the top of your game over the next couple of days."

When they reached his room—the epitome of black leather manliness—he stopped and turned toward her. The way his lips curled up at the corners and the glimmer in his eyes sent a rush of warmth from her heart down through her core. She barely resisted a lusty shudder.

"So you're saying you're willing to share a bed?" he asked.

"I . . . uh . . ." she sputtered.

"It's a king-sized bed. You won't even know I'm there."

"You're a little hard to miss."

He set her bag on the bed and moved so close she could smell his clean, manly scent. "I could keep you warm if you got cold."

The idea of having his big, warm, muscular body wrapped around hers sounded very appealing.

"There's nothing to eat in here." Nicole's shout rattled from the kitchen throughout the apartment.

"Try the top shelf in the cupboard. It's where I keep the forbidden food," Jordan shouted back to his sister, then his attention zeroed right back in on Lucy. Strong arms surrounded her and drew her against his hard-muscled body.

"You keep thinking on my offer." He lowered his head and delivered a sweet and deadly kiss that was way too quick for Lucy's liking. "It won't be the last time you hear it."

"What about the teenager in the other room?" Although Lucy liked the way he staked his claim because she'd never had a man do that before, she had to bring up the obvious. "I'm her teacher. I need to set a good example."

"You're an excellent example. And she'll have to find her own snuggling partner," he said. "Maybe I should get her a cat."

At their feet Ziggy swept his tail back and forth.

"What do you think about that, Zigmeister?" Jordan asked her dog, who gave a growly bark in response. "Unless he eats cats."

"The only things he eats are Frisbees, Beggin' Strips, and the best brand of dog food on the market. Which obviously does not help his *wind* problem."

"Ah. So you're one of *those* pet mommies."

"Yes. I spoil him. Is there something wrong with that?"

"Nope. Just trying to figure out how to get in line for some of that spoiling."

She grinned. "All you have to do is sit and lie down when you're told. Don't chase your tail. And warm my feet when they get cold."

"Done." He grinned back. "And as a bonus I'm already housebroken."

"You're a strange and funny man."

"I can show you a whole different side of me." He wiggled his eyebrows. "Preferably a naked one."

"We'll see." Playful really wasn't her thing. Neither was flirting. But she decided to give both a go. "It all depends on how well you perform your tricks."

His responding grin told her she'd hit a home run.

"Lucky for me I've got a bagful."

With a playful wink he told her to go ahead and use whatever drawers she wanted to put away her things, use as much space in the closet as she needed, then pointed to the adjoining bathroom for her to put out her toiletries. And then he slipped from the room to help Nicole, who complained loudly that forbidden food did not include all-natural granola bars with no sugar.

Lucy stood in the middle of the room surrounded by his massive bed and his personal items. It smelled like him—delicious, clean, and manly. This was where he bathed, dressed, slept, and God only knew what else. Yeah. She wasn't even going to think about *that*. She did not want to think about him in that big bed wrapped around the perfect body of one of those gorgeous blondes she'd seen photographed with him in the magazines.

Lucy carried her toiletries into the bathroom and inhaled the delicious aroma of his trademark aftershave. When she walked back into the bedroom, she looked at the bed again. Unsure of exactly what he expected from her, she knew one thing and one thing only. Jordan looked like a man who knew how to give a woman what she wanted and needed. Lucy was a woman who'd never wanted or needed before.

Until now.

Chapter 11

*O*ver two weeks had passed since Jordan had walked into a locker room. He expected to feel like an outsider. To be given the cold shoulder. After all, he'd let his team down.

Letting people down seemed to be the thing he did best.

If anyone doubted his expertise in this area, all they had to do was ask his sister. She'd verify it in a red-hot second.

"Good to see you, man." Center Tyler Seabrook stood and shook his hand the minute he walked into the locker room. Likewise did defenseman Beau Boucher, goalie Jack Riley, and forward Scott O'Reilly who'd recently married the nurse who stitched him up when he'd busted his face on the boards.

They asked about his family. Gave him their condolences. Apologized for not being able to attend the funeral. And proved, once again, they were good men off as well as on the ice. Of all the players on the team, the four of them were his closest friends. They partied, shot pool, played poker, and golfed together. Until two weeks ago they'd had everything in common.

Seabrook pushed a hand through his hair and scratched at the beard stubble on his jaw. "You up for a couple of beers after practice?"

"Wish I could. I brought my kid sister back with me. She's been having a pretty tough time since our parents died." Jordan shrugged. "She's seventeen and full of attitude on a normal day. But right now she's breaking my heart. I didn't feel good about leaving her behind."

"Maybe while she's here I could have my cousin Bridget give her a call. She's seventeen too, a little nerdy, and kind of a genius. But she's really nice."

"I like smart girls."

"Oh yeah?" Seabrook grinned. "Since when?"

Jordan shoved his jacket inside his locker, opened his duffel bag, and pulled out his practice jersey. "Since I was a punk-ass kid."

"What happened to your passion for long-legged blondes with IQs smaller than their bra size?" Seabrook asked.

"My tastes have recently changed to glasses-wearing brunette schoolteachers."

"Every man's fantasy."

"Yeah, but this one's mine."

"Does she know that?"

"I'm working on it."

"What?" Seabrook laughed as he slipped his jersey

over his shoulder pads. "You have to do more with this one than snap your fingers?"

"It's complicated." Jordan pulled out his skates and set them on the bench in front of his locker.

"I think I'm looking forward to meeting this mystery schoolteacher."

"Yeah. Well, hands off when you do."

"Oooh. This just keeps getting better and better." A grin that had women falling at his feet spread across Seabrook's face as he grabbed his stick. "Good to have you back, buddy. Hope you can still pass the puck."

"Ha." Jordan hoped so too. He'd never gone so long without strapping on his skates before.

While he finished putting on his gear he noticed that not everyone was happy to see him back. The vibe he picked up from the Rock was more than just a passing state of pissed off.

Not that Jordan didn't understand the man's frustration.

The team had needed him to help them toward winning the Cup and he hadn't been there. And now they were falling short of what they needed to go all the way. But enough was enough with the dark glares burning holes in his backside. Jordan had his own frustrations. Like his grumpy little sister who currently sat in the stands above the locker room tunnel, and Lucy who was in such foreign territory she almost backed out.

When he finally shushed out onto the ice it was like he'd never missed a beat. He looked up and gave Lucy and Nicki a wave just as the Rock gave him a big shove. Had Jordan not been prepared for it, he would have gone flying. Because his sister and Lucy were watching he ignored the vicious push, skated to his position, and readied for the warm-ups.

"Nice to have you back." Coach Reiner gave him a friendly nod that contradicted the harsh texts he'd sent just a day ago.

At the other end of the line the Rock stood with at least twenty guys between them. However, with each relay the big man with an angry, battle-scarred face only a mother could love, drew closer. By his aggressive glare Jordan knew his teammate was looking for a fight.

By the time they got around to practicing shots and passes, Jordan ignored the heat coming his way and focused on his job.

Forward Scott O'Reilly passed the puck on a long drive toward the blue line. Jordan got in position to slap the puck into the net. The next thing he knew he was flat on his back and the Rock was standing over him.

"Get up, you backstabbing fucker," the Rock snarled.

Backstabbing?

Jordan had been called many things. Most had been appropriate. The Rock's slur was not.

The stress and the frustration of the past two weeks blew wide open like a lit box of TNT. Jordan came up off the ice, dropped his gloves, and grabbed the Rock by the front of his jersey. The Rock grabbed back but couldn't get a good grip.

A scream reverberated through the arena and Jordan snapped his head around to find Nicole pounding on the glass.

"Get your filthy hands off my brother, you ugly dipwad!"

At the moment Jordan had the advantage with one hand wrapped in the Rock's jersey and the other fist pulled back ready to deliver a haymaker. Misplaced or not, pride burst through his chest that his temperamental little sister wanted to come to his defense.

The Rock turned his glare back to Jordan and sneered. "You pussy. You have to have a little baby bunny save your ass?"

"Not this time." Jordan delivered the punch and knocked the Rock off his skates.

"Yeah!" Nicki shouted.

Jordan winced as he heard his sister yell. When he looked up to the stands, Lucy had her hand over her mouth and his sister was doing some kind of crazy touchdown dance.

As he stood over the Rock, who was laid out on the ice grabbing his sore jaw with an ungloved hand, Jordan pointed a finger. "Enough. If you have a legitimate complaint with me, you bring it to me like a man. Not like some backyard brawler waiting to catch me off guard. I'm sorry that it inconvenienced you when my parents were burned alive in a helicopter crash, but my family comes first. You don't like it, too fucking bad."

Heart pumping, Jordan skated off to rejoin his team.

"You done?" Coach folded his arms and lifted a brow.

Jordan nodded.

Seabrook leaned over and chuckled. "*Really* fucking nice to have you back."

Standing on the ice with his team felt great. Jordan had missed it. But as he looked up into the stands one more time and found Lucy and Nicki with their heads together, obviously talking about what had just happened, Jordan knew he'd give up everything to make things right.

"**D**id you see that?" Nicole was practically bouncing out of her Ugg boots.

Lucy wondered at the enthusiasm Nicole displayed over the violence. As she gave a simple nod, it worried her.

"That was badass." Nicole flopped down into the seat next to Lucy.

For obvious reasons Lucy hated violence. She hated confrontation of any kind. Oh, she had no problem standing up for herself these days, but that didn't mean she liked to engage unless it was absolutely necessary. She'd watched the big man push and taunt Jordan, and she knew Jordan wasn't the type of person to take it for too long. When the man had used his stick to whack Jordan across the chest and knock him off his skates, like Nicole, she'd felt a needy rush to retaliate. Instead she'd closed her eyes and prayed he was okay.

Fighting was a huge part of what he did for a living.

How he managed to deal with such aggression on a regular basis she didn't understand. She'd not seen that side of him until now. Knowing it wasn't the same as seeing it. Not that it made her afraid of him; it was just one more facet of his personality.

"Should I be worried that seeing your brother fight excited you?" she asked Nicole.

"No." The teen dropped her shoulders and sighed. "Nobody gets me. Why is that? I have five brothers. Five! And not a single one of them has a clue who I am."

"I think you have to actually talk to them rather than snarl at them for them to understand. I know they want to."

"And that's why Jordan brought me along?"

Lucy nodded. "You can think what you want about him but he truly loves you. And he's worried. I think if you give him a chance he'll surprise you. He won't quit on you. He wants you to be happy and he can't figure out what's wrong."

"It's a long story." Nicole leaned back against the seat like all hope was lost.

Lucy's heart sank.

"I'm not who my brothers think I am."

"Then maybe you should enlighten them."

"I don't want them to hate me. Which is dumb because they probably already do. But . . . they're all I have."

"They would never hate you. Nothing you tell them is going to change the fact that they love you and they want the best for you." Lucy couldn't imagine what could possibly be tearing apart this beautiful young girl. Losing her parents hadn't started this problem, but it had certainly added to the enormity. "I know it's scary when you're about to graduate from high school because you feel like you're just being tossed out into the world unprepared. So if you have feelings of ambiguity, I think you shouldn't worry so much. Your brothers will help you make the right choices. All you have to do is let them know what's going on."

Nicole scoffed. "I wish it were as easy as being afraid to step out into the world past graduating from high school. Which—I know, I know—I won't get to do unless I bring my grades up."

Lucy knew she was walking a fine line between teacher and friend. But she'd wanted to be a teacher so she could help kids. And right now, this one in particular seemed to need her friendship.

She put her arm around Nicole. "I promise I'll help you graduate if you promise you'll at least put in the effort to do the work."

The girl looked up, her blue eyes watery. "Why do you want to help me? I've been such a . . ."

"Brat?"

That brought the hint of a smile.

"I was seventeen once," Lucy said. "It was one of the hardest years of my life. Or so I thought. When I look back now it wasn't so bad. I don't know what's going on that's making you so miserable, and I'm not asking you to tell me—although I've got a soft shoulder you can cry on whenever you need it. All I want to do is help you get through it. I think you're a wonderful girl. You have talent, and brains, and you're strong. I know you are."

"I am?"

Lucy nodded.

"Everyone else just tells me I'm pretty."

"Well . . ." Lucy chuckled. "You're that too. But

you're so much more. Don't ever judge yourself or let others judge you solely based on your looks, Nicole. You should judge yourself on your heart, your integrity, and your willingness to step outside the box others want to paint you in, so you can just be you."

"Is that what you've learned?"

"I learned a long time ago that I'm not the Miss America type, but I'm smart and I have talents maybe not a lot of other people have and I'm totally okay with that."

"What kind of talents?"

"Well . . . I can tie a cherry stem with my tongue. I can write love stories. I can even start and finish the entire book I've written without editing chapter one a hundred times. I can do a triple back flip that would make most cheerleaders green with envy. And I can make treasure out of trash I find at flea markets."

Nicole smiled. Then she did the unexpected. She melted into Lucy's embrace and returned the hug.

Chapter 12

After Jordan's practice, Lucy and Nicole took his Range Rover and went in search of dinner while he soaked away the aches from the hard hits he took on the ice. It surprised him how much he'd gotten out of shape in just two weeks. But other than the nights he'd gone to the gym, he'd spent no time doing the exercises he normally did that kept him in top condition. Not that he'd gone soft by any means, but the hard charging he did on the ice for the duration of a game necessitated a certain type of endurance.

While the jets pounded his tense muscles, he laid his head back, closed his eyes, and wasn't at all surprised when a vision of Lucy—naked—flashed in his mind. He hadn't actually seen her without her clothes, but he'd seen enough of her for his imagination to take flight.

He wanted her.

The question was, would she want him?

Seabrook had been right when he'd said Jordan had never needed to work hard to get a woman's attention. Call it what you wanted; he'd been lucky and blessed with the family's looks. But while looks might draw women in, a little finesse was required afterward.

Over the years, he'd learned how to treat a woman right. He'd also learned how to keep an emotional distance. He'd never had the time or need for someone on a more permanent level.

He felt that need now.

Whatever walls he'd put up, whatever bullshit line he'd told himself that he didn't need anybody, everything was quickly changing.

He'd never had a hard time reading a woman, but with Lucy it was different. Lucy had a tender heart, but in her past she was a woman who'd been badly mistreated. She'd found the strength to overcome her situation, to rebuild her life. And though she was a strong woman, he didn't want to do anything to break the trust he'd hopefully gained. She was a complicated puzzle he was trying to put together one piece at a time.

All he needed—wanted—was the chance.

Through the closed bathroom door he heard the chatter of female voices. Lucy and Nicki were back. Anxious to join them, he turned off the jets, dried off, and threw on a pair of sweats.

The moment he walked into the kitchen the chatter stopped. While Lucy pulled items out of a grocery bag and set them on the counter, Nicole pasted on her usual glare. When Lucy's question to Nicki was met with silence, she turned around. Her gaze skimmed past his sister. When it reached him, it came to a screeching halt.

Lucy didn't often get to view perfection. Seeing Jordan wearing only a pair of sweatpants, a tribal tattoo that spread over his shoulder, and a few drops of water slowly sliding down the center of his immense chest and tightly rippled stomach, was better than anything she would ever see at a fine art gallery. The sweatpants hung low on his narrow hips. He'd slicked his wet hair back and a day's worth of stubble covered his square jawline. Lucy barely held back a sigh. She hoped he wouldn't put on the T-shirt he held in his hand.

"What did you guys come up with for dinner?" A genuine smile flashed to his sister and then her.

Like the pasta she held in her hand, Lucy felt noodly all over. Like she'd been hit with a hot dose of testosterone that melted all the bones in her body. A new reaction for her.

A good reaction.

One she wouldn't mind having over and over.

She held up the bag of whole-wheat penne. "I thought I'd make one of my favorite pasta dishes with fresh tomatoes and zucchini, and a romaine side salad with avocado and caramelized pineapple. Unless you'd like something else?"

"That sounds great. But I thought you were just going to grab pizza or something." He slipped the blue cotton shirt over his head, then tugged the bottom into place. "I don't want you to go to all the trouble."

"It's no trouble. And since I usually just cook for myself, it will be nice to feed someone else. Plus Nicole has offered to help."

Jordan's surprised gaze shifted to his sister. "That's great, Nicki."

She gave him a shrug with attitude. "It's no big deal."

"It is to me."

When he hugged Nicole, Lucy could see the girl's uncertainty whether to hug him back or not. At least she was thinking about it.

A step in the right direction.

Ziggy danced at Lucy's feet and she laughed. "Yes, I got you some treats too."

"Can I give one to him?" Nicole asked.

"Sure. They're in the bag over there."

Nicole's beautiful face came to life as she dangled the Beggin' Strip and Ziggy showed off his tricks.

"Have you ever had a pet?" Lucy asked.

"No." Nicole's smile turned to a frown. "My father was allergic and my mother didn't want animal hair all over her furniture. Which is stupid because we've always had leather furniture and you can just wipe it off."

"Nicki," Jordan said in a warning tone. "Be careful what you say about Mom. She isn't here to defend herself."

"I know that," Nicole snapped.

Uh-oh. Lucy sensed their nice moment was about to head south.

"Can you come wash the lettuce?" she asked Nicole as a deterrent.

"Sure." And the dark cloud was back in place.

For several minutes they all worked together in the kitchen in silence. Uncomfortable to say the least. Lucy realized that not only was it her job to keep an eye on Nicole and try to help figure out the problem, but she also needed to be the Band-Aid between brother and sister.

"Do you have a stereo?" she asked Jordan.

"Just the music channels on the TV. You can listen to just about anything you want there."

"How about you put on some music while we get dinner together. It might . . . lighten the mood."

As soon as Jordan disappeared into the living room and the music came on, Lucy leaned in and whispered to his sister. "Talk, Nicole. Barking is for dogs."

When Nicole looked up, she smiled. "So you're saying I do a bad impression of a Rottweiler?"

"Sweetie, you aren't even a good Schnauzer."

When Nicole laughed, it lifted Lucy's heart and she kept her fingers crossed for a more peaceable evening.

An oldies station came on and Jordan came back into the kitchen looking doubtful. "Is that okay?"

"I love old Beatles stuff," Nicole said while she tore the romaine lettuce and dumped it into a bowl Lucy had found in the cupboard.

"So do I." Jordan moved up to the counter between Lucy and his sister and began slicing the tomatoes. "Do you like country music?"

"It's my favorite." Nicole grabbed a knife to slice the zucchini.

"I thought kids your age just liked rap and hip-hop."

"My friends do. But I like music with a softer rhythm and a meaningful story."

Jordan nodded while the Beatles sang about strawberry fields.

"I'll bet you didn't even know I play guitar," Nicole said. "Or write music."

Both Lucy and Jordan stopped what they were doing, looked at each other, then looked back at Nicole.

"Nope." Nicole sighed. "I didn't figure you did."

"That's amazing, Nic. When did you start doing that?"

"About two years ago. I bought an old pink guitar I found at a thrift shop as a decoration for my room." Her slim shoulders came up in a shrug. "One night I was bored and just started goofing around with it and I got interested."

Jordan slanted a glance at Lucy that made her heart stand still. He'd just discovered more information about his sister in one minute than he probably had in seventeen years.

"I'd love to hear your music some time," Lucy said.

"I'd love to hear it right now," Jordan said.

"I didn't bring the guitar with me."

"But you'd play it for us if you had it?"

"Sure."

"Then let's go." He grabbed his sister by the hand. "Lucy? Do you have this under control until we get back?"

Lucy smiled at the exhilaration on his face and nodded.

"Where are we going?" Nicole asked as he grabbed their jackets off the hook by the door.

"There's a music store a couple blocks away. I want to get there before they close."

"Why?"

"Because I'm buying you a guitar."

When the door shut behind them, Lucy leaned back against the counter and wanted to cry. Jordan had seen the opportunity to become a part of his sister's life. He'd found a connection. And he'd seized the opportunity to make things right. Just like he'd done on the ice today.

Only in a much softer version.

*H*ours later, Jordan sat beside Lucy on the sofa listening to his sister play her guitar from down the hall. She had God-given talent. Best of all, she'd been forced to talk to him while they'd been at the music store, where she'd picked up several acoustic guitars and strummed until she found a Gibson Hummingbird that had felt right. When he'd started to take it to the cashier to pay for it she'd tried to stop him.

"You can't buy that," she'd insisted. "It costs two thousand dollars."

He halted in the middle of the store. "Do you like it?"

"Yes."

"Will it make you happy?"

She'd hesitated and looked away to where a separate room housed numerous drum sets. "I don't want you to buy me anything."

"Why not?"

She'd shrugged.

"Because you think you'll owe me something?"

Another shrug lifted her shoulders.

He'd taken her by those slim shoulders and made her look at him. Blue eyes exactly like his own had stared back at him, verifying the reason he wanted to help.

"You will owe me nothing, Nicki. I'm not buying it for you because I want something to hold over you. You're my little sister. I love you. I want to see you happy. And if somehow this guitar will make you smile, then it's worth every penny. Come on."

When he'd tucked his hand beneath her elbow and guided her to the cashier, he'd sworn he could hear her heart pounding.

After he'd paid for the instrument and handed her the black carrying case, she gave him the first real smile he'd seen since he'd come back home.

His heart melted.

When they'd come back to his apartment it smelled amazing from the pasta Lucy had made. They'd all sat at the dining table and actually had a conversation while they ate Lucy's delicious meal. Jordan figured buying the guitar had probably only given him a one-night reprieve from the baby dragon's temper. But he'd take what he could get. Because for the first time, with Lucy and Nicki there, his apartment felt like a home.

Now, as he sat next to Lucy on the sofa, listening to Nicole play something that sounded like a soulful Miranda Lambert song, he sighed and reached for Lucy's hand. "She's really good."

"*Really* good." Lucy nodded. "Who knew?"

"Not me, that's for damn sure. Nobody—not even my mom or dad—ever mentioned that she played."

"Some of her song lyrics are just breathtaking. I wish she'd have turned those in for an assignment instead of a review for *Pretty Little Liars*."

He chuckled. "Me too."

"When we talked today she didn't mention anything about writing songs."

Jordan turned to look at her, noticing—not for the first time—just how beautiful she was without a stitch of makeup. Earlier when she'd taken her shower, she came back into the living room sans makeup, hair pulled up into a mess of silky curls piled up at the top of her head, and smelling like fresh peaches. Somehow he'd managed to keep his hands to himself when all he'd wanted to do was bury his face in her neck and take a bite. He'd wanted other things too but he was still trying to take things slow.

Hardest damn thing he'd ever done.

"You talked today?" he asked.

Lucy nodded.

"About?"

"How strangely excited she got when you decked that guy."

"Oh. Sorry."

"Don't be," she said. "I was thrilled that she let her emotions rule and that she appeared to want to protect you."

"I hate to admit it but I was damn proud of that." His heart gave a crazy little thump at the memory. "What else did you talk about?"

"About how she should trust you and talk to you so you can help her with whatever's bothering her. And that you're a good brother who loves her very much."

That Lucy had come to his defense touched him deeply. He lifted her hand to his mouth and kissed the backs of her fingers. "Thank you."

Sincerity flashed like gold glitter in her brown eyes from behind those dark-rimmed glasses. "I wouldn't have said it if it wasn't true."

Her soft voice floated over him like a gentle caress that tightened every muscle in his body with awareness. Craving to touch her, he brought her hand to his lips again and kissed the soft skin on the inside of her wrist. When she didn't pull her hand away he drew her in so he could kiss her sexy mouth. When she leaned into his kiss, he lifted her onto his lap so she straddled his thighs with her cute little unevenly cutoff sweats, which she probably thought were unattractive and a safe choice in sleepwear. Yet all he could think about was slipping them off her curvy legs and touching all that bare skin and everything in between.

When he cupped his hands over the firm curve of her ass and swept his tongue across her full bottom lip, she leaned into him. On a sigh she parted her lips and he took possession of her sweet, minty mouth. Her plump breasts pressed against his chest, and the scent of peaches drifted from her warm, soft skin. It was the most intimate they'd ever been. And he wanted more.

But wanting and having were two different things.

He didn't want her to think he'd brought her along to *service* him and he didn't want her running out the door because he'd scared her. Though she responded to his touch and his kiss, he didn't know exactly where she stood with the whole sex thing.

Maybe because of her past she wasn't receptive to the idea. He needed to be careful about that. Though he'd been a man who'd always taken, this time he had to give. And with Lucy that meant he had to give her time to decide if this was what she wanted, not that she felt she'd been forced into anything.

Reluctantly he ended the kiss without being abrupt, then he made some lame-ass excuse about it might be better if they stopped in case Nicki walked in, which was a complete one-eighty on what he really wanted to do.

Lucy lay in Jordan's giant bed between ultra soft, luxurious sheets, staring up at the ceiling wondering why he'd abruptly ended such an amazing kiss.

Maybe, like he said, it really had been because Nicole was just down the hall and could walk in at any moment. Or maybe Lucy just didn't push his buttons dressed in a pair of raggedy cutoff sweats and a T-shirt. Of course, if he'd gone a little further he would have discovered her newest Victoria's Secret lace undies. Those were certainly sexy, if she had to say so herself. And of course she did because no one else had seen them.

Or probably ever would with her luck.

Lucy had never had the opportunity to be the aggressor in a relationship. Her ex and whatever this was going on with Jordan was all the experience she had in the world. It wasn't much. Especially since her ex had been so callous and selfish in bed. Not to mention very, very speedy.

Thankfully.

Unlike many women who'd gone through abusive situations, she wasn't turned off toward sex. Just the opposite. She was very curious. She wondered if there really was such a thing as multiple orgasms. Or even if it was possible to have an orgasm with a real live man and not a battery-operated boyfriend.

She readjusted the pillow, giving it two punches just for good measure.

Why was she lying there thinking about that kind of stuff when all it would do was bring her another frustrated night of tossing and turning? She needed to think about something else. She ran her fingertips over the fluffy comforter and her thoughts immediately shifted toward guilt.

How could she lie there all night in that gigantic bed—alone—while Jordan, who was well over six feet tall and built like a god—was probably uncomfortable sleeping on the sofa? Especially when he had to get up the following morning and hit the ice for another grueling practice.

She sat up, pushed her hair off her face, and got out of bed. She couldn't let him sleep out there. He was right. The bed was big enough for both of them. They'd just have to make sure Nicole didn't find out.

She'd tiptoed into the darkened living room before she realized she'd left her glasses on the nightstand.

Though moonlight filtered through the curtains, she couldn't see anything but a blur because of her nearsightedness.

Too late to go back and get them now.

Careful she didn't stub her toe, she made her way toward the sofa. Jordan was stretched out on his back with one arm thrown over his eyes. The other arm was hugging a blonde stretched out between him and the back of the sofa.

Lucy stopped.

Squinted.

Her heart pounded. Maybe he'd ended their kiss earlier because he had someone else in mind and she was on that sofa with him right now.

No.

He wouldn't do that.

Would he?

She took another step closer and squinted again. Between the dim light and her horrible eyesight she couldn't see much. Just a mop of golden hair. Beneath her foot a floorboard creaked. The head popped up and relief poured like sugar through her when she realized it was only Ziggy.

Not wanting to startle Jordan, Lucy crept closer. She reached out her hand to touch his shoulder and gently wake him. Like a bullet his hand shot out and he pulled her down on top of him. Ziggy escaped over the back of the sofa.

Lucy let out a giggle. "You scared me."

Suddenly his hands were on her behind and he was grinning up at her.

"I didn't know you had it in you to be so sneaky," he whispered. "I like it."

His hands pressed her down and she figured he must really like it, because his sizable erection surged against her most sensitive area.

Want and need sprang to life.

"What were you sneaking in here for?" He smoothed his hands down her entire backside.

"To get you to come to bed."

He lifted his head to get a better look at her through the moonlight. "Why do you want me to come to bed, Lucy?"

His voice sounded hopeful. And though she hadn't intended for him to come to bed for *that*, she had to admit that subconsciously maybe she'd done exactly that very thing. But she'd never be able to say it out loud.

"It's not fair for you to sleep on this sofa when you have to work so hard tomorrow. Now that I've seen a little bit of what it is you do I feel selfish being in that big bed all by myself. You're right. There's plenty of room."

"Is that the only reason?"

When she didn't answer—because she couldn't without lying or being completely embarrassed—he cupped the back of her head and brought her face down to his.

"Tell me you want me, Lucy. Because I sure as hell want you."

She could lie, but her nipples were aching and hard and pressing into his chest. And surely he could feel the tingle between her legs where his erection was pressed.

She could lie.

But why would she when she'd wanted him since she was seventeen years old.

"I want you."

"When I make you come . . ." He brushed her hair away from her face and gave her a smile that sent an extra jolt between her legs. "And I will. I want to hear you scream my name from that sexy mouth of yours."

Oh. My.

He rolled her beneath him and with the buttery leather at her back he pressed his erection into the soft spot between her thighs. A hot tingle danced down her spine as he lowered his face and kissed the side of her neck.

No man had ever kissed her neck. Or licked the shell of her ear. Or nipped playfully at her throat. Jordan was a lot of man. She just hoped she could handle him.

"I love the way you smell." He ran his nose up her throat, then he gently sucked her skin.

Panic started to set in. Not that she didn't want this. She wanted it more than she'd ever wanted anything. But even though she'd been married, she had no real experience at sex. That relationship had never been give and take. On second thought it had been. She'd given and he'd taken. In a hurry. Unlike her ex, Jordan didn't seem like he was in much of a rush to get to the end result. As embarrassing as it might be, she needed to let him know.

"I . . . don't know how to do this," she whispered.

He lifted his head. "What?"

"Sex. I really don't know how. Not in a loving manner. Not in . . . how to give real pleasure to a man."

"And I'll bet you don't know how to receive pleasure either."

She sighed and looked away. Even though it was dark she could feel his gaze on her face. "This is so embarrassing."

"*You* have nothing to be embarrassed about. A sexual partner is supposed to discover the other person's needs. Their desires. What makes their blood rush, their heart race, and their toes curl. If your past partners—"

"Partner. Singular."

"Partner, didn't take the time to get to know you or take care of you, that's not on you, Lucy. That's on him."

"So you don't think I'm sexually stunted?"

A smile lifted his lips. "I think you're a strong, sensual, fascinating woman who deserves to know what real lovemaking is like."

Thought stopped. Desire and curiosity took control. She'd never thought of it in those terms before. One of the great things about Jordan was he opened doors to new things. So far they'd all been pretty good. God help her, she trusted him.

She rolled out from under him, stood, and held out her hand. "Come on."

The brief confusion darkening his eyes brightened as he looked up at her. "Where are we going, Lucy?"

"I want to learn what real lovemaking is like." She crooked her finger in a come-here-big-boy way. "Time for you to learn a little bit about me, and for me to learn a whole lot about you."

$\mathcal{T}$he minute she put her hand in his, Jordan knew he had her trust. But he wanted more than that. He wanted her to relax, enjoy, and completely give herself over to him. He didn't need to hear the details of what went on in the bedroom when she'd been married to know that her jerk of a husband had been harsh and selfish.

To Jordan, Lucy was like one of those brilliant blue orchids—rare, delicate, and ready to bloom under the right conditions. He had all night, and everything he knew, everything he had to give, was hers for the taking.

She led him into the bedroom and quietly shut the door. Then he opened the heavy drape over the window so the moonlight filtered through the sheer white curtain. By the time he turned around she was hugging herself and looking very unsure. The carpet was soft beneath his feet as he made his way back over to her and cupped her shoulders with his hands.

"Do you trust me?"

She nodded without hesitation.

"Good. Because I would never ask you to do anything you feel uncomfortable with and I would *never* hurt you. Clear?"

She nodded again.

"First rule . . . no more nodding. I want you to talk to me. Tell me what you want. What you like. What makes you feel good."

"Oh God." She snagged her bottom lip between her teeth.

"Nope." He smiled to reassure her. "It's just me and you. Close your eyes."

When she did, he cupped the side of her head with his hand, letting the soft, silky curls fall over his forearm. He used his other hand to grasp her hip and bring her closer. Then he whispered against her lips. "Tonight is all about you."

He brushed feather-light kisses down the side of her neck, inhaling her sweet scent along the way. When he reached her shoulder he gently pushed the loose material of her T-shirt aside and continued his descent. He could hear her heart pounding as he lifted the shirt over her head. She breathed a small gasp when the cool air touched her skin and she lifted her arms to cover herself.

"You're so beautiful, Lucy. Let me see you." He moved her hands away, then gently cupped the fullness of her breasts in his hands. When he stroked his thumbs across her nipples they peaked into tight rosy buds. "Do you like that?"

Eyes still closed, she started to nod, then obviously remembered the rule. "Yes."

"I want to touch you all over. I want to know what makes you feel good. And then I want to touch you again to be sure."

"I like you touching me." She spoke in a breathy whisper that was so sexy his cock hardened more with a deep, needy ache. He couldn't remember a time where he'd been so turned on just leisurely touching a woman. Most women wanted to get right to the action. Lucy didn't even know what the action was. But she was about to find out—the slow and seductive way.

He took her hands and placed them down at her sides. Then he took his time kissing her mouth, throat, and shoulders. He kissed her arms, lifted her hair and kissed the back of her neck and all the way down her spine. He touched her smooth skin with the gentlest of hands, and she rewarded him with soft sighs and throaty moans. When he reached her hips he tucked his thumbs in the waistband of her cutoffs and slid the fabric down her legs. He lifted each foot to remove the pants, then sat back on his heels to look at her standing there in a high-cut lacy pair of pink panties and nothing else but skin.

"Damn."

"What's wrong?" Concern tinged her voice but she managed to keep her eyes closed.

"Not a thing." He smoothed a hand down over her hip and thigh. "You just take my breath away."

"No I don't. I hear you breathing just fine."

A smile touched his lips before he leaned in to kiss her firm belly, cup her sweet, rounded, lace-covered ass with his hands, and slick his tongue across her belly button. Her skin tasted sweet like honey. He could only imagine how delicious the rest of her would be.

Slowly he lowered his hands down her hips in a smooth caress, letting his long fingers dip into the warm, damp apex of her thighs. Just enough to test.

To tease.

Her long, hungry moan coincided with the weakening

of her knees. Without missing a beat, he scooped her up in his arms and laid her on the bed.

"Are we done now?" she asked.

The disappointment in her tone made him smile and a chuckle rumbled deep in his chest. "Baby, we're just getting started."

*E*yes closed, Lucy grasped the fluffy comforter as he trailed his fingers from the base of her throat down between her breasts to the top of the lace on her panties.

"Relax." His fingers brushed and swirled, sending chills—the good kind—through her body. "Use your hands for something better than gripping the bedding. Use them on me."

He leaned down, his bare chest pressed into her breasts as his hot breath whispered in her ear. "Or better yet, touch yourself. Show me what feels good."

She'd touched herself before, but not with her bare fingers. A vibrator gave her what she needed without it becoming too . . . personal.

This definitely went beyond personal.

The low, sexy tone of his voice kept her calm and made her want to do as he asked. She wanted to please him as much as apparently he wanted to please her.

When his lips found her throat again he kissed his way down to her breasts where his tongue flicked her pebbled nipple before he sucked it into his warm, wet mouth. A hot ache of need shot down between her legs. She arched into him, and a gasp she couldn't control slipped past her lips.

"Does that feel good?"

"Yes." He sucked again and the need tripled. "More. Please. More."

With a murmur against her skin he moved to the other breast, and instead of instantly sucking her nipple into his mouth, he circled it with his tongue, then flicked it and rolled it gently between his teeth. Her hands came up off the comforter and dove into his hair, holding him at her breast, silently begging him to continue. Between her fingers his hair was silky and long enough to grab and hold tight if the need arose.

And boy did she ever hope it arose.

She'd never had a man's tender touch. Never had her breasts paid attention to in a sensuous manner. Never knew they could be so fabulously sensitive when the right man was in command.

Her entire body was on fire. Tingling. Craving more. *This* kind of control she was willing to hand over.

Only one problem existed. She wanted to see him. He was a gorgeous man with an incredible body and a sexy tattoo running over his broad shoulder and chest that she wanted to lick. Keeping her eyes closed seemed unfair. Currently he was busy rocking her world so she snuck a peek. Seeing him at her breast, concentrating on what he was doing to make her feel good intensified the sensation.

"Oh."

He looked up. "You cheated."

"It's so much better with my eyes open. I want to see you. I want to touch you."

"Believe me, there's nothing more I want than your

hands on me. But right now, there's something I've fantasized about doing to you."

"You've fantasized about me?"

"From the minute I walked into your classroom. You looked so prim and proper and sexy as hell. All I wanted to do was strip you down and get you messy."

"Messy?"

"Hot. Wet." He gave her nipple a lazy stroke with his tongue. "And sweaty."

"Sweaty?" Totally new concept for her.

"Mmm hmm. But right now let's focus on . . . *wet.*"

He slid his way down her body, kissing her stomach, her hips, and sliding her panties off. Then he cupped his hand beneath her bottom and kissed her pubic area. She didn't panic, but she froze.

"Jordan . . . I've never . . ."

"I know, baby." He kissed the apex of her thighs and . . . hmmm . . . fancy that. Her legs just parted all on their own like they knew exactly what was about to happen.

"And I promise I'll make it good for you," he said.

When he kissed the inside of each thigh she held her breath. Then he gently parted her feminine folds with his thumbs.

"Mmmm." He moaned. "So pretty." His warm, wet tongue slowly licked across her slick flesh, and a jolt of white-hot pleasure curled all the way up into her chest and down to her toes.

So, so, *so* much better than a vibrator.

His moan of approval pulsated against her skin while he teased, licked, and sucked the sensitive flesh.

He made her come alive and she grasped at everything she could get her hands on—his hair, shoulders, the bedding, her own hair. A sizzling heat caught fire to all the nerve endings in her body and she exploded. The jolt rendered her speechless but for a lusty groan that came from somewhere deep inside she never even knew existed. As she spiraled even higher, one single word burst from her lips.

"Jordan!"

Moments later as every muscle turned to jelly, he moved back up her body and propped himself over her. His huge erection pressed against that flesh he'd just caught on fire and he moved his body in a way that kept the sensation going. He kissed her and she parted her lips to let his talented tongue slide inside.

While they kissed, he moved that hard-muscled sexy body against hers and it didn't take long for that needy ache to reappear.

She filled her hands with his strong back and firm buttocks while he moved against her. But when she thought he'd push inside, he didn't.

"That was a first?" His deep voice rumbled against her breasts, waking them up like they had a connection straight between her legs.

"Yes." Should she feel embarrassed? She didn't. She felt . . . amazing. But she wanted more. She wanted him.

He grinned down at her. "Then here's your second."

Before she could move, he slid down her body and stirred up a whole lot of magic again that answered her long-wondered question.

Yes, there was such a thing as multiple orgasms.

Chapter 13

$\mathcal{F}$rom somewhere in the apartment an alarm beeped. Jordan jolted awake, once again on the sofa. After he'd given Lucy several orgasms, she'd fallen asleep in his arms. He'd held her all night until the wee hours of the morning when he'd slipped from bed and gone into the bathroom to take a shower.

Holding off from slipping his aching cock inside her sweet, slick body had been the hardest thing he'd ever done. But he wanted Lucy to know that he wasn't just thinking about himself. In more ways than one she came first. He'd never been a man who'd given before but he'd excelled at taking. With Lucy, he wanted to give. He wanted to feel her relax in his arms and make those sexy sounds that told him she'd left her past at the door and trusted him enough to let him go places no man had ever been.

He'd never cuddled before in his life. Yet when he got out of bed, he wanted to crawl right back in next to her.

The middle-of-the-night shower had been a necessity to relieve the ache of wanting her. His own hand had been a poor substitute, but making Lucy happy came first. Because he didn't want Nicole to wake up in the morning and find him in bed with her teacher, he'd gone back to the cold sofa and eventually fallen asleep with Ziggy snoring by his feet.

When the alarm buzzer shut off, he knew Lucy would soon make an appearance. He got up and folded the blanket. Then he went into the kitchen to turn on the coffeemaker and start throwing something together for breakfast. If it had just been him a protein shake would do, but he had two females to think about right now.

That knowledge made him smile.

He'd never had to think about anyone else's needs before. It made for a nice change.

The only blonde in the place just needed a bowl of kibble to keep him happy. Jordan rubbed the dog's head as he reached into a bottom cupboard for a skillet. Several minutes later Lucy shuffled in wearing her big fluffy robe, bed hair, and a confused look. She stopped at the end of the counter as if she didn't quite know what to say or do.

"Good morning." He pulled her into his arms and kissed her. "Sleep well?"

She nodded. "I'm not sure I've ever slept that well before."

He gave her a knowing grin. "I'm glad to know you were satisfied."

"Obviously several bone-melting times. But you . . . ?"

Ah. There was the reason for the confusion.

"I slept good too," he joked, trying to pull her from her state of concern.

"But you didn't . . . I mean we didn't . . . I mean you—"

"Last night wasn't about me." He pulled her close. Kissed the top of her head while the coffeemaker gurgled. "We have lots of time to figure things out. I don't want to push you into something you don't want to do."

"Jordan?" She curled her fingers into the front of his shirt. "I want to. I really really want to."

"Ah. I love the sound of my name on your lips."

A cute little frown wrinkled between her brows. "You're dodging the subject."

"I'm not. I was about to say that if my sister wouldn't be walking in here in a few minutes— which is why I went back to sleeping on the sofa last night—I'd be carrying you off to the bedroom for lesson number two just so I could hear my name on your lips again."

A sleek dark brow lifted from behind her glasses. "Just?"

"Just one of the many reasons." He slipped his hands down her back, gripped her rear end in his hands, and gave her a little squeeze. "We still have tonight."

"Can you have sex before a game?"

"Absolutely."

"Good." She lifted to her toes and planted a kiss on him that made him rethink the whole waiting thing.

"I'm taking a shower," she said as she sauntered away. "Just in case you're interested."

"You're killing me, Lucy," he said, but the grin on his face said he liked the new, playful Lucy.

He liked her a hell of a lot.

Though Lucy had sworn she didn't mind cooking dinner again, Jordan insisted on taking her and Nicole out to a place called Peach Magnolia Grill. When they walked into the converted Victorian house, Lucy immediately liked the traditional Southern décor. The aroma from the food at the surrounding tables made her mouth water. Nicole, however, looked slightly unsure.

"They have everything here from fried chicken to alligator," Jordan told his sister. "I'm sure you'll find something you like."

"Alligator!"

He grinned as he pulled out a chair for her. "Tastes like chicken."

Lucy wanted to laugh at the horror on Nicole's face but decided nothing that seemed to be a form of making fun of her would be a good idea. They wanted to have a nice evening. And while Jordan and his sister had made some strides last night, things were still touchy.

"I've been thinking about turning vegan," Nicole said. "Now might be a good time to start."

"They also have pan roasted duck if you change your mind."

"Oh sure, make me think of Daffy at a time like this."

Lucy smiled. Watching brother and sister tease each

other was like getting hit with the warm rays of the sun.

The server appeared at their white linen–covered table—a gorgeous blonde with a narrow waist and long legs in a pair of perfectly fitted black pants. Her bustline filled out the simple white shirt like nobody's business. She arrived at their table with a smile that let Lucy know before the woman even spoke that she was on very familiar ground with Jordan.

"Hey, handsome. I haven't seen you for a while. I thought you were going to call me when you came back into town."

"He's been busy," Nicole snapped. "Our parents were killed in case you didn't know."

The server's flirty smile fell. "I'm sorry. I didn't know."

Jordan's expression shifted between the amusement of his sister's response to the server's flirting and the horrifying truth of their parents' deaths.

"Well now you do," Nicole grabbed her cloth napkin from the table, settled it on her lap, then looked up at the blonde with big innocent eyes. "So maybe we could have another server who doesn't know our personal business?"

"Of course." The woman turned on her heel and disappeared into another part of the restaurant.

"Nicki, that was rude." Jordan's stern look failed to impress.

"I don't know." Nicki lifted a shoulder. "Her coming on to you when she didn't know who either me or Ms. Diamond were was pretty rude if you ask me."

Jordan looked at Lucy who shrugged. "She has a

point." Not that *she* was really anything to him, but the blonde didn't know that.

Lucy knew Jordan had been with women like the server. She'd seen dozens of pictures of him out on the town with similar females—women who were long-legged, busty, and gorgeously blond. But last night he'd been with *her*—kissing her in places that had never been kissed. Licking her in places she'd never imagined. He made her see stars and rainbows by giving her the most unbelievable orgasms she'd ever had. From now on, her battery-operated boyfriend didn't stand a chance.

Afterward he'd held her in his arms and made her feel special. Cared for. Wanted. Thanks to him, she now knew what sexually satisfying for both partners meant. Tonight she'd make sure she gave Jordan just as much satisfaction as he'd given her.

They had a long time to look at the menu before the new server appeared at their table, a young man this time, who humorously appeared equally as smitten with Jordan as their previous server had been. After Jordan ordered roasted pecan salads with fried green tomatoes for all of them, Nicole excused herself to use the restroom. Once she disappeared, Jordan reached across the table and took Lucy's hand.

"Nervous?" he asked with a cagey smile.

"About what?"

"What I'm going to do to you tonight when we get home."

Lucy thought about the server who'd flirted so openly. She thought about all those other women who'd caught Jordan's eye. Before she became completely intimidated she dismissed them. Because for the first time she was living in the moment. Reaching for the brass ring on a quickly spinning merry-go-round. It was time she stepped outside her comfort zone and grabbed hold of a dream, even if she woke up in the morning and everything disappeared. At least she'd have taken a chance.

"Maybe . . ." She squeezed his hand. "It's about what I'm going to do to *you* when we get home."

Okay. Forget about stepping outside that comfort zone.

She'd freaking leaped.

*D*inner had been a Southern feast without the grits and fried chicken. Jordan had selected an Italian rosé for their meal while Nicole grumbled about having to drink a virgin mint julep. The conversation mostly centered on a new song Nicole was creating and Jordan's upcoming game. Lucy had little to add to the discussion other than that she'd like Nicole to hand in her lyrics for extra credit on her final grade. She didn't mind her lack of participation in the conversation. Because watching the man she cared so much about reconnecting with his sister was like opening an early Christmas present.

It was late by the time they got back to the apartment. Mildly tipsy from the delicious rosé, Lucy followed Jordan and Nicole inside, where they were greeted by a happy-to-see-them tail-wagger. While brother and sister discussed plans for the following day leading up to the game, Lucy escaped by taking Ziggy outside to do his business. The break was what both she and her dog needed—for drastically different reasons.

Every minute spent in Jordan's company only increased her want and need for the man. She knew she was dreaming of the impossible; their lives were too completely different. But trying to tell a heart what it couldn't have was like explaining to a two-year-old that ice cream was bad for them.

The breath of fresh air helped clear her mind a little so she could still grasp the fact that while she might want and might take whatever Jordan wanted to offer right now, it was short-term. Eventually he'd go back to his regular life and so would she.

When she came back into the apartment both Nicole and Jordan were absent from the room. One look at the sofa where last night Jordan had pulled her down on top of him created a crazy tingle inside her body before reality shoved it aside and her earlier bravado shriveled like a rotten apple.

How did she compare with the other women Jordan had been with? His celebrity allowed him to attend exclusive parties and red carpet events. He dined in the finest restaurants and dated supermodels while she was accustomed to home-cooked meals and not dating at all. She had no worldly experience. Even when she'd been married to a man with money, she'd never fit in with his family, his friends, or his colleagues. So how in the world did she think she could ever fit in with Jordan's?

Not that he'd asked her to.

The women he dated were gorgeous and far more experienced at pleasing a man than she'd ever be. Last night he'd pleased her multiple times. But really, what did she know about turning the tables? Yes, she was an eager student. But what if she did something wrong? What if he laughed at her?

When nerves got the best of her she escaped to the bedroom where she could hear the shower running in the adjoining bathroom. Trying not to imagine him in there naked with soap bubbles on his perfectly muscled body; she pulled on her sweats, grabbed a pillow and blanket, and headed for the sofa.

A few moments later he came out into the living room with a towel wrapped and knotted at his waist. Moisture clung to all the dips and ripples of muscles, and a drop of water slipped from his wet hair and trailed over the tattoo on his shoulder.

"What are you doing?" he asked.

Curled up beneath the blanket on the sofa, she tried to keep her gaze steady and not let it wander all over his body.

Tried and failed.

"I'm not letting you sleep on the sofa tonight." She punched her fist into the pillow. "You need to get your rest."

His head tilted. "You want me to *rest*?"

While he stood there looking like some kind of sun-kissed god with his bare chest and rippled abs on full display, Lucy swallowed hard and nodded because, really, that's about all she could manage.

"Well, I guess you're right. I could use a good night's

sleep," he said while he stalked closer. His clean scent waved before her like an aphrodisiac.

Not that she needed one where he was concerned.

"My thoughts exactly," she said in a reasonable tone even while her heart pounded and her blood rushed through her ears like an ocean wave. "So I'll sleep out here. You can have the bed."

"I always sleep better after I've worked out a little."

"So you're going down to the gym *after* a shower?"

Coming closer, he gave her a grin that said, *Nice try*.

The towel knotted at his hip looked like it was about to slip as he stopped right in front of her. Which put her at eye level with . . . whoo boy.

"*Not* the kind of exercise I had in mind," he said with a chuckle.

Lucy squeaked when he picked her up, easily tossed her over his shoulder, and carried her into the bedroom.

As soon as they reached the door his towel slipped off and she had a perfect view of his tight and rounded gluteus maximus—a true thing of beauty.

Though she appreciated the visual, and though a large dose of estrogen sent her awareness into overdrive, doubt and anxiety dug in their heels. "But . . . Nicole's not asleep yet."

"She's all the way on the other side of the apartment." He gently tossed her on the bed and leaned over her; completely aware he was naked, and confident with the exposure. "Plus earlier she recorded the music to her new song. And right now she's wearing the headphones I bought her and listening to the track while she's working on the lyrics. So you can moan and scream all you want. She won't hear a peep."

"I won't scream." Because she knew with him, she had nothing to fear except maybe falling for him fast and hard.

A smirk lifted his mouth. "We'll see about that."

*J*ordan wanted her with an urgency he couldn't ever remember feeling before.

Maybe it was just the chase. Maybe he was being too bold to assume she wanted this. If she'd told him no instead of confirming she wouldn't scream he'd never have gone caveman. Fortunately he wasn't so far gone that he couldn't slow down or stop. It was still all about her. If tonight was a repeat of last night and he ended up taking matters into his own hand afterward, so be it. But the way her hungry eyes roamed his body and the fact that she was voluntarily staying put on that bed gave him a proceed-until-otherwise-noted signal.

"You want to run, Lucy?"

She shook her head. "But tonight I do want to touch."

Had she not licked her lips at the end of that statement his knees wouldn't have nearly buckled from the white-hot flash of need.

"Tonight it's your call." He lifted his hands in surrender. "We do anything you want."

"*Anything?*" She looked up at him from behind her glasses. "Even if I'm not sure what I'm doing?"

"Baby, as long as it makes you feel good, that's all that matters."

"So I can explore all I want?" She came up to her knees and ran her soft palms up his chest. "I can be the boss?"

Holy shit.

Stuttered breath clogged his lungs and every muscle in his body tightened.

"You can be and do whatever you want." He threaded his hand through the side of her silky hair and pressed his mouth to hers in a tongue-tangling, teeth-nipping kiss. The little purr that came from her throat went straight to his head like a double shot of Patrón. "As long as it's with me."

Her head tilted as she dropped her gaze to his chest. "So it's okay if I do this?" With a hum of pleasure her fingertips walked down his pecs, circled his hard nipples, and gently plucked them. Her touch sent a jolt of urgency into his erection and it was all he could do to keep from taking her hand and wrapping it around his cock.

"You're the boss," he managed through gritted teeth. Her sensuous experimental touch was probably going to kill him. But at least he'd die with a smile on his face.

"Oh good." Next her fingers danced down his abs and gripped his hips. "I think I'm going to like being in control."

He would have expressed his delight but she leaned forward and slowly licked his stomach from his belly button downward. Then her fingers tentatively touched his cock. It jumped at the contact and she gasped.

"Did I do that?"

"Uh-huh." Oh good, he was reduced to muttered responses. Pretty soon the anticipation would melt him into a big needy puddle at her feet.

She touched him again, this time wrapping her fingers around him with one warm hand while cupping his testicles in the other. His need for her was ruthless. Primitive. But with the eager curiosity on her face he knew he'd suffer to give her whatever she wanted, whenever she wanted it, and for however long she needed it.

If he could manage to hold out that long.

In a momentary break that allowed him to catch his breath, she took off her glasses and set them on the nightstand. "I've never done this before . . . of my own free will."

"I'd never force you to do anything you didn't want to do." He cupped her chin in his hand, looked into her eyes, and captured every subtle shift and flicker of emotion. "You know that, right?"

She nodded. "I've never *wanted* to do this . . . until now. With you."

Jesus, she was killing him.

He wanted to wrap her up in his arms and just hold her. Protect her. But then she surrounded the base of his cock with her fingers, lowered her head, and licked the full length. A moan rumbled from his chest and he felt her smile against his tight skin.

For a while she touched, tested, and teased until he was nearly out of his mind with voracious need. When she finally took him into her mouth and swirled her tongue around him, he nearly exploded. Miraculously he kept his hands to gentle touches of her arms, neck, and shoulders. He didn't grab her by the hair and push into her mouth. He let her control what she wanted and how much.

For the first time in his life he had to try and think of something else so she could explore him at her leisure. Toughest damn thing he'd ever had to do when everything male inside him wanted to push her back on the bed and bury himself between her legs.

While he'd mentally recited the broad range of his penalty minutes over the years, she kissed her way back up his chest.

Being with Lucy made him feel brand-new. Like everything they did was the first time for him. Luckily he was smart enough to realize that the way he felt had a hell of a lot more to do with his heart than with his nerve endings.

Even if those were about to explode.

"Will you touch me now?" Her lips glistened and her eyes were dark and seductive.

"Baby, anything you want. It's yours."

"Then I want you."

He cupped her face between his hands and kissed her. Then he slid his hands down to caress her breasts. To slip his fingers between her legs and touch her the way he now knew she liked to be touched. When he did so, her head dropped back on a long, lusty moan, exposing her pretty neck for him to kiss. The more he touched her, the more she pressed against his hand.

He could tell she was on the verge when he whispered in her ear, "I'm going to lick you so you'll come."

"No." She grabbed his shoulders as he began his descent. "I want you inside me."

Now she really had his attention. "Are you sure?"

She gave a quick nod. "Don't make me wait. I really need you. I want this. I want *you*."

Relief and lust collided as he yanked open the nightstand drawer and pulled out a condom.

"Let me put it on." Her voice was eager as she reached for him. "Show me how."

His hands were shaking with anticipation as he tore open the package and showed her how to roll it down over his erection. Having her watch so intently was a double turn-on. But even as much as he wanted to just push inside her and get moving, he wanted to savor every stroke. Every second. Every sigh. Every moan.

She lay back and opened her arms for him. For the first time in his life he felt like those open arms were more than just an invitation to fuck. They felt like an invitation into her heart.

He leaned in and kissed her thoroughly, then he gazed into her eyes while his fingers slipped into the slick folds between her legs. His careful attention arched her back and made her moan.

"Take me now, Jordan."

To know she wanted him after everything she'd been through made his heart race. He rocked his erection against her slick opening and kissed her thoroughly while he slid slow and deep into her incredible heat.

Not a doubt entered his mind. Being with Lucy was exactly where he wanted and needed to be.

Thinking stopped and pleasure took over as Jordan slid deep into her body. Lucy had worried that she might not be able to do this. Worried that her past had left too many mental and emotional scars. His warm, clean, manly scent washed over her as she closed her eyes and just enjoyed the amazing sensation of having him inside. Whatever she'd fantasized about Jordan Kincade didn't come close to the real thing.

While he made love to her she filled her hands with the solid muscles of his shoulders, back, and buttocks. She felt his muscles release and contract as he surged deep inside her. She'd never experienced anything like this before, and the overwhelming emotion of it made her want to cry.

Like he could read her mind, he captured her lips in a kiss that stole her breath.

"You feel so damn good," he whispered hotly against her ear as he lifted her leg over his hip and pushed in deeper. "I'll never get enough of you."

The shift in position brought a new sensation that delivered an onslaught of hot tingles where their bodies were joined. It was the most incredible thing she'd ever felt. Her friend Claudia often complained that she'd never had an orgasm during actual intercourse. Lucky for Lucy, Jordan had all the right moves.

The more she moaned, the more he whispered dirty words in her ear. The more he whispered, the faster the pace of their lovemaking. What had started out slow and sensuous had built into a fiery passion that had them both panting. Sweating. And then the heat detonated.

She shattered, clutching his back, and screaming his name. His entire body tensed and he pushed into her a final time with a shudder and a long groan.

Hearts pounding together, he kissed her tenderly. He did not pull out and roll off. He did not leave her feeling as though she'd been used. When he rolled, it was to his side, and he took her with him.

And she felt loved.

He wrapped her in his arms, kissed her neck, and chuckled. "Told you I'd make you scream."

She smiled because she never knew sex could be so fulfilling and so much fun.

"Okay, but next time it's my turn to make *you* scream," she said. "If there is a next time."

He rolled her to her back, leaned over her, and kissed her forehead and the tip of her nose. "You're not getting rid of me that easy."

He did get up then and disappeared into the bathroom to dispose of the condom. Moments later he reappeared and dropped down onto the bed, trapping her between his big arms and body. She laughed at the big, sexy, satisfied grin on his face.

"And just so you know . . ." He kissed her and gently caught her bottom lip between his teeth. "*Next time* starts right now."

Chapter 14

*G*ame two in the series between the Carolina Vipers and the Philadelphia Flyers turned out to be a free-for-all brawl within a hockey game. While Nicole leaped to her feet to root for the Vipers player to win in the scramble, Lucy turned her head. Especially when Jordan had been involved in a bout that had drawn blood.

His.

Glorified violence was something she'd never get used to—not after what she'd experienced. Not that she wasn't willing to fight for what was right, just that she'd choose words over fists. Of course, in a hockey game, with the clock ticking, there probably wasn't much time to talk things out. And that little black puck moved pretty quick across the ice.

The penalty box seemed a place Jordan enjoyed because he sure ended up there a lot. As she watched him in that glass-enclosed time-out, the intensity on his face revealed a completely different side of the man who'd whispered such passionate words while he made love to her.

All around her people screamed his name when he rushed the puck toward the net. They screamed his name when he dropped his gloves on the ice and duked it out with an opponent. They screamed his name when he slammed an opponent into the boards. She'd known he was a fan favorite, but seeing the frenzy in person was something else. She couldn't imagine what it would be like to have such fans. To have women throwing themselves at you wherever you went.

Not that he probably minded that part.

Before the game the PR department had arranged a meet-and-greet for the fans. It had been the first time Lucy had stood near Jordan when he'd been in uniform. He was a big, muscular, tall man made even more breathtaking by the added height from the skates and the shoulder pads he wore for protection. A true warrior on ice.

There had been little boys wearing Vipers hockey jerseys who looked up to him. Little boys who wanted to be him. There had been beautiful women who wanted him in their beds and who'd curled around him like cats while having their picture taken. They'd pressed their breasts against him and looked up at him with *good time guaranteed* flashing in their eyes.

While Nicole beamed with pride and inserted herself into the pre-game activity, Lucy had stood back in the crowd, taking it all in. Invisibility had its advantages, but when the shield shattered, it did it in a big way.

One of the busty blondes who'd cozied up to Jordan in the meet-and-greet and had done everything in her power to grab his attention had walked up to Lucy afterward and shoved an open newspaper at her.

"Is this you?" she'd said.

Lucy looked down at the sports page headline and the photo below it.

KINCADE HOT FOR TEACHER?

The photo was of them leaving the Peach Magnolia Grill. His hand was at her back and he was smiling down at her.

Lucy felt her heart stop, then trip trying to get started again. She didn't have time to read the short article because the sneering blonde pulled it away.

"You're not his type, you know," she'd said. "Someone like *you* could never give him what he needs."

Nothing earth-shattering about that. Lucy knew that fact painfully too well.

"We've been together," the blonde said. "Often. I'm sure if he has anything to do with you it would just be a pity fuck. So why don't you do us both a favor and back the hell away. Jordan and I belong together. And now that he's back, we can pick up where we left off. I'm sure the next headline you see will be our engagement announcement."

Stinging from the verbal assault, Lucy had watched the woman walk back toward Jordan, where she pushed aside a little girl in a hockey jersey to plant a kiss on Jordan's mouth. The smug look she flashed Lucy afterward claimed him like he was a piece of property to be owned.

Uncertainty again rose like smoke from a fire.

Even if Jordan had already stolen her heart, she had to be honest with herself. The blonde was right. They'd never fit. No matter how much she wanted it to be so.

She was a schoolteacher who lived a quiet, boring life compared to his fast-paced and exciting existence. He traveled for most of the year while she preferred the safety and security of home. She abhorred violence. He played a violent game and loved every second of it. Jordan was wonderful, sensual, and patient. But he'd grow tired of someone like her—even if he'd never made her feel that way. Her life was in a small town, his was on the world's stage.

They were boarding a plane directly after the game to go back to Sunshine. Between his sister and the rest of his family, he had a lot on his plate. Tonight needed to be *their* last night together. As much as she wanted it to be different, her sensible side knew she had to let go.

Even if it broke her heart.

After the second game of the series, the locker room was abuzz with conversation, congratulations, and the beat of Iron Maiden's "The Trooper" pounding through the sound system. With two more wins under the team's belt the Vipers had advanced toward the playoffs. The incident with the Rock had barely been a blip on his radar as the two of them worked together on the ice to create a win.

In the midst of players removing skates and giving the media post-game interviews, Jordan took a look around the room, and pride beamed through him. They'd been warriors out there tonight. Next week they'd come together to do it all over again. He felt damn good about what they'd accomplished. Damn good about being back where he felt the most comfortable. Even if there was still plenty to deal with, along with the promises he'd made to his family. No matter what, he intended to honor every single one.

In the meantime, he'd chartered a jet to take him, Lucy, Nicole, and Ziggy back to Sunshine. He'd have the weekend to get caught up on what was going on at home. Then Monday he'd catch an early morning flight to Dallas, where they'd play the next series of games. If they made it through that, they'd advance in the chase for the Stanley Cup.

Playoff schedules were grueling. With a game approximately every other day until they either moved forward or were eliminated, they had little time for rest, recreation, or private matters. Which meant he'd have a hell of a time getting back to Sunshine between games.

By now he hoped Nicole understood what he did for a living and that he had no plans to leave Sunshine on a permanent basis—even though the playoffs might make it seem that way. He couldn't take her with him on the road but he didn't want to break the momentum they'd gained in their relationship either. He'd have to find a way to be there without actually being there. Skyping seemed the best avenue if she'd agree to it.

And then there was Lucy.

He'd spent the past several nights making love to her and sleeping with her wrapped in his arms. Even if she snored like a buzz saw he wanted to be right there beside her. He wanted to wake in the morning and watch her stretch like a cat before she rubbed her pretty eyes, then smiled at him like he'd given her something special. He wanted to stand beside her in the kitchen while they made coffee and scrambled eggs. He wanted to hear her singing off-key in the shower. He wanted to see her side-by-side with his sister making headway on school assignments and building more than just a teacher-student rapport.

Somehow they'd been able to keep their relationship from Nicki, which, being in the same apartment for days, had been tricky. Especially if his sister had caught the way he looked at Lucy—which he did as often as possible—or if perhaps she might have heard Lucy's passionate sounds. He didn't know how he was going to juggle everything while he was on the road; he only knew that everything he had to balance was important.

"So you're heading back to Washington?" Tyler Seabrook ran a towel over his wet hair, then draped it around his neck.

"Yeah. I'll meet up with the team in Dallas."

"You're pretty brave to let your little sister loose on the rest of the world while you're gone." The comment was made with a smile, and Jordan knew the reference came from Nicki yelling at the Rock.

He laughed. "She is fierce for such a small fry."

"I think Colton is going to be sad to see her go. He's been checking her out in the stands every time he skates by."

The rookie was twenty-one, only a few years older than Nicole. Still, Jordan didn't want any hockey guys looking at her. Hell, he didn't want *any* guys looking at her, period. "I'll have to have a talk with him about that," he said knowing there was no way in hell he'd let the horny kid anywhere near his sister.

"How are things going with your teacher?" Seabrook asked.

Jordan smiled. "Time will tell."

*J*ordan watched Nicole board the plane with her guitar case in hand until she disappeared inside the cabin. Behind her, Lucy began to climb the stairs, then turned and stopped, putting a hand on his arm. He took it as an indication that she wanted a kiss before they got on board and had to act like there wasn't anything going on between them. But when he reached for her she stepped back.

"What's wrong?"

The fact that she wouldn't look at him spoke loudly.

"I'm so happy that you and Nicole are working things out," she said, her hand caressing the sleeve of his jacket.

"It wouldn't have happened without your help."

"That's not true." She looked down at her feet. "You'd have done just fine without me. You love her. It was only a matter of time before she accepted it."

"Lucy?" He tucked his finger beneath her chin and forced her to look up. "What's wrong?"

"This has been fun, and I'm so glad you asked me along."

"But?"

"But now that you have things working in your favor with Nicole, it's time we move on."

"Move on?" A cold chill pricked the back of his neck.

She nodded. "Not that I don't appreciate everything. But I guess I never really believed anything would ever happen between us and—"

"But it *has* happened," he reminded her. "And it's great."

"Maybe on the surface." She pushed her glasses up with her index finger, and the shuttered look in her eyes sent another chill up his back.

"On the surface. Between the sheets. Wherever you want to take this, Lucy. You can't deny we're good together."

"I agree it's been nice but—"

"*Nice?* Is that what you want to call it?"

"Be reasonable, Jordan. You and I both knew this was temporary."

"It doesn't feel temporary."

"But it's what's reasonable," she said, like repeating the word would make more sense. "Do you really think you're the type to carry on a long distance relationship?"

She tilted her head and gave him a moment to think about that. A few weeks ago he'd have said a big hell no. But now . . .

"You have a busy life to get back to. And so do I," she said. "Between your family, your sister, the trouble with the winery, and your career, you already have way too much going on."

"And you think I won't have enough time for you?"

She turned her palms upward. "Why would you want to add one more thing?"

"News flash. You're not a *thing*. You're a woman I'm very interested in."

"For now. But we both know distance does not make the heart grow fonder. It makes it more difficult. So isn't it easier to say good-bye now before things go any further?"

"Why do you think we'll say good-bye at all?"

"Isn't it obvious?"

"Not to me." He slammed his hands down on his hips. Now she was pissing him off.

"We're too different," she said, sidestepping his remark. "We run our lives completely the opposite. And . . . it's also a good idea to keep our time together just between us."

"Why?" And now she didn't even want anyone to know? What the hell? "Do I embarrass you?"

"I'm thinking about Nicole. After all, I'm her teacher. It might make things uncomfortable for her if anyone at school found out. And your sister is already going through enough."

"And that's the *only* reason?"

"No." Her jaw twitched. "Other than you, no one in Sunshine knows anything about my personal life. I'd like to keep it that way."

"Seeing me has already thrust you in the spotlight."

Her lips tightened. "No one in Sunshine is going to read a paper from all the way across the country."

"The paper has an Internet site, and I'm sorry for that. But I don't see why it should make you doubt us."

Her shoulders lifted with a sigh. "You don't understand."

"Then make me understand." He tossed his hands up. "Because right now I'm confused as hell."

She looked away. When her gaze came back to him, he could see the shadows from the past emerge.

"When I went through the divorce my name was dragged through the mud. His family hired the biggest, baddest attorney in town—who also happened to be a close family friend. The man made me look ridiculous. Like I asked for the abuse because if I hadn't liked it I wouldn't have stayed with him for so long. It was like the rape cases you hear about where, because a woman wears a short skirt, she's asking for it. The judge also happened to be a close family friend so I was in a lose-lose situation."

Jordan never understood how that could happen in a court of law—how a victim could be made to look like the one at fault or how a judge wouldn't be recused because he knew the players in the case and couldn't be impartial. When she put it in those terms he began to understand a little more what she'd gone through. And he got a big clue that maybe for Lucy, this really wasn't about how much he had going on, but more about how his life operated in the limelight.

"People called me a liar. They said I was making

up stories just so I could get a big divorce settlement. I didn't want money; I just wanted my life and my dignity back. I didn't want to see my name in the newspapers anymore. It took me a long time before I regained my confidence and could look people in the eye again. I walked away with a suitcase of clothes and a hefty bill from my attorney. But I can tell you that no amount of money I might have received would have made up for what I'd been through."

"Jesus, Lucy. Who *was* this guy you were married to? Didn't you ever file a police report?"

"Who would have believed me?"

"No one? Not even your mother?"

"My mother and I haven't spoken in years. Her life revolves around cigarettes and a bottle of her poison of choice. If she never came to my defense when I was a kid, how could I ever hope she'd do so now?"

"I'm sorry, Lucy."

"You have enough on your plate, Jordan. You don't need to be worrying about me." She closed her eyes. "Devote your time to your career and your family. They need you."

"What about you?"

"It doesn't matter."

"Then what about what *I* need?" He clasped her arms. "I need *you*, Lucy."

"Jordan." She turned her head. When she faced him again there were tears in her eyes. "Please. This is the way it has to be."

Jordan dropped his hands.

Inside he was absolutely ripped apart; devastated

that she didn't have enough confidence in him—in
them—to see things through.

When she leaned in and kissed his cheek his heart
shattered in a million pieces.

On Saturday morning Jordan woke up in the bed at
his grandfather's cabin in a foul mood. Last night he
and Nicole had dropped Lucy off at her house on their
way home. After he'd gone inside to check and make
sure there were no bogeymen hiding in her closets, he'd
wanted to take her in his arms and kiss her good-bye,
but she'd kept enough distance between them to make
that impossible. Unless he'd tackled her. Which, as bad
as his heart ached, had been a possibility.

On the flight home she'd sat at the back of the
plane with Nicole, listening to a new song his sister
was working on. When the music ended, the two of
them put their heads together and chatted about this
and that, completely excluding him. He was sure that,
once again, he'd be the bad guy. A fact proven when
he drove Nicki up to the main house, carried her bag
inside, and was given a snippy "Thanks" for his efforts. He didn't know how the hell he kept getting
himself in that predicament but apparently all those
penalty minutes he'd racked up during the games had
leftover karma.

A nasty one at that.

After two strong cups of coffee he wandered over
toward the main house to sit down with his brothers
and go over the newest details of the missing money

and exactly who was going to live in the house with Nicole until she went off to college.

When *hopefully* she went off to college.

On his way to the house he walked up and down a few rows of vines. The first buds had started to appear and the ground was moist from the early morning rain. He walked up to the event center and went inside. Any signs of the night he'd taken Lucy to the prom had long ago been cleaned up, removed, and delivered back to the high school. But even with everything gone, he could still picture her in that lovely gown, looking up at him as he danced with her in his arms.

Presently there was a full staff decorating tables with blue and purple flowers and peacock feathers for an afternoon wedding reception. A large white tent was being constructed outside to keep the wedding party and guests dry from the light rain that had been predicted for the afternoon.

Usually he never paid attention to things like weddings. For some reason the sight of one being set up on his family property coiled around his heart. The only one of them who had tied the knot or even gotten close had been Ryan. None of them ever thought Laura was the right woman for their oldest brother, and she'd proven them all correct. Still, they'd supported Ryan a hundred percent before the wedding and after she skipped town.

Jordan had never thought much about marriage other than he figured it would eventually happen someday. He'd never gotten the right feeling for or from a woman.

Until Lucy.

It hadn't been even twenty-four hours and he already missed her so much it ached deep in his chest.

He needed to keep walking. Find something to distract him from fighting the need to go over to her house and kiss some sense into her.

With his hands on his hips he took a good look at the property—the rolling hills, the creek, the rows upon rows of grapevines, the buildings in need of updating. What he saw was potential. There were so many ways they could make this a destination instead of an afterthought.

While he'd been on the plane last night with no one to talk to except Ziggy, who'd abandoned him as soon as Lucy called his name, he'd made notes about investigating wine production in the area. A few new local winery tour companies had sprouted up, and he wondered if Sunshine Creek was on their map. He'd have to make sure he asked Ryan. Wine-tasting tours were a great way to bring in revenue.

When he opened the front door to his parents' house, Ryan, Declan, and Ethan were already settled around the dining room table with a carafe of coffee in the middle and various breakfast pastries piled up on a plate. The acid from the two cups of coffee Jordan had drunk clawed at the empty pit of his stomach. He figured what the hell and grabbed two bear claws before he poured another mug.

"Dieting again?" Declan smirked. "Or drowning your sorrows in sugar?"

Jordan looked up. His brother couldn't possibly know that Lucy had kicked his ass to the curb.

"Exactly what sorrows would I have to drown? Our team is one step away from the playoffs."

"And you're front-page news too. Gee, aren't you lucky."

"What the hell are you talking about?"

Ryan shoved the newspaper in his direction. When Jordan picked up the *Talk of the Town* and read the headline his blood pressure blew through the roof.

KINCADE HOT FOR TEACHER?

"Are you fucking kidding me?" He couldn't believe the North Carolina article had made it to front-page news in the local trash paper. "This is bullshit."

Lucy's worst-case scenario had transpired.

"Is it?" Ryan lifted his cup of coffee and looked at Jordan over the rim.

Arms folded, Ethan asked, "Does this have anything to do with your tux-wearing apology?"

"I don't want to talk about my personal business." Jaw tight, Jordan bit off a piece of bear claw and nearly choked on the glob of sugary icing.

"Too damn bad," Parker said as he came into the room. "You start making trouble around here, you have to answer to us."

"How the hell did I start trouble?" He shoved the rest of the pastry into a napkin, wrapped it up, and squeezed it in his hand. "I merely asked Nicole's favorite teacher to come along because I thought she could help watch Nicki while I worked and maybe she could help her out with her assignments too."

Parker laughed. "That's the lamest bullshit story I've ever heard."

"What do you want me to say? That I took Lucy along for my own personal reasons?"

United, his brothers said, "Yes."

"Okay." He wiped the sugar from his fingers with another paper napkin. "I'll admit it was half and half."

"And are you hot for teacher?"

"If you're worried about Ms. Diamond's character, don't. She's too smart for that."

"Meaning?" Declan's eyebrows jacked up his forehead.

"Meaning whatever I thought we might have had, she showed me the error of my thinking."

"Stop dancing around." Parker poured himself a cup of coffee. "What the hell happened?"

"Are you asking out of genuine concern?" Jordan asked. "Or are you just being nosy?"

"Nosy," Declan admitted.

"Gee. Just when I was starting to love you again you go and get nasty."

"Did she dump you? Is that what crawled up your butt this morning?"

Fuuuuck. He did not want to talk about this.

"He did say she was smart," Ethan reminded them.

"She's probably way out of his league," Parker quipped. "I don't think Mensa allows hard-hitting hockey players."

"I'm glad you think this is so funny."

"It's only because we love you, bro." Declan smiled, and Jordan had a hard time staying mad at the person he'd once built sheet tents with so they could stay up all night building stuff with Tinkertoys.

"I'm going to keep that in mind when a woman takes you down to your knees," Jordan said.

"Only one reason a woman will ever have me on my knees." Declan grinned. "And I can guarandamntee there won't be any clothes involved."

"Right, Mr. Celibate."

"Celibate!" Heads turned in Dec's direction while he cringed and flipped them all the bird.

"All right. Let's stop joking around," Ryan said. "This sounds serious."

It *was* serious.

But how could he tell these yahoos he was related to that the woman he'd fallen hard for had decided he wasn't worth the effort? He knew she felt something more for him than just the pleasure of great sex. Still, she'd found it pretty damn easy to give him the boot. He needed to investigate how serious of a problem this article was for her. He didn't want her to lose her job or respectability because of him. And he certainly didn't need to lose any more points in his favor.

Aunt Pippy came through the door too late to rescue him, but she did brighten the room with a purple and yellow geometric print dress with a wide vinyl belt, silver shoes, and dangly earrings in the shape of bananas and oranges.

"Sorry I'm late," she said, dropping her big yellow bag on a nearby chair. "Had to hit up the farmers' market first. Heard Mountain Ridge Cellars was having a wine tasting. Thought I'd go incognito and check out the goods."

Incognito?

His aunt's outfit glowed bright enough to be seen from outer space.

"You've been hitting the bottle already?" Parker teased. "It's not even ten o'clock in the morning."

"Just a nip." She sat down across from Jordan and snapped up a powdered sugar donut. "They're charging ten bucks for five wines and they aren't even filling the glasses a quarter full. That's some profit they're going to take home."

"Maybe we should be following suit," Ethan said.

"I say we expand the wine-tasting room right here," Ryan said. "Bring them to us instead of us going to them."

"How are we going to do that when we're in the red?" Jordan asked. "Have we found out any more about the missing money?"

Aunt Pippy had just taken a bite out of her donut. Powdered sugar lined her lips when she popped up out of her chair. "Anyone need more coffee? I'll make a fresh pot." And away she went, disappearing into the kitchen without even waiting for a response.

Jordan noticed that whenever they started to talk about the missing money she found a reason to vanish. But there was no way she could have stolen the money. She never dealt with the finances of the vineyards. Sometimes she helped out with picking the grapes at harvest, but for the most part, she didn't have much to do with the business.

Still, her behavior made him curious.

Ryan frowned. "We hired an investigator and a

fresh pair of accounting eyes. We should have a report in the next week or so. Until then, we need to discuss what we're going to do about having someone live here in the main house with Nicki. Obviously she needs a full-time in-house guardian. She doesn't turn eighteen for several months, and even then, until she goes off to college, she can't be left alone. I can't uproot Riley from her home and routine. She's had a tough time of it already."

"No shit," Ethan said. "Poor kid."

"I can stay the nights when the food truck doesn't run," Parker offered. "But driving here every single night from Portland and being back at four a.m. would be a bitch."

"I can come back in a couple of weeks and help out," Declan said.

"I can stay for a few weeks." Ethan ran a hand through his newly cut hair. Jordan was happy to see the beard gone too. "Fire season doesn't start for a little while. I got an offer to fight fires down in Florida this month but I'll just take a leave of absence."

"I want to help," Jordan said. "But everything rides on what's going to happen next week in Dallas. If we win the series we go to round one of the play-offs. Then there's a game every other day for almost a week at a time. But I don't want to let Nicki or you guys down."

"We're big boys," Ryan said. "We can take care of ourselves. The playoffs are a big deal for you. We'll manage until your season is over. Then we'll reestablish where we stand."

"You sure? I'd walk on my contract but it would cost me around four mil. And I figure we could probably use that money around here for upgrades."

"Jesus." Declan's eyes widened. "Four million? Don't you dare walk away from that. We'll make this work."

"I'm just worried about Nicki feeling like we're tossing her around like a ball," Jordan said. "Like none of us can stick long enough to make her feel like she's important. But she is."

Aunt Pippy wandered back into the room without a new pot of coffee, giving them all the idea that she'd been in the kitchen eavesdropping.

"You boys have got your hands full right now. Best thing is for me to stay with her," Pippy said. "She's a might touchy these days. Maybe having a woman around full-time will give her someone to talk to."

It made sense for their aunt to stay with Nicole. She'd been retired for several years and didn't work at anything other than keeping up with the local gossip. But that didn't make Jordan feel any less guilty for not being able to step in to help out like he said he would. He was doing exactly what he'd sworn he wouldn't do because he'd yet to find a way to make everything work.

Maybe Lucy was right. Maybe he needed less to focus on.

Only one problem with that.

Walking away from Lucy took away a whole lot of inspiration. He not only wanted her in his life, he needed her.

*B*eing home felt good, but odd. Lucy hadn't slept in her own bed for almost a week. That had *never* happened before. And she never thought she'd hate sleeping alone. But she did. She missed having Jordan curled up against her, his warmth, and feeling safe when he had his arms around her. She'd only been with him a few days, yet it felt like a lifetime. She'd have to get used to things without him. And that didn't sound like much fun either. Even poor Ziggy looked a little sad. Not that he'd liked being in an apartment, but the extra attention he'd gotten from both Jordan and Nicole had been pretty great.

But life now had to go on without Jordan, and in order to handle that reality, Lucy needed to streamline her focus on things other than tall, dark, and hunky.

She needed to check on Mrs. B. Yes, Lucy knew the sweet old lady's children could take care of her, but that didn't stop Lucy from worrying or caring. The stack of mail and newspapers on top of her kitchen table weren't going to get any smaller if she kept walking by and ignoring them, so she grabbed a cup of coffee and sat down to go through everything. Junk mail, pizza coupons, and other delightful garbage were stuck in between her gas and electric bills. When her phone rang she considered it a saving grace from the rest of the envelopes.

"Do *not* read today's issue of *Talk of the Town*." Claudia's voice on the other end of the line sounded panicked.

"Why?" Curiosity soared; she pushed aside the mail

to grab the local paper buried beneath. Reading the headline, she choked on a gasp.

"I told you not to look."

"Oh my God." Her eyes scanned the article but she couldn't comprehend anything past the shock. Her nightmare had come true.

"I'm so sorry, Lucy. I know you're a very private person. Although I can't help being a bit miffed that you didn't tell me there was something going on."

"There isn't. I just went along to help out with his sister." Lying really wasn't her thing, and yet, in this circumstance, telling the truth would only hurt more.

"That's not what the look he's giving you says."

"Don't misinterpret that for anything other than gratitude."

"Sure, go ahead. Ruin my fantasy that you finally found someone to love."

She had.

Her chest tightened as she tried to end the call before she broke down in tears. "I guess I'll see you on Monday. *If* I still have a job."

"You didn't break any rules," Claudia said. "You're an adult. It was spring break. You're allowed to spend the time any way you want."

She'd slept with a student's brother. There had to be a rule against that.

"Even if you say otherwise, I do hope you managed to have a little fun," Claudia added before she hung up.

For once, she'd had more than fun.

And now she had to pay the price.

Hot tea burned her throat as she reread the article.

When she read the part the editor/pathetic-excuse-for-a-journalist had interjected into the story, the words burned like acid around her heart.

For some reason, Margaret Brickridge had dragged the Kincade family name into the slop by questioning the behavior of *all* the brothers.

Lucy wasn't a person who normally lost her temper, but at that moment she needed a fire extinguisher to put out the flames.

$\mathcal{T}$he old building on Main Street that housed *Talk of the Town* had a deceptively businesslike exterior. Yet most of the garbage they printed was nothing but outrageous tales and gossip without any verification. As Lucy pushed open the door, she wondered why anyone would want to lie and stir up a hornet's nest.

Margaret Brickridge appeared as ancient as the mountains surrounding the town when she came to the front desk with a walking cane and a stiff back. The woman had been editor of the gossip rag for over fifty years, and from what Lucy could see, she needed to retire.

"What can I do for you?" Mrs. Brickridge asked in a bitter tone that let Lucy know she was accustomed to people showing up in her office ready to unload.

Lucy set the morning's paper on the counter and gathered up her courage. No wimping out. No backing down. No taking no for an answer. "You need to retract this story."

"Now why would I do that?" The woman looked up through squinted hazel eyes.

"It's garbage and lies."

"Says who?"

Lucy gritted her teeth. "If you're going to print such absurdity you should probably be more aware of who you're writing about and take the time to get some clarification on matters."

The woman leaned closer, took a good look at Lucy, and snickered. "So you're the teacher."

"Yes, I'm the teacher who has nothing romantically going on with Mr. Kincade." At least not anymore.

"Well, once a story is inked I've got no recourse."

"Of course you do. You can print a retraction."

"The article originally ran in the *North Carolina Observer*. So why would *I* want to retract it?"

"Because you added to the original story. Why would you do that?"

The woman shrugged her stooped shoulders. "It's a local interest story. I've always had a hankering to be one of those *Weekly World News* journalists. Figured I'd just spice it up a little."

"At the detriment to a local family?"

"Haven't you heard the old sayings, 'If it bleeds it leads' and 'Scandal sells'? A retraction now won't mean spit."

The door opened behind her but Lucy was too fired up to care.

"A retraction *will* matter." Lucy inhaled a deep breath. "Look. You can make up all the lies you want about me, I'll survive. But I won't let you drag the Kincade family's good name through the mud. They're nice, respectable people who've recently suffered an unspeakable tragedy. They run a successful business in this town and they don't deserve your acid tongue. Why do you want to be so mean anyway? Does causing people heartache make you happy? Do you sleep well at night knowing you've made someone's life miserable?"

The newspaper editor opened her mouth, then snapped it shut when Lucy continued her rant.

"If you don't print a retraction and apologize to the Kincade family, I will personally sit outside your office and protest, as I'm sure will some of the others you've offended over the years. Gossip is vicious and the damage done never goes away. Someone needs to show you how it feels to be on the receiving end. I don't mind being that person."

Lucy exhaled, straightened her shoulders, and gave the woman her nastiest glare. "Now what do you have to say?"

"I say bravo." The comment came not from Mrs. Brickridge but a deep male voice directly over Lucy's shoulder. Though she'd know that voice anywhere, she spun around.

"What are you doing here?"

Something crazy fluttered in Jordan's chest as he smiled at the woman who seemed to have changed everything in his life. "Watching you stand up to a town menace."

"Some people deserve it." She turned back to the newspaper editor and pointed a finger. "I meant what

I said. Push me and you'll find out how fast I'll push back."

A wave of emotion washed over Jordan as Lucy stepped around him and marched out the door. His immediate instinct was to follow. But like her, he'd come to the newspaper office for a reason.

"You run this place?" he asked the elderly woman with features so pinched he couldn't imagine that face would ever crack a smile.

"That's right. Don't tell me you've got a gripe too."

He gave her his negotiating face—the expression he used when he found himself sitting across the desk from someone he knew was going to try and screw him over.

"I'm not the type of person to *gripe*." He planted his hands on the counter. "I'm the type of person who takes action. I don't know how you've gotten away with spreading lies and gossip for so long, but it's time for it to stop."

The woman folded her sagging arms across her drooping breasts. "Is that so?"

"Yes. That's so. Tomorrow I expect you to print a special edition of your rag paper with a retraction for your addition to the story and an apology to Ms. Diamond."

"And who are you to tell me what to do?"

"You really should know the subjects of your lies better. Like, maybe take a look at the photos you print."

The woman looked down at the paper lying on the counter. When she looked up at him, he knew she had it figured out.

"The way I see it, I don't figure many people have

the means to hire the biggest badass attorney on the planet to sue you. I do. And if I don't see that apology tomorrow, I'll shut you down so fast you'll see stars spinning over your head."

He didn't give her a chance to respond. He'd said his piece, now it was time to catch up with the woman who, at her own expense, had taken a bold stand on his family's behalf.

*L*ucy unlocked her front door, threw her purse in a nearby chair, and flopped down on the sofa. Her heart pounded like a trapped rabbit and her throat felt as dry as a summer day in Death Valley. Ziggy wandered in and settled his big head on her leg, waiting to be petted.

She hadn't given much thought to what she'd say or do once she got to the newspaper office; she'd been running on pure emotion.

Something she seemed to be doing a lot these days.

Since Jordan had come back into her life, she'd been jumping in all different directions. Behaving like she normally wouldn't. Stepping outside her comfort zone. Agreeing to things that were a huge risk.

Especially to her heart.

If anyone had tried to tell her that on a whim she'd go to an unfamiliar state in an unfamiliar situation with a man who embodied the word *dangerous*, and jump in bed with him, she'd have told them they'd bonked their head too hard. If anyone had told her she'd do all the naked things she'd done with Jordan—happily and willingly—she'd have told them they were a quart low in the gray matter department. If anyone had told her she'd march into the local newspaper office and threaten the proprietor, she would have put them on the waiting list for counseling.

Everything had changed.

It scared her.

And yet, at the same time she felt good. The worst thing had happened. She'd faced it and won. She didn't crumble or cry. She'd stood up to wrong and it felt very right. The only thing that didn't feel right was walking away from Jordan.

She'd told him they'd never fit. But they did. So why was that so hard for her to accept?

How could she go on with her life status quo when she now knew what it felt like to share special moments with him? What it felt like to be in his arms? What it felt like to wake up beside him?

A car pulled up in front of her house and she squeezed her eyes shut. Prayed it would not be him because she needed some time to think. Time to accept that she'd gone down to the newspaper office to stand up for Jordan because she loved him.

She swallowed.

Yes. She was crazy, heart over head in love with a man she had no business loving.

A knock on the door had her peering through the curtains.

Of course it was him.

"Go away," she shouted. "There's nobody home."

"Open the door, Lucy."

"Lucy's not here."

"Open the door or I'll huff, and I'll puff, and I'll blow your door down. I'm not leaving until I see your face."

"It looks the same as an hour ago."

"Open. The. Door."

She sighed. Went to the door. Opened it a fraction and stuck her face in the opening. "Satisfied?" When she went to close the door he stuck his foot in the way.

She sighed again and backed up to allow the inevitable. As expected, Jordan pushed his way inside.

"I know what you're doing." Eyes sharp and focused, he advanced toward her and forced her to back up into the living room.

Ziggy barked a welcome and Jordan briefly reached down to pet her dog on the head. Kindness in a heated moment. Moments like that totally melted her heart.

"What is it you *think* I'm doing?" Besides hiding like a coward from the plethora of feelings she'd developed for him.

"You're trying not to care because you think it will keep you safe," he said. "But you walking into that newspaper office and taking on the person who printed that article? You were thinking more of me and my family than you were thinking of yourself."

Emotionally drained, she shrugged like it didn't matter.

"You care, Lucy."

"So sue me." Her chin tilted in a show of defiance.

"Oooh." A grin flashed across his face. "I like it when you're feisty."

"I'm too exhausted to be feisty."

"Really?" The tilt of his head told her he didn't believe her. "So you're too exhausted to fight if I do this?" He pulled her into his arms.

She gave a feeble attempt to push him away, but it felt so good to be in his arms she caved in a blink.

Silly weak woman.

"You can't walk away from this," he said.

"*This?* What's *this*? You overpowering me?"

"Baby, you know I'd never do that." He loosened his hold but didn't let her go. "I'm talking about whatever this is developing between us."

"Nothing's developing. You know we don't fit."

He pulled her in tighter to prove her wrong.

"I'm not talking about body parts," she said.

"Neither am I."

"Jordan. You live an exhilarating full-steam-ahead life. You know you'd get bored with me. You need to find someone more exciting."

"What if I don't want anyone more exciting?"

Great. He agreed she was as dull as rust.

"Sorry. That didn't come out right." He tucked her head beneath his chin. "I need you, Lucy. I need your calm. Your patience. Your ability to cut through the bullshit and get right to the point."

"A good therapist can do all that."

"See how quick you get to the point? I don't need a therapist. I need *you*. The woman who's wrapped up my heart and made me think of things that have never even crossed my mind before."

She looked up at him, not exactly expecting to see humor on his handsome face, but certainly not expecting to see sincerity either. "What kind of things?"

"Forever things." His long fingers came up to smooth her hair away and cup her face between his hands.

Forever? She didn't dare let herself fall into that fantasy.

"Until now all I've ever thought about was hockey. The next game. The next win. But that's not all that occupies my thoughts now." He lowered his head and kissed her so tenderly it brought tears to her eyes. "Don't walk away, Lucy. Don't throw away what's growing between us because you're scared or because you've judged me wrong. I know you're strong. Stronger than me in a lot of ways. All I ask is that you give us a chance."

She should say no.

But when he pulled her tight against him and kissed her deep, wet, and bone-melting hot, her hesitation, doubts, and fears evaporated like rain on a summer sidewalk. When he lifted her into his arms and carried her upstairs, she knew the word *no* wouldn't find its way into her dialogue. Because once he got started the only word she'd know would be *more*.

More.

More.

More.

Chapter 15

After passing through the wedding taking place in the event center and the outdoor tent, Jordan felt more strongly than ever that they needed to introduce some fresh ideas into Sunshine Creek Vineyards. They had a gorgeous area surrounded by shade trees that they never used. If they constructed a stage on the grassy knoll, they could have outdoor concerts with wine and picnic supplies available to buy. With dark wood and heavy curtains, the inside of the event center was a bit dated. He felt sure there was a way to bring it back to life without costing them a fortune. Hell, he and Ryan could put in the sweat and labor themselves.

Tiered wine club memberships that included a concert series could provide them with enough revenue to push them far away from the financial red zone.

Leaving the bride and groom to their wedding toast, he walked into the main house more determined than ever to do the right thing. Outside the sun shone high in the sky and he'd just spent several hours in bed with Lucy. There had been no pillow talk, just long, satisfied moans interspersed with laughter.

He didn't know how he'd missed it the first, second, or even third time, but during his afternoon explorations he'd discovered his sexy little schoolteacher had some ticklish spots. Though the one behind her knee intrigued him, it was the one at the very lowest area on her spine— just above her sweet rounded bottom—that tempted him the most. It had been the very spot he'd kissed just before he got out of bed and left her to finish her nap.

Knowing he'd worn her out and left her with a smile on her face was like being given a piece of his favorite candy. Hell of a good way to spend a Saturday afternoon.

Inside his parents' home he found Aunt Pippy folding laundry on the kitchen table. Never in his life would he refer to his mother's sister as a domestic goddess. A lovable psychedelic outspoken wacko maybe. Lately she'd become a little secretive. He still hadn't figured that one out.

"Well, fancy seeing you here in the middle of the day." She snapped out a pair of women's bikini panties before folding them, and Jordan wanted to cover his eyes. He didn't know if they belonged to her or his sister and he didn't want to find out.

"I've only got two days to get things worked out," he said, turning his back when she snapped out another pair of women's underwear.

"Exactly what are you working out?" A brown eyebrow that did not match her carrot top head lifted.

"I need to talk to Nicki. Is she around?"

"She woke up late. She's been up there playing that guitar you bought her. Hasn't eaten a darned thing all day."

"Mind if I grab some of those breakfast pastries to take up to her?"

"Go ahead. You're lucky those brothers of yours left any of them. I think they were even putting them in their pockets."

He didn't want to tell her that the powdered sugar circling her lips pointed the donut burglar finger at her.

"I'll get a plate for you."

"Aunt Pippy? Is there something you know about the missing money you're not telling us?"

"Me?" Her eyes widened like she'd seen a polka dot baboon. "Wha-huh-pffft. No."

"You sure? Because every time the subject comes up you hightail it out of the room."

"I'm a busy woman. I got things to do. Stuff to take care of."

Like what? he wanted to ask.

Yes, he and his brothers were fortunate she'd stepped in and agreed to live in the main house with Nicole for the time being. It was obvious by her suddenly trembling hands that the question made her nervous. Whatever it was, she just needed to tell them so they could fix it. If she had anything to do with it, they'd forgive her. She was family.

"Well, if you can think of anything you think we should know, you'll tell us, right?"

"Of course." Her nervous laughter raised an even

bigger question mark. "Well, I'd better get that plate. Your sister's probably starving."

A few minutes later, sugar-laden plate in hand, Jordan knocked on Nicole's door and the strumming of the guitar stopped. He waited for the proverbial snotty teen response but to his surprise she opened the door and said, "Hey."

Thank God they'd moved on from "What the hell do you want?" Although with his luck, the reprieve was probably temporary.

"I brought you breakfast."

She smiled. "It's afternoon, you dork."

He could hardly tell his sister that he had happily lost track of time between the sheets with Lucy today, so he shrugged. "There's never really a bad time to eat donuts, is there?"

"No. But now I'll have to exercise." She snatched one off the plate and bit into it. "Mmmmm. I love maple bars."

"You sleep okay after we got home last night?"

"Why wouldn't I?"

"No reason. Just trying to look after you. How's the song coming along?"

"I'm putting it in my repertoire."

"You have a repertoire now?"

"Yeah. For when I go to Nashville."

"Nashville! What the hell are you talking about?"

"My birthday is in a couple of months. So whether I graduate or not, I'm packing up my stuff and heading to Music City. You can hardly start a country music career here."

"Whoa. Whoa. Whoa." He put his hands up. "Let's back this train up for a second."

"You're not talking me out of it." She sat on her bed and pulled the guitar onto her lap. "Besides, what do you care? I heard you guys talking this morning. Apparently I'm a giant pain in the ass you feel someone needs to babysit. This way you won't have to worry."

"Are you shitting me?" Panic raced inside his chest. "You take off to a city you've never been to, all alone, and I'll worry even more."

"*You* took off at eighteen."

"I was drafted by the NHL when I was eighteen. Big difference."

"Maybe to you. Besides . . ." She smirked. "I never said I was going there alone."

"What?" His head whipped around so fast his neck cracked.

"A friend is going with me."

God, now he was getting a freaking cramp in his brain. "Does this *friend* happen to be a boy?"

"Does it matter?"

"Hell yes it matters." He sat down on the bed next to her.

Now he knew how fathers of stubborn, wild teenage girls felt. And he had a feeling that talking sense into her was going to be like catching a fish barehanded.

"Picking up and moving away without a plan, or money, or a job is crazy," he said. "Doing all that with a guy who has expectations makes it worse."

"Who said I don't have a plan or money?"

"You don't think Taylor Swift made it big the minute she rolled into town, do you? She had parents to take care of her needs. Who's going to take care of yours? Where are you going to live? How are you going to pay rent? Buy food?"

Holy shit. He sounded like an old fart.

"I'm going to play in bars until I get discovered."

"You're not even old enough to go into a bar. And I wouldn't count on that instantly getting discovered thing. It's not easy to make it in the music industry. There are people who've been playing those bars for years and have barely made enough to buy a McDonald's hamburger."

"How do you know? You've never been in the music industry."

"No, but I dated an award-winning country singer at one time. Gave me a little insight to the business."

"You dated a country singer?" Her eyes popped open wide. "Who?"

"I'm not telling."

"Come on. No secrets."

He laughed. "Look who's talking."

"Well, if you won't tell me who she is, tell me what color hair she has."

"Blond."

"Carrie Underwood?"

"Little sister, do you really think someone like Carrie Underwood would ever date someone like me?"

"She married a hockey player."

"Yeah, but he's a nice hockey player. I'm mean."

She giggled, and the sound rippled through him like

a happy wave. "You do like to spend a lot of time in the penalty box."

"And *you*"—he bumped her with his shoulder—"like to try and change the subject."

She dropped her head and nodded. "I just don't want to argue anymore. You've been . . . really nice to me. And I'm pretty sure I don't deserve it."

"Listen." Taking a chance she wouldn't retreat, he wrapped his arm around her. "The teen years are hard enough without suffering the loss of your parents. I'm barely dealing with it, so I don't have a clue how you're coping. Everyone grieves in their own way. There's no time limit."

"Jordan?" When she looked up there were tears in her pretty blue eyes. "That's not why I've been so angry. Losing our parents makes me unbelievably sad. But it's . . ."

"Go ahead." He gave her a side hug. "You can tell me. I won't judge. I promise."

A heavy sigh pushed from her lungs. "It's because of what I said to Dad just before they left for Hawaii."

"Did you have a teenage meltdown?"

"No. I had an I'm-tired-of-being-ignored meltdown."

"Ignored?" From over three thousand miles away, he'd thought Nicki was probably being spoiled and growing up like a little princess.

She dropped her face into her hands and sobbed. He pulled her into a full hug and just let her cry it out. She wiped her nose on his shirt and he didn't even care. He wanted to know what was wrong. He wanted to help. At the moment he just wasn't sure how.

When the tears started to subside, he left her long enough to grab the box of tissues from her dresser. She pulled out a half dozen and tried to mop up the damage.

"S-sorry about your shirt." She hiccupped.

"I don't care about the shirt, baby girl. I just care about you. Please tell me what's going on. I can't help if you don't."

"You can't help anyway." She sniffed, then decided to blow her nose. "I got tired of Dad always having something else to do when it involved me. He'd practically run out of a room when I'd walk in."

"Nicki. That can't be true. He loved you."

"I don't think he did." Her face crumpled and the tears started to flow again. "I'm not even sure I'm really your sister."

"What?" Where the hell had she gotten that idea? "Of course you are. You look just like the rest of us except prettier."

She shrugged. "I finally asked Dad why he ignored me. I hoped—like Mom—he'd tell me I was imagining things and give me a hug to make me feel better. But he didn't. Instead he admitted that something in his past had affected him negatively where I was concerned. And that while he didn't blame me, he just didn't know if he could ever move past it to be the kind of father I wanted."

What the fuck?

Everything was starting to crumble and Jordan felt a cold chill slice up his back. He'd always thought his parents were perfect and that they had the perfect marriage. But now . . .

"I don't know what he meant," his sister said. "Now he's gone and I'll never find out."

"Nobody else knows about this conversation?"

She shook her head. "I wanted to tell Ryan but he's so busy and he's got to take care of Riley all on his own. I didn't want to burden him with my problems."

"Why didn't you ask Mom?"

"There wasn't time."

"God, Nicki, I don't know what to say." He gathered her up in a hug and she finally hugged him back. "But we'll figure this out, okay?"

She nodded. "What did you come in here to tell me before we got sidetracked?"

Do the right thing.

Jordan took a deep breath. "Don't worry about anything, Nicki. We're going to get this all worked out. I've made a decision and family comes first."

*T*he nap Lucy had taken earlier revived her so that now when she should be thinking of going to bed she was wide awake. Waking alone had been both disappointing and a blessing. There was nothing she loved more than looking at Jordan's sleek, toned muscles when he was naked. She loved the heat that radiated from his body. His always clean, masculine scent. And the feel of his soft hair beneath her fingers. But the discussion they'd had just before he'd hauled her off to the bedroom had been uncomfortable.

For three years she'd been in control of her life. Of every step she took and every move she made.

She'd made healthy decisions and she'd set healthy boundaries.

Jordan ripped all that control to shreds.

Not in a nasty way by any means. He did it with sweet talk, compassion, and a whole lot of hotness. She didn't fool herself for one minute, though. When it came to Jordan Kincade, she *wanted* to lose control. She liked the way he made her feel safe, cared for, even sexy. Until he'd come along she'd *never* felt sexy. Never felt beautiful. Never in her life would she have thought he'd beg her to give *them* a chance.

Lifting the wineglass to her lips, she paused the Oozma Kappa *Party Central* from the *Monsters University* DVD to find a snack that wouldn't bypass her breasts and go straight to her thighs or hips. She had to step over Ziggy, who'd stretched out at her feet.

The doorbell rang and she stopped midway to the kitchen, wondering who could possibly be at her door at this time of night.

She looked down at her plaid pajama bottoms and baggy white T-shirt and prayed to God it wasn't Jordan. He'd seen her looking bad enough. And then she remembered the avocado mask on her face. Wonderful. No time to go wash it off, she went to the door, nudging tail-wagging Ziggy aside with her foot.

A Kincade stood there, but not Jordan.

"Nicole? What are you doing here?"

The teen stood there wearing a PINK hoodie, jeans, and Ugg boots, hugging herself against the cool night air.

"Come in," Lucy said, and then she remembered. "Excuse the mask. I wasn't expecting company."

Ziggy did his usual happy dance and Nicole rewarded him with an affectionate stroke of her hand over the top of his head.

"I'm sorry to bother you."

"You're not. Have a seat. Would you like something to drink? Maybe something hot since its cold outside?"

"No thank you." She sat down on the edge of the sofa like she was ready to run.

Lucy could see Nicole's hands were shaking, and her concern ignited.

"I probably should have gone to my brothers. But . . . I really thought you'd be the one who could help the most."

Lucy sat next to her and put an arm around her shoulders. "Honey, what's wrong? You're trembling."

"It's Jordan."

Oh dear. What did the man do now?

"Earlier when he came to talk to me I told him I didn't want to go to college and that I wanted to go to Nashville to be a musician."

"And he got upset?" The news made Lucy sad because she knew how far Nicole could go with the right education. But she also realized that college wasn't right for everyone.

"Well, yes. He told me how dangerous and risky it was. And he tried to tell me how hard it would be. But he didn't yell. Although he looked like he might when I told him I wasn't planning on going alone."

"Going with someone else didn't make him feel any better?"

Nicole scrunched her nose. "I kind of made him think it would be a guy."

"Oh."

"And then I told him something I haven't shared with anyone else. I told him the reason I've been so . . . angry."

As much as Lucy wanted to ask about the problem, it was none of her business. If Nicole wanted her to know she'd tell her. "And what did he say?"

"He said he'd made a decision and family comes first." Nicole squeezed her eyes shut for a second, when she opened them the blue was swimming in tears. "Ms. Diamond, I think he's going to quit hockey, and it's all my fault."

"Oh, honey." Lucy pulled her into a hug even as she wanted to go find Jordan and ask him what he was up to. "If he does quit after this season it's not your fault. Your brother's a big boy who knows what he wants. Even if it doesn't make sense to anyone else."

"No. I think he's going to quit right now because of what I told him. I should have kept my mouth shut. I'd never dream of asking him to quit. It's what he does. It's what he loves. I could see that when I watched him play. I could see it at the meet-and-greet when he was with his fans. I don't want him to stop doing what he loves because of me. I couldn't live with that."

"That's a heavy burden for you to bear. And, sweetie, you've been through enough lately." Lucy pushed a lock of hair off Nicole's forehead. "Did he actually say he was going to quit?"

Nicole shook her head. "He didn't have to. I could

see it in his eyes and it was heavily implied. The deter-mination on his face pretty much confirmed it."

"Then you're right, he can't quit." The thought of the man not doing what he loved twisted Lucy's stomach up in knots.

"I know. That's why I came to you. To see if you could try and talk some sense into him."

"Why would you think he'd listen to me?"

"Because you two have something going on."

Lucy felt like she'd been hit with a shovel. She'd tried so hard to be careful so Nicole wouldn't know. It would make things extremely awkward between teacher and student.

"I know you tried to hide it from me," Nicole said. "But it's pretty unmistakable with the way you guys look at each other. Plus . . . I got up one night to get a glass of water and he wasn't on the sofa. I knew he was in the bedroom with you."

"Oh my God." Lucy covered her face with her hands. "I'm so sorry."

"It's okay." Nicole touched Lucy's shoulder. "I think it's pretty cool."

Lucy lowered her hands and peeked over her finger-tips. "You do?"

Nicole nodded. "I think you're good for him. He needs someone like you in his life. And . . . I like you. Even if you make me do hard assignments in school." Nicole's grin went straight to Lucy's heart.

"Only because I know you're very smart and can ace anything you want if you'll just try."

"I aced laying a guilt trip on Jordan when he first

came home. I just always thought he was gone because he didn't care about us."

"You know he does."

"I do now. But that was before I saw him doing what he loves. And I can't let him give it up because of me. I'm selfish, but I'm not *that* selfish. I know he wants to do what's right. But staying here out of obligation isn't right."

"I don't think he'd stay just out of obligation, Nicole. I think he loves his family and he wants to be here for you. He wants to be a part of your life. He's missed a lot over the last fifteen years."

"You can't make up for lost time," Nicole said sadly. "And if you give up something because you think that's what you need to do to try, it's wrong in too many ways to count. Before my parents died, quitting never entered his mind. Doesn't that tell you it's wrong?"

Lucy knew she was the wrong one to give out advice. Especially where a family was concerned. She didn't have one. She never really had. Her parents had quit on life way before she'd even entered high school. And for her to even try to step in and interfere with something she had no business doing scared the life out of her. But for a seventeen-year-old girl, Nicole made sense. And if Jordan was going to make such a gigantic decision, he couldn't do it at the risk of making everyone else feel guilty because he'd done so.

"It tells me he should give this a lot more thought," Lucy said. "I think he's just looking at it the way he does business on the ice. Out there he slams, punches, and pushes his way to get what he wants or needs. He doesn't have time to think it over. He just makes an abrupt decision."

"Then will you please talk to him?"

How could Lucy refuse the concern in Nicole's eyes? "I'll give it my best shot."

Relief washed over Nicole's face. "Thank you." She hugged Lucy, then leaned back and wrinkled her nose. "Although you might want to wash that mask off first. You're cracking."

Lucy chuckled. "Story of my life."

The idea of taking the tiger by the tail and trying to convince Jordan he shouldn't do something he probably really thought he should do would be a challenge bar none. Lucy hated confrontation. Of any kind. So she needed to come up with a disarming way to approach the matter. Catch him a little off guard. Then hopefully he'd see reason.

Then again, she'd seen his deciphering on the ice, and Lucy knew that meant things probably wouldn't bode well for what she needed to do. And the fact that she'd never been in this type of situation before guaranteed that no one should bet on her success.

Jordan Kincade was a man with a will and a mind of his own. And *that* was only a part of what made him so darned sexy.

Time to step out of her comfort zone.

Again.

Chapter 16

After his talk with Nicole, Jordan spent a couple of hours with Ryan in the bottling room, learning about the new vintner arguments on corks versus screw tops. He didn't have an opinion either way. But to him, it just didn't seem right to open a bottle of Dom Pérignon with a screw top.

Nine-year-old Riley tagged along, scuffing her tennis shoes and sighing with boredom so often that Jordan told Ryan they'd talk about the subject another day. He needed and wanted to learn the business, but family came first. And with the circumstances what they were, Riley needed her father's attention more often. Just one more reason that solidified Jordan's decision.

No one felt like making dinner so he'd picked up burgers in town at Mr. Pickle Buns and they all ate at his parents' kitchen table.

During the course of the meal the house had been intensely quiet and the glaring absence of their parents had been painful. Ordinarily his mother would be fussing about preparing food or working on a project for one of her favorite organizations. His father would have been rambling about fixing this or that or talking about a new blend for the wines. All of them at the table felt the void but no one said a word. They all knew—like it or not—it was an aching emptiness they were going to have to learn to live with. The realization did nothing to ease the knot in his stomach.

He'd cried for his parents. Lost sleep over the visions of the horrific way they'd died. And now he knew he had to honor them by doing what was right for the family.

Once they'd finished dinner, Jordan strolled around a section of the several hundred acres that made up Sunshine Creek Vineyards. With a fresh eye, he noticed things he'd forgotten from his youth. Like the peaceful sound of the creek bubbling over rocks, sand, and the occasional waterfall. Or how the deer came down to the pasture across the creek to graze on freshly sprouted grass. He noticed how much property stood vacant and available for the possibility of expansion while still maintaining the integrity of the serene surroundings.

When he finally got back to his grandfather's cabin he showered, threw on a pair of sweatpants, and grabbed a bottle of Naked Blonde Ale from the refrigerator. Mulling over the ideas he'd come up with for the vineyards, he turned on the TV and flipped through the channels. He finally stopped on *Tombstone* where Doc Holliday was once again stealing the show with his huckleberry line.

The sudden pounding on the door came as a surprise. Figuring Ethan had decided to come over for a beer, he opened the door.

Not his brother.

Instead Lucy stood there in a knee-length buttoned-up sweater and black boots. Her hair fell in loose curls over her shoulders and her dark eyes behind those dark-framed glasses took a slow ride over his body.

"Oh good." She settled her fingers on his chest and pushed him back into the room. "You're already half naked."

Jordan's heart jumped when her hands were suddenly all over his bare chest and shoulders. They dipped provocatively beneath the waistband of his sweats and sent a hot shot of lust straight to his dick.

"Not that I don't like what you're doing," he said, sliding his hands to her hips and holding on, "but what are you doing here?"

Head slightly tilted, she looked up at him and her luscious lips tipped in a beguiling smile. "Seducing you."

"Sweet." He pulled her against him. "But I have to warn you that you probably won't have to work all that hard."

"Maybe you could pretend."

"I don't think so. You feel what's going on beneath these sweatpants?"

Her hand slid south and she gave him a squeeze. "Feels like a promise of good things to come."

"Oh, it's a promise all right. But I'll try to behave and let you take control."

"Or . . ." While one hand stroked him, she slipped the other soft hand around the back of his neck and pressed her firm, plump breasts against his chest. "You could be bad and still let me take control."

"I like the way you think, schoolteacher."

"That's good. But do you like the way I do . . . this?"

She lifted to the toes of her boots and kissed him.

Slow.

Wet.

Delicious.

She tasted like butterscotch candy and desire. Then her soft, moist lips traveled to the side of his neck, where she sucked the flesh into her warm mouth, and a hot mass of tingles shot through his blood. He couldn't remember ever being seduced. He'd always been the one who made the moves. With Lucy, he was enjoying the hell out of the other side. For a woman who'd seen her share of misery, he liked knowing she felt confident enough with him to be assertive. It was a hell of a turn-on.

He moaned. "I love the way you do that."

Her palms flattened against his chest as her lips moved downward. Kissing. Tasting. Licking.

He wanted to touch her so bad it hurt. But he'd promised to be good. Then again, she'd told him it was okay to be bad. He hooked his hands around her waist, pressed her back against the wall, and leaned in for a kiss that went from hot to scorching in 0.2 seconds. Their tongues tangled and danced. Swept, withdrew, and plunged. And then she reversed their positions. Suddenly he had his back against the wall.

When he reached for her she stepped away, licked her lips, and looked up at him from beneath those thick, sooty lashes. He didn't know exactly what she had in mind, but he was game for anything.

Her fingers went to the top button of her sweater and unbuttoned it. Then slowly she made her way down to the rest of the buttons. It soon became clear that his sweet little schoolteacher was completely naked beneath that prim and proper garment. She held out her arms and shrugged the sweater off. As it pooled on the ground, his woman stood before him in nothing but sweet-smelling skin and a pair of black high-heeled boots.

"Damn, baby. You're making me so hard I can't think."

"Good." She came closer. "I don't want you to think. I just want you to touch." She took his hands and placed them on her breasts.

Almost out of his mind with an aching need to have her, he caressed those perfect breasts and lightly pinched the nipples as her head dropped back and she sighed her pleasure. Then her head came back up and she licked her lips again.

"That's good," she whispered. "But not nearly enough." She tucked her fingers beneath the waistband of his sweats, pulled them down his legs, and helped him step out of them.

She looked up at him as she slowly ran her hands first up his calves, then his thighs. On her way up she took his erection in her hand, sucked him into her warm mouth, and stroked him with her tongue. It felt so damn good he saw stars.

What started out slow shifted into a sense of urgency. It wasn't enough that he was receiving unbelievable pleasure, he wanted to give it in return. With his hands cupped over her smooth shoulders he urged her up to her feet.

"I want you." His voice came out rough and breathless. The words caught with the pounding of his heart. "More than I've ever wanted any damn thing in my life."

"Then it's a good thing I came prepared." She came up with one last slow lick, then reached into her boot and pulled out a condom. "Magnum, right?"

All he could do was nod as she tore open the packet and rolled on the condom. Then she took his hand and placed it at the apex of her firm thighs. "Touch me."

Kissing someone never unbalanced him. It was a simple thing—the touching of lips, mingling of breath, a rush of blood, a beginning to increased awareness. Kissing Lucy as he slipped his fingers into her slick heat, and found the spot he knew made her go a little crazy, filled him with hunger for more.

The scent of her skin, her long sigh, the feel of her silky hair against his chest, completely rocked his control. He stroked her until her breaths whispered through her lips in pants and moans.

"Take me," she pleaded. "Take me now."

Changing places, he eased her against the wall, hooked his hands beneath her butt, and lifted her. She locked her high-heeled boot–covered legs around his hips, and at last he plunged into her with a satisfied groan. He looked down between them and watched as his cock moved in and out of her. This wasn't making love slow and easy like they'd done before; this was unleashed passion and hunger. He thrust deeper and faster until, groaning his name, she came hard and his own climax bulleted through him. Panting, he leaned into her, holding her firm against the wall as their hearts beat together and their bodies pulsed where they were joined.

A minute later he chuckled. "I don't know what got into you tonight—"

"You did."

He chuckled again, lifted his head, and kissed her. "Well, I sure as hell liked it." Reluctantly he withdrew, but figured they'd have another go-round as soon as he recovered. She unlocked her legs and he let her feet touch the ground. Needing to dispose of the condom he said, "Give me a second."

When he came back into the living room she'd put her sweater back on and had it buttoned up all prim and proper again. Trouble was, on her it looked sexy as hell. Especially since he knew she was naked under all that finely knitted cotton. He grinned, thinking of the possibilities. "Do I get to take that off next time?"

"What makes you think there will be a next time?"

$\mathcal{L}$ucy's heart had never plunged so far as it did with the way he looked at her, dark brows colliding over intensely sharp blue focus.

"What?"

"I try not to associate with quitters," she said, trying

her hardest to remain calm and sound like the stern schoolteacher. Right now she couldn't talk to him as his lover. She needed to be tough so—if Nicole was right—he'd realize the mistake he was making. "So this will be the last time we're together. I wanted it to be memorable. And it was. I thank you for that."

He folded those muscular arms across his wide chest and looked down at her with what she now knew as his intimidation glare. An angry naked man was quite intimidating indeed. But probably not in the way he might imagine. Her imagination, however, was running at full speed.

"What the hell are you talking about?"

"I've heard rumors that you're quitting hockey. Tell me I'm wrong."

"How the hell did you know about that?" He grabbed his sweatpants, shoved his legs inside, then dropped his hands to his hips.

"Nicole. She came to me earlier and begged me to talk to you because she thinks you're quitting hockey right now when you could be skating toward the Stanley Cup. Something you've dreamed of your whole life. Why doesn't that make sense to me?"

"You don't understand, Lucy. I've always put hockey first. Now it's time to put my family first. Nicole was mouthing off about not going to college and moving to Nashville and I need to stick around to make her see that the choices she makes now are going to affect her for the rest of her life."

"Kind of like the choices you're making now are going to affect *you* for the rest of your life?"

When he didn't respond she knew she'd made him think.

"Nicole said she'd feel horrible and guilty if you gave up what you love to do for her. She's seen you play. And she knows how much the game means to you. I have to agree."

"I can't be a brother if I'm never here. And I already have a fifteen-year track record of not being a good brother. I don't even know my own twin anymore. We used to be so close. And now . . . all I know is he's great at making money. The first time I walked into my parents' house after their funeral I noticed the photos they have around the house. All of them are group photos. The only one with me is my roster photo from last year. I'm not in any of those candid family shots. None."

Her heart ached for him. She knew he was in a tough spot. She also knew it wasn't easy living with regrets. Any way he turned he was going to have some kind of guilt, whether it was giving up hockey or continuing to play and leaving his family once again.

"How much longer is left in the season?"

He shrugged. "Anywhere from a couple of days to several weeks."

"And you don't think your family will understand if you take that time to complete what you've started? What are you teaching your sister if you quit?"

"That family's important."

"Wrong. You'll teach her that guilt overrides giving up a dream. And if that's the case, why should she bother having a vision for her life whether it's obtaining a master's degree or signing with a record label?"

"It's more than that, Lucy. Something happened before our parents died and I told her I'd try to help her figure it out."

"And you will. She knows you'll be there for her."

"If she leaves as soon as school's out that gives me no time."

"She's not going to do that."

"How do you know?"

"Let's just say that I think I understand her. I know she's searching for herself. But I'm pretty sure she really doesn't want to do it alone."

He glanced away. "I don't know."

"Look. Everyone I know quit on me and I even gave up on myself many times. I won't let you give up on you. No one expects you to give up everything for them. Talk to your family. I'm sure you'll see that they support you and your career a hundred percent. You've worked all your life for this opportunity. Take it. Everyone will still be here when you're done."

Because she could say no more, because she was silently begging him not to quit on *her*, and because it was breaking her heart to stand there and see him so torn up inside, she knew she had to leave.

"Don't quit on Nicole," she said in parting. "Be her champion by giving her guidance, even if it's from miles away. Show her what hard work and determination can accomplish. And let her know that love doesn't have time or space limits." She kissed his cheek and headed for the door.

"What about you?"

She turned. "What about me?"

He crossed the floor and stopped in front of her. The masculine scent of his warm body, soap, and sex drifted up like a wonderful perfume that made her head spin.

"If I don't quit, will you still be here when I'm done?" he asked.

"In the beginning, everything inside of me told me to run. That you would only hurt me again. That a man as perfect as you would never truly find anything special about someone like me. But I took a chance anyway. As much as I tried not to, I've fallen in love with you. So prove to me you're not a quitter and yes, I'll still be here."

She reached for the door and he stopped her with a hand on her arm.

"Promise me," he said. The haunted look in his eyes verified it was important for her to do so.

"I promise. Now you have to prove it."

Before she could change her mind, she opened the door and walked out.

She just hoped it wouldn't be forever.

Chapter 17

Sleep came in short spurts. Jordan finally got up at six o'clock after looking at the clock radio for what felt like every hour on the hour. All night his mind had whirled with the dilemma. No matter which way he turned, he'd end up letting someone down. Whether it was Nicole, Lucy, his brothers, his teammates, or his fans. And he had no one to blame but himself.

Trying to work things out in his head, he went for a run, then to the gym. Then he busted all his hard work to hell by stopping at Sugarbuns and satisfying his sweet tooth with an apricot-almond breakfast pastry. Halfway through his workout Ryan had called another family meeting, so he also picked up a dozen donuts but only managed to make it home with eleven. Somewhere along the way a glazed old-fashioned had disappeared.

When he walked into his parents' house, the place was silent. He set the donut box down on the kitchen table and wandered back into the living room, once again looking at the endless array of group photos and the solitary photo of him. One day he'd change that.

Sooner than later, he hoped.

As a start he took his picture off the mantel and shoved it into a side table drawer. He'd rather not be there at all than be there alone.

Ethan and Declan came into the kitchen as he was making a pot of coffee.

"Don't take this personally, Jordy." Declan snatched a coffee mug off the counter. "But you look like ten miles of a bumpy road in hell."

"Too much stress." Jordan snapped the lid closed on the coffeemaker. "No sleep."

"And now another family pow-wow," Ethan said, grabbing his own coffee cup.

"Yeah. Hopefully Ryan has some good news."

At that moment Ryan and Riley—still in her footie pajamas and looking sleepy—strolled into the kitchen. Ryan handed his daughter a donut on a napkin, gave her a kiss on the forehead, and sent her off to the den to watch cartoons. Judging by the look on Ryan's face, Jordan figured the news was going to be anything but good.

"This couldn't have waited until later?" Jordan asked. "Riley still looks half asleep."

"Yeah." Ryan glanced toward the doorway his little girl had disappeared through. "She's not too happy with me right now. But things need to be discussed so we can start moving forward. And since everyone has lives to get back to, it needed to happen."

Jordan agreed, but his heart still went out to little Riley. Admittedly, until he'd come back home he'd never put much thought into his niece other than she was adorable and she'd gotten the shit end of the stick when her mom took off.

Jordan saw her in a whole different light now. She was a sharp little cookie with a sweet smile that melted his heart. He'd never thought much about having kids. He'd just figured someday they'd come along when he finally decided to settle down. Now he could picture himself with a couple of cute little brainiacs that looked just like Lucy.

"Your little girl deserves a break."

Ryan nodded. "I figured once everything settled down a little I'd take her somewhere like Disneyland to take her mind off things. In the meantime . . ." He tossed a thin newspaper on the table. "Looks like you made a visit to *Talk of the Town*."

Only after Lucy had already taken a stand.

Jordan lifted the paper and read the headline story that was a retraction and apology. "Yeah." He chuckled. "I threatened to sue her nasty ass."

Ethan cocked his head and looked over Jordan's shoulder at the paper. "Looks like she took you seriously. That paper doesn't have a Sunday edition."

"Told her she wouldn't have *any* edition unless she apologized. We all have enough to worry about without some mean old biddy trying to stir up a hornet's nest."

"Who's stirring up trouble?" Parker came into the room looking like he might be dealing with a hangover as he reached up into the cupboard and grabbed a coffee mug.

"Jordy single-handedly took down the wicked witch at *Talk of the Town*," Ethan drawled while he perused the selection of donuts.

"Not single-handedly," Jordan said. "Lucy got there before me and took her down a couple of notches before I even got warmed up."

"My kind of woman," Declan said.

"*Not* your kind of woman," Jordan shot back. "*My* kind."

His brothers raised their eyebrows because even though back in the day they'd often been in competition, he'd never before claimed a woman.

"Duly noted," Dec said, selecting a regular glazed donut from the box. "Hands off the schoolteacher."

"Hey," Ethan complained. "That's the donut I was going to take."

Parker scoffed. "You've been in this family for thirty-one years and you still haven't learned to act fast when there's food around?"

Jordan chuckled. He'd missed the banter with his brothers. When they'd been younger they'd all tried to prove who was bigger and badder by basically beating the crap out of each other. One or the other had often sported a black eye or a busted lip. Their mother had always shaken her head in disgust and complained about too much testosterone in the house. Now, Jordan realized, he was grateful to have his brothers. And he was grateful to have the chance to get to know them again.

"So . . . a schoolteacher, huh? Never figured you for the type. Unless she's like one of those you see in *Playboy*." Parker sipped his coffee and grinned. "Is she?"

In Jordan's opinion, despite her choice of plain outerwear, naked Lucy far surpassed anyone in the pages of *Playboy*. "Doesn't matter. She's hands off to you."

Aunt Pippy bounced into the room like a ball of energy in a retro bell-bottom jumpsuit made of a blue, green, and yellow paisley print. Once again, plastic fruit dangled from her ears.

"As soon as Nicki comes down we can get started," Ryan said.

"I'm here." Nicole came into the room wearing her grumpy baby dragon face. Jordan handed her a cup of black coffee.

"Eeew." She handed it back. "I only drink caramel macchiatos from Starbucks."

"Starving musicians can't afford caramel macchiatos from Starbucks." Jordan leaned in and grinned.

Nicole grinned back. "They do if their big brother is a superstar hockey player."

That got a laugh out of him. "Good one, sis." He grabbed her in a one-armed side hug.

"Everyone take a seat," Ryan said.

Wood chairs scraped against the tile floor as everyone chose a place to land.

Ryan sat at the head of the table. "Sorry about the short notice," Ryan said, folding his hands together on the tabletop. "I wanted to discuss your ideas for improving the business and give you some updates before we all started going in different directions."

Parker leaned his forearms on the table. "I'm still all in for a trattoria."

"I like the idea of renovating the event center and creating a wine club," Ethan added.

"I took a look around the property and there's no identity. No theme," Jordan said. "Some of the buildings look Old West and others look European. We need to figure out what we want it to be and stay the course."

"We also might consider hiring an in-house event coordinator," Declan suggested. "Someone who is really enthusiastic about what they do and will keep the place booked year round."

"Great idea," Parker said.

"I also think we should put in a stage over by the grassy knoll with priority seating for concerts which can be obtained by joining the wine club," Jordan added. "There's plenty of room to add a picnic market for folks to purchase everything they need right here instead of dragging it all in with them. There's also room to add another couple of cottages by the creek for guests. A spa isn't out of the question either. I agree we need to turn this place into a destination instead of just a vineyard. No other winery in the area has that much going on. They might copy us, but at least we'd be able to build the clientele first."

"Great ideas," Ryan said. "As soon as we get the report from the financial investigator we can figure out the priorities and costs so we can come up with a budget."

"Ryan and I think the man we hired is getting close to an answer," Declan added.

"Oh my." Aunt Pippy made a big show of looking at the gigantic watch on her wrist. "I've lost track of time. I was supposed to be at . . . church . . . yeah . . . church. Ten minutes ago." She pushed back her chair and headed toward the door mumbling, "Hope Reverend Collins didn't start without me."

"Since when does she go to church?" Parker wanted to know.

"She doesn't," Ryan answered. "Mom always said she was afraid the roof would cave in on her for all the things she did during the 'Make Love, Not War' era."

"Then what the hell was that all about?" Jordan asked. "Come to think of it, whenever we talk about the missing money she finds a reason to leave. She's starting to look suspicious."

"Dude, she still dresses like it's the 1960s," Ethan piped in. "Maybe she's just getting old and senile."

"You're around her the most, Ryan. You have any idea what's going on?"

"I try not to delve too deep into Aunt Pippy's mind. I'm afraid I'll tap into a bad acid trip."

"This is bullshit." Jordan stood and shoved his chair away with the backs of his knees. He caught Aunt Pippy before she reached the stairs.

"Hold on there, turbo," he said. "You're holding out on us."

"Don't know what you're talking about." Aunt Pippy placed her hand on the stair rail but Jordan caught her by the back of her jumpsuit before she could escape.

"I think you do. Because if you were going to church you'd be heading out the front door, not sneaking up to your room," he said, taking her by the elbow and leading her right back to the kitchen. "So how about we all sit down at the table and you can enlighten us."

Panic widened her eyes. "I don't have anything to say."

"Don't make us get the interrogation light and smoke cigars in your face till you break," Parker joked, even though it was no joking matter.

"Have a seat." Jordan pulled out the chair she'd been sitting in.

Pippy looked at the chair, then at all of them. "He *had* to do it," she announced, then burst into tears.

Jordan's heart sank. What the hell was going on?

Ryan's brows pulled together tight. "He who?"

"Not sure I even want to hear this," Nicole said.

"But we're going to." Jordan handed his aunt a napkin to wipe her tears. "Aren't we, Aunt Pippy?"

"I can't tell you who," she said between sniffs. "I'll be betraying him."

"I don't care if you're talking about the president of the United States," Ryan said. "This family's future depends on your answer. So yes, you *will* tell."

Fingers curled over the backrest, she stared at the chair they expected her to sit in. Finally she looked up. "Your father took the money. I can't tell you why. Don't ask. I can't betray him any further. He was a good man but he wasn't perfect. And neither was your mother. God rest their souls."

She heaved a huge sigh. "And now I *will* be going to church so God doesn't strike me dead for my disloyalty."

As their aunt escaped the room without giving them

further details, they all sat there stunned, staring at the half-empty box of donuts like it held the answers they sought.

"Oh my God." Nicole started to cry. "It's starting to make sense now."

"What is?" Ryan asked.

Nicki tossed Jordan a panicked look and he knew he had to step in.

"Nicki told me something that I haven't been able to share with any of you yet," Jordan said, his heart breaking for his sister. Because no matter what she said, the truth was none of them knew much more now than they did when they'd first entered the room.

Declan slid his hand over the back of her chair. "What's up, buttercup?"

"Seems there's some confusion about a conversation she had with Dad before he and Mom left for Hawaii. And that's why she's been so . . . touchy."

Expression apologetic, Ryan looked at Nicole. "I'm sorry, sweetheart. I've felt something was out of place but I never knew what or why. And I never asked. I guess I just got too wrapped up in my own problems."

"Me too." Ethan nodded. "I should have paid more attention."

The more they discussed, the more Nicole slunk down into her seat with tears streaming down her face.

"But how does Dad pilfering money have anything to do with Nicki?" Declan asked.

No sense tiptoeing around the subject. This had to come out. Not just to help Nicki, but to try and put to rest one more mystery.

"Nicki doesn't seem to think she's our real sister," Jordan said.

"What?" Every confused head, including Ryan's, turned toward her.

Ethan stood up and faced Jordan like he was looking for a fight. "What the hell are you talking about?"

"*I* didn't say that," Jordan said to make it clear in case his brother started throwing punches. "*She* did. Dad admitted to her that something in his past had affected him in a negative way where she was concerned. He said he didn't blame her. But he did tell her that he didn't know if he could ever move past it to be the kind of father she wanted."

Nicki broke down in tears again. The poor thing was surrounded by five men who were reduced to pansy asses at the sight of a woman's tears. Even their own sister's. Then as if a glass wall shattered, they were all up and hugging her.

"There's no way you're not our sister," Ryan said. "You look just like us."

"That's what I told her," Jordan added.

"We love you, Nicki." Ethan squeezed her tight and Parker pushed him out of the way.

"Best little sister ever," Declan added.

"That would be totally crazy," Parker said. "But even if it were true, you're still our sister no matter what."

Riley heard the commotion and shuffled into the kitchen. As soon as she saw her aunt crying and all her uncles hugging her, Riley started crying too. Ryan opened his arm and his little girl dove right into the mix.

"We're a family." Emotion clogged Ryan's throat. "And we always will be."

Jordan had intended to tell them all about his decision for his future, but family came first. They all had enough on their plates to have to worry whether he planned to continue playing hockey or not.

*J*ordan jammed a hand through his hair as he drove back to his parents' house after a quick trip into town later that day.

Holy shit.

Their father had stolen money from his own business. But why?

What could cause a man to basically steal from himself or the welfare of his own family? Why would he risk endangering the business he'd worked so hard to make prosperous?

No doubt there was more to the story and more they needed to find out. Which was just one more reason Jordan came back to the house to explain the decision about his future to Nicole.

When he climbed the stairs to her room, he smiled when he heard the melodic chords from her guitar and the sweet sound of her voice. She had talent, and he'd support her whether she wanted to spread her wings and fly or devote the next four years to a college education. Whatever made her happy.

Especially after Aunt Pippy's bombshell had them all guessing.

He knocked, and the music stopped while she told him to come in.

"Hi." Like a Gypsy girl, she sat on her bed in a colorful skirt, T-shirt, and scarf wrapped around her head. All that was missing were dangling gold earrings and bracelets.

"Hey." He leaned down and kissed the top of her head. "I wanted to come tell you that I'm going to finish out the season."

"I'm so glad." She hugged his neck when he sat beside her. "I'd never want you to quit on my behalf."

"If and when I do leave the game, I want you to know it will be the right thing to do for me. Not because I feel forced into it. Okay?"

She nodded.

"And I want you to know that no matter where I am, I'm never too busy for you."

"Unless you're punching the Rock in the nose, right?" She grinned.

"Even then." He kissed her forehead. "I love you, Nicki. And as sorry as I am that I haven't been there for you in the past, I'm glad I'm here now."

"Me too."

"But . . ." He reached down and picked up the box he'd carried into the room. "Just in case you miss me too much, I brought you this to keep you company."

"What is it?"

The excitement in her eyes squeezed his heart in a good way.

"Open it and find out."

She pulled up the cardboard flaps and a smoky gray kitten jumped out and into her arms. A squeal of delight filled her room as she nuzzled the kitten. "He's mine?"

"He's all yours. I have all his accessories—including an auto cleaning cat box—down in the car."

She snuggled the kitten and smiled. "I'm going to name him something that reminds me of you."

He laughed. "Like what?"

She rubbed noses with the kitten. "Fezzik."

"Like from *The Princess Bride*?" He figured he'd get extra good brother points for even knowing that. "Why?"

"Because Fezzik is a gentle giant. And that's how I see you."

When his baby sister hugged his neck and cried tears of joy, Jordan knew that whether he ever won the Stanley Cup or not, home was where his heart belonged.

And nothing could ever be better.

*S*unday afternoon Lucy sat at her kitchen table preparing her lesson for the following day and fanning the fumes from Ziggy's particularly raunchy toot.

"Good Lord, dog. What is it you eat that makes you stink so bad?"

Ziggy looked up with his tongue lolling out of his mouth and his tail wagging the stench. When the doorbell rang he scrambled to his paws and headed for the door. Lucy wasn't particularly surprised to see Jordan standing on her front porch. And, as always, he looked good enough to eat.

"Can I come in?"

"Of course." She stepped back but he caught her up in his arms and planted a kiss on her mouth that immediately kicked into high gear. Before she could say, "Let's go upstairs," he broke the kiss and held her face between his hands.

"I'm heading to the airport right now."

Her heart raced. "You're going to Dallas?"

He nodded. "I wanted to come say good-bye and . . ."

Relief danced through her veins. Then her heart went all jittery. Did he mean *good-bye* good-bye?

"And?"

"And I know I didn't say anything last night when you told me you were falling in love with me. I'm sure that stung. But I've never said that to a woman before."

"I understand." Being in love by yourself sucked. But she'd had a talk with herself when all this began and she guessed she never really expected him to fall in love with her.

"I don't think you do." His thumbs gently stroked the high bones of her cheeks. "There's been so much going on that the thoughts all started scrambling in my head. All my life I've taken. I've never given. I wasn't even sure I knew how."

"I do understand, Jordan. You have a lot going on. One person can only handle so much and—"

"I love you, Lucy."

"What?"

"I love you." The smile he gave her washed over her like a fountain of sparkling happiness. "I not only know I *can* give, I *want* to give. I have no doubt whatsoever."

"I love you too," she said. "And I'm not just falling, I'm totally in."

"Then promise you'll wait for me until I get back."

"Where would I go?"

"Promise me."

"I promise."

With another bone-melting kiss he got in the SUV and drove away. Lucy waved until the taillights disappeared. Then she closed the door, sank to the floor, and cried tears of joy.

Ziggy crawled into her lap and spoiled the moment by doing what he did best.

On Monday morning Lucy drove toward school with nerves coiled up like rattlesnakes in her stomach. She didn't know what to expect when she walked into the building. Gossip about educators didn't set well with the school administrators. They might view her as a bad influence for the students.

Would she be fired?

Suspended?

Whatever the punishment for falling in love, she'd pay without argument. Because not for one minute did she regret going to North Carolina with Jordan and Nicole. She'd met the man of her dreams—even though she'd once considered him a nightmare—and she'd somehow managed to help and understand a young girl who seemed to be in such need after the loss of her parents.

She'd been grateful for *Talk of the Town*'s apology, even if it didn't sound too sincere. But what take on the situation would the school administrators have?

Guess she'd soon find out.

Parking in her usual space, she gathered all her supplies and headed toward the brick building amid students chatting about what they did for spring break. As soon as she opened her classroom door the snakes in her stomach reared their tongue-flicking heads. Waiting for her at her desk was Principal Brown in his usual black pants, white shirt, and expertly styled comb-over.

"Good morning, Ms. Diamond. Welcome back."

"Good morning, sir. Thank you."

"Quite a stir the newspaper created."

"My only intention on going to North Carolina was to help a student."

"I figured."

"You did?" Her heart slammed against her ribs.

"I've known you for three years. I think you have excellent character. And I'd never doubt your decision to help someone after they'd suffered such a loss as has Nicole Kincade."

Relief weakened her knees. "Thank you, sir."

"You can thank the young lady herself. She came into my office this morning. Told me how you helped her with her grief and her schoolwork. She told me how you helped her find the courage to talk about her music and how you encouraged her songwriting. She's very excited to come back to class."

"She is?" Lucy wished the girl was there right now so she could hug her.

The principal nodded. "She said you were also able to help her brother deal with his grief."

Lucy sighed. "Mr. Brown, not everything in that story was a total fabrication."

"Oh?"

"Jordan Kincade and I have known each other since high school. I used to tutor him. We were . . . friends."

"And now it's something more?"

"How did you know?"

"You're glowing, Ms. Diamond." He smiled and patted her hand. "Love has a way of doing that to people. My Maisey had that same look when we were courting."

"I was afraid I'd come back and find out I'd been fired."

"You have a job here for as long as you want." The school bell rang. He got up out of her chair and headed to the door. "In the meantime, enjoy yourself. It's nice to see you smile."

As soon as he left the room Lucy wanted to drop down in her chair and cry with relief, but her students started filing in, chattering like mice, and she just felt too darned happy to cry.

In the final game of the series against the Stars, the Vipers were down by a goal with a minute left on the clock in the third period. Jordan stood in front of the bench rocking side-to-side on his skates, anxious to get back on the ice.

When he'd skated on earlier to warm up everything had felt different. *He* felt different. He'd never been in love. Never had someone waiting at home for him. Still he played a fast and furious game.

Tonight the Stars were on. Their passes were accurate. They didn't bullshit around with extracurricular pushing and shoving. They were in it to win it and the Vipers were fighting back with everything they had.

With the shift change, Jordan threw his legs over the wall and skated into the face-off determined to help the team to a win. They'd overcome a deficit in this short amount of time before; they could do it again.

The ice in the Stars' stadium was hinky. Slushy in places. Not everyone who played could handle the inconsistencies that had been a part of their problem all night. When the puck dropped, Jordan slid it across the ice to Seabrook. Seabrook pushed forward and passed to O'Reilly, who'd had a hard time getting a stick on it all night. The puck skittered across the ice as the clock wound down to five seconds.

Jordan yelled, "Shoot it."

O'Reilly pulled his arm back, swung, and the puck flew right of the net. The buzzer rang.

Game over.

No playoffs. No Stanley Cup.

While the joyous Stars gathered at center ice, the defeated Vipers skated off to the locker room.

Once they'd all gathered, Coach Reiner gave his spiel about there always being next year. They'd worked hard. Tried hard. Things just didn't go their way. Blah blah blah. Once he wrapped up, the media converged like sewer rats. Usually the reporters went straight for the victor's locker room but apparently the Stars' doors were locked and they had time to kill until entry was granted.

Jordan sat down on the bench in front of his locker. While taking off his skates he noticed a pair of pressed khakis in front of him.

"Brett Beaver from FOX 4 News. Can I interview you?"

Jordan looked up to the man holding a video camera who looked like he never went out in the sun or had learned to properly knot a tie. "Sure."

"How do you feel about losing the chance to go to the playoffs? Are you depressed?" The man stuck the microphone in Jordan's face.

*H*eartbroken for the Vipers, Lucy sat next to Nicole on the sofa in her living room watching post-game interviews. After Jordan had left for Dallas, she and Nicole had spent more time together. They'd grown closer. And when Nicole finally explained the cause of her anger and the situation with the missing money, Lucy's heart ached.

Right now the young girl sat on Lucy's sofa wearing a huge frown because her brother's team had lost. Lucy felt bad because they'd fought a good fight out on the ice. But at least he'd given it a try. That's what mattered.

At their feet lay Ziggy and the kitten Jordan had given Nicole. The cute little gray fluff of fur Nicole had named Fezzik had perched himself along Ziggy's back and lay purring while he slept.

Suddenly the camera went to the Vipers' locker room, where Jordan's gorgeous face filled the screen.

With a slight tilt of his head, Jordan replied to the reporter's question. "Am I depressed?"

Nicole chuckled. "Jordy's going to punch that guy."

Lucy chuckled because she'd bet that's exactly what

Jordan felt like doing. "No he's not. He saves the fists of fury for on the ice."

"I feel bad for the team." Jordan's broad shoulders plus padding came up in a shrug. "They've worked hard to get this far. Plus they had to cover for me while I was gone."

"Family matters, right?" the voice behind the camera said.

"Both my parents were killed."

"My condolences."

"Yeah." Nicole snorted. "He sounds real sincere."

Lucy had to agree the guy sounded like he couldn't care less.

"Thanks." Jordan ran a hand through his soaking wet hair. "Being back home gave me a lot of time to think."

"I can imagine," said the voice behind the camera. "So how did that feel when O'Reilly completely missed that last shot on goal?"

"Can't think about that right now." Jordan shook his head. "I've got more on my mind than what someone did or didn't do on the ice tonight. You can't rewind time and change things. You have to move forward. That's why this is my last season. I'm retiring."

"What?" Nicole and Lucy said at the same time, then looked at each other like maybe they hadn't heard right.

"Retiring?" The voice behind the camera perked up like he knew he'd just caught an exclusive moment. "It's not like you're too old to play anymore."

One side of Jordan's mouth quirked. "I've been

playing hard for fifteen years. That's fifteen years of busting my ass, my knuckles, and my face. Fifteen years of tearing ligaments and cracking ribs. I'm not going to miss any of that. I'm leaving the game with 668 goals and 934 assists. I'm proud of that. But to accomplish all of that I missed a lot of time with my family."

"But you love the game, right?" the reporter asked. "The competition?"

"He does," Nicole said to Lucy. "So why would he quit?"

Lucy shook her head and a sinking sensation hit her in the gut. "We have to trust he knows what he's doing."

"He did tell me that when he leaves the game, it will be the right thing for him," Nicole said. "Not because he felt forced into it."

"Then we definitely need to trust him," Lucy said.

"I do love the game," Jordan said to the reporter. "And there might be times when I'll miss it. But there are other things I love just as much or more. I don't want to be a Kincade in name only anymore. I want to be an actual part of my family. I can't do that if I'm never around. So, back to your question. Am I depressed about losing this game and the chance to go to the playoffs? The answer is no. I have something better to do."

"Anything specific you have planned for your future?"

"Yep." Jordan looked into the camera and grinned. "I'm going home to ask my girl to marry me."

Lucy and Nicole looked at each other, screamed, then hugged each other until they cried.

Nicole's kitten sprang off Ziggy's back.

Ziggy cocked his head and completely ruined the moment.

*J*ordan had texted Lucy while she'd been teaching a class to say he was on his way home via commercial flight. A feat that could mean he'd arrive home on time or possibly end up sleeping on the floor of the Phoenix airport. She'd texted him back saying she couldn't wait to see him. Since she hadn't made any reference to it, he wondered if she'd watched his last game. Wondered if she'd seen the interview afterward.

A grin lit him up inside and replaced any doubt about walking away from his career. With his skates and jersey in his suitcase, he knew he'd have days of doubt. Possible days of regret. Days where he just missed the fast pace of the game and the camaraderie between teammates. He also knew that he was heading into unfamiliar territory.

And that excited the hell out of him.

The possibilities were endless.

He had no idea what he might do with the rest of his life except for one thing. He wanted to be with Lucy during the good times and the bad. He wanted her to be the last thing he saw at night and the first thing he saw each morning. He wanted to plan their future together, have children, and grow old together. And the faster he got to her house, the faster he could make it all happen.

Finally, at ten minutes after seven he rang her

doorbell. The front door flew open and Lucy rushed into his arms.

"Yes. Yes. Yes, I'll marry you."

He planted a long, sweet kiss on her luscious mouth, then chuckled. "So I guess you saw the post-game interview?"

She nodded and her glasses slipped down her nose a little before she pushed them back in place with the tip of her finger. "I saw the whole game. And I'm so sorry you lost. But I'm so glad you're home. And . . . yes. Oh, I love you, Jordan."

Something wound around his heart that he'd never experienced before. Not even the first time he'd slapped the puck between the pipes.

Absolute pure joy.

Lucinda Nutter loved him.

"Can I ask you properly anyway?" he asked with a grin. "Just for the record."

"You can do anything you want."

"*Anything?*"

Her fingertips danced down the buttons on his shirt. "*Anything.*"

"Exactly what I wanted to hear." He backed her into the house and kicked the door shut. Then he scooped her up and tossed her over his shoulder. She giggled all the way up the stairs and the entire time he stripped her naked.

He took off her glasses and set them on the night-stand. Then he pulled off his own clothes in fast-forward speed.

When he eased her back onto the bed she was still

chuckling. "I thought you wanted to do this properly."

He kissed her deep, hot, and wet. The kiss set him on fire. He wanted her. Needed her. Loved her like crazy. When she moved her legs apart he slid inside, filling her body while she filled his heart.

"*This* is *my* version of properly." He framed her face with his hands. Kissed her forehead. Kissed the tip of her nose. "I love you, Lucy. You're everything that matters today, tomorrow, and forever. You've made me a better man. Will you marry me?"

"I love you, Jordan." She sighed dreamily. "Yes, I'll marry you."

Once upon a time, Jordan's wishes had been about hockey goals, fame, fortune, and life in the fast lane. Somewhere along the way he'd learned to be careful what he wished for. But if he'd known Lucy would come into his life and fulfill his dreams for a happily-ever-after, he would have made different choices a long time ago. Together they were about to create a life together where the sky was the limit.

And in that new world, loving Lucy was everything that mattered.

Don't miss Candis Terry's next fantastic
Sunshine Creek Vineyard novel

Coming early 2017

*I*n Declan Kincade's world the real problem with leisure time was finding the time for it.

At the window of his Newport Beach high-rise office, he watched the sunset glisten across the ocean waves. Down on the beach–like a ritual changing of the guards–the sun worshipers packed up their beach towels, tanning lotion, and umbrellas to head home while the locals grabbed their boards for their moment in the sand and surf. Early summer was the perfect time of year for Californians to play along the coastline before the hoards of vacationers swamped the beaches and local bars.

Not that Declan knew much about having fun these days. In fact, he hadn't had fun in . . . hell, he couldn't remember. He'd spent nearly eight non-stop years working on his career. Not that he was complaining, but he had started to feel the wear and tear on his brain. At the age of thirty-three, he felt like he was entering his golden years without all the significant life experiences. And that was not okay.

The recent tragic deaths of his parents had taught him one thing—life was too damn short.

Hands in pockets, he settled back on the heels of his black oxfords, wishing instead he was in a more casual shoe and strolling down the Newport pier. He imagined the sound of the waves crashing against the pier's massive pylons. He imagined watching the fishermen bring in their daily catch while the gulls hovering overhead screeched for scraps. He imagined stopping at the oyster bar for a cold brew and a quiet moment to watch the last of the bikini-clad beauties shuffle back to their cars. Instead he would spend one more evening within these office walls in a meeting scheduled to start in . . . He glanced down at the Citizen Signature watch clasped to his wrist . . . four minutes.

Imagining life was no longer enough. He'd reached a point where he needed more. He needed to participate instead of just being a part-time observer. The problem was, he'd kind of forgotten how.

Behind him the door opened.

"They're here. Are you ready?"

The husky female voice caused him to turn instead of just nodding his head. Over the past four years he'd heard that voice a million times. But today, as his assistant peeked around the door, Dec couldn't help consider his twin brother's recent observation.

She's hot as hell.

It wasn't that Declan had never noticed Brooke Hastings's bikini bod, long legs, and deep brown eyes.

It wasn't that her bubbly personality hadn't made him laugh at times when he really wanted to pull his hair out. And it wasn't that he didn't have an appreciation for her high IQ that never failed to create a solution that would benefit the financial investment company he'd built from the ground up. But Brooke was his assistant and mixing business with pleasure was a very bad idea.

Even if his newly engaged brother insisted he chose pleasure over work.

"Dec?" Brooke's head tilted slightly and a waterfall of honey blonde hair fell over the shoulder of her silky white blouse. "Are you okay?"

Hell no, he wasn't okay.

Because right now, even though he knew it was wrong, he couldn't help wonder how all her soft shiny hair would feel wrapped around his hands while he pulled her in and seduced her right out of that hip-hugging skirt.

"Dec?" When she stepped inside his office he blinked to take his eyes off all those curves that made a simple button-down blouse look like something that should be removed.

Slowly.

One button at a time.

With his teeth.

"Yeah." He took a breath. "Bring them in."

"You sure?" Her head tilted in an are-you-positive-you-haven't-gone-off-the-deep-end way.

The only thing he was sure about was he was going to kill his brother for planting ideas in his brain that had no business being there.

"Yep. Let's do this."

Before she disappeared to escort their clients into his office, Brooke flashed him a grin that showed off a perfect set of dimples. He'd seen those dimples five days a week for four freaking years. So why, all of a sudden, did he have the urge to press his lips against them and then follow up with a slow slide of his tongue down her long, delicate neck?

Less than a minute later she escorted James and Josh Flavio into his office. The father-son duo was looking for investment advice on a beachside Caribbean-style restaurant.

"Gentlemen. Welcome." Declan extended his hand. With the perfunctory introductions made, he gestured to the conference table. While the men chose their seats, Declan watched Brooke settle into the leather chair at the end of the granite table and cross her legs.

Her bare, tan, smooth, shapely legs.

The black high-heeled ankle strap sandals she wore bordered on dominatrix and that intrigued the hell out of him. Not that he was into the whole Christian Grey red room thing, but he sure as hell wouldn't mind seeing Brooke in a little black lace and leather.

When she opened the file folder she'd placed on the table, he noticed the length of her fingers and the pale pink polish on her nails. A white-gold band graced the ring finger on her right hand and a silver bracelet with a charm that said *Fearless* encircled her left wrist.

What made her fearless? Extreme sports? Overcoming anxieties? Taking risks?

And why was he wondering these things now?

He had plenty of other things to think about. Like the fact that he had clients sitting at his conference table. Or that his parents had been killed barely three months ago and he and his brothers were struggling to keep the family vineyards afloat. Yet here he was, eyeing his assistant like she was a five-star meal he couldn't wait to devour.

Damn his twin.

This was all Jordan's fault.

For four years Declan had kept his mind to business and his hands to himself. Aside from knowing he'd be lost without Brooke, he knew virtually nothing personal about her. He didn't know what she did in her spare time. He didn't know if she was vegetarian or if she liked her steaks rare. He didn't know where she'd been born or what kind of upbringing she had. He didn't know if she lived in a rental house or one she owned. He didn't know if she lived alone, had a roommate, or lived with a boyfriend. Hell, he didn't even know if she had a boyfriend.

For four years he'd kept everything on a strictly business level. Now all he could think about was how much he'd like to caress Brooke's shapely curves in a very non-businesslike manner.

"Would you like me to record the meeting?"

Caught daydreaming, Dec's head snapped up. "What?"

Her lips tipped in a saucy smile. Okay, maybe it was just a regular smile. But for what he'd just been imagining, saucy fit the scenario better.

"I asked if you'd like me to record the meeting."

"Gentlemen?" He glanced at the two men at the table. "It's your choice."

"Josh can take notes," the father said.

"I'll be happy to do that for you," Brooke said. "That way you can focus on the discussion."

"Then let's get down to business, shall we?" At that moment, Dec made the mistake of looking at his assistant again. While she reached for her laptop, her breasts pushed together just above the buttons of her shirt. Then she looked up at him and licked her lips. And for the first time in his career, he couldn't give a shit about anything other than how badly he wanted a taste of her.

Damn.

As soon as he got back to the vineyards, he was going to beat the shit out of his brother—one punch for each insane thought he'd planted in Dec's head.